THE CHILD LEFT BEHIND

THE CHILD LEFT BEHIND

by

Gracie Hart

Magna Large Print Books
Gargrave, North Yorkshire,
BD23 3SE, England.

British Library Cataloguing in Publication Data.

A catalogue record of this book is
available from the British Library

ISBN   978-0-7505-4742-0

First published in Great Britain in 2018 by Ebury Press

Published in Large Print 2019 by arrangement with
Ebury Publishing

Magna Large Print is an imprint of Library Magna Books Ltd.

Printed and bound in Great Britain by
T.J. (International) Ltd., Cornwall, PL28 8RW

Acknowledgements

With grateful thanks to Gillian Green of Ebury Publishing, for having faith in me when others didn't. Also her wonderful team of editors, copyeditors and all the staff that are involved in the publication and distribution of my books.

And as ever my thanks to Judith Murdoch, my agent, for having patience with this lass from Yorkshire.

Chapter 1

Woodlesford Village, near Leeds, 1866

'Bastard, bastard, you're nothing but a bastard.'

The schoolchildren's taunts echoed in Victoria's ears as she ran down the cobbled street. She brushed away the tears from her eyes. She hated them all. They would never let her forget that she had no father and that her own mother had abandoned her, even if she had left her in the loving and capable hands of her Aunt Eliza. She sniffed and snivelled and clutched her snap tin close to her along with her chalkboard as she rubbed her hand across her snotty nose and tear-stained cheeks. She wanted to put on a brave face before returning to her aunt in her small dress-maker's shop. She loved being at the shop, but her classmates made her life impossible. She wasn't the only one who didn't have a father, but she was the only one who wasn't allowed to play roughly on the streets and the only one who had someone at home spending time encouraging her to get a good education. In class, she was the teacher's pet. This gave her jealous classmates an op-portunity to pick on her when they felt aggrieved by the attention shown to her. That was exactly what had happened that afternoon, when she had recited a poem word for word without fault and the teacher, Mrs Kirk, had given her the apple from her desk that everyone had coveted for showing so much promise.

Victoria knew as soon as the school bell was rung by the headmaster that she would be bullied on her way home. Especially by brash Tilly Harrison, whose head had been shaved to get rid of nits and had impetigo scabs on her face. Tilly was part of a family of ten, and they all lived in one of the slum houses down by the canal. Victoria knew she was no different from Tilly – she and her Aunt Eliza were also poor – but as it was just the two of them she did not want for love and attention, which was probably why Tilly hated her so much.

'Now, what's all this about? You look as if you've been crying again, my sweetness.' Eliza dropped her sewing and went to comfort her niece as she entered the small dress shop.

'I didn't want you to know, but I can't help it, they make me so sad and that Tilly Harrison is just a bully.'

Victoria sobbed as soon as she felt the comforting arms of her Aunt Eliza around her. She'd really tried to hold back the tears, but as soon as she had seen the concern on Eliza's face the tears had welled up again.

'Oh now, don't you let her get you down. Remember what I told you: one day you will be the princess of Woodlesford and you'll want for nothing and she'll not even dare to look at you, let alone talk to you.' Eliza pulled an offcut of material from one of her shelves and placed it on Victoria's shoulders like a royal cloak. 'There, Princess Victoria, here I am your faithful servant.

12

And if I may suggest, your highness, going home for some supper? Perhaps caviar and salmon will be on the menu this evening. Followed by who knows what for a pudding.'

Eliza wiped her niece's tears and kissed her brow before putting away the dress she was working upon. 'I've had Grace Ellershaw in today, my love; she ordered a new dress from me, so that will keep the wolves from our door for another month or so. I must say, I was ever so thankful. I didn't have much work on the books until she made her appearance.' Eliza tidied her sewing away and reached for her shawl and bonnet and placed them both on as she watched Victoria looking gloomily out of the window.

'In fact, it was so quiet that I made you this out of some old rags. I thought that it might cheer you up a little, although now you are nearly nine, you are perhaps getting too old for dolls.' Eliza reached for a floppy rag doll from under her sewing, which she had quickly put together from scraps of left-over cloth. 'She's got a real happy face and blue eyes.' Eliza put her arm around her niece. 'She's just short of a name. Can you think of one for her?'

'She's lovely, Auntie, I'll call her Tilly, to remind me of Tilly Harrison, because I swear I will not let her bully me again. And whenever I look at my new doll it will remind me to smile because Tilly never does.' Victoria held the doll tight and looked at it as it flopped over her arm, the face smiling at her from underneath the black wool Eliza had used for hair.

'That's it. Never let anyone get the better of you.

13

Think why they are being so nasty and usually you'll find that they are either jealous or their lives are just downright terrible. There will always be Tilly Harrisons in the world, Victoria, we just have to learn to live with them. Now, let's go home and get the fire lit and the kettle on.' Eliza guided Victoria through the door and locked the door of the small lean-to behind her before walking down the main street of Woodlesford with Victoria by her side. 'I can't really promise caviar and salmon but I think there's still a little blackberry jam left...'

'Did George come with Miss Grace to the shop?' Victoria asked Eliza as she quickly walked beside her.

'No, he didn't, he'd be busy having lessons like you,' Eliza said sharply.

Victoria glanced up at Eliza. 'George is too old to go to school! I like George, he always talks to me and sometimes even gives me a piece of spice.'

'He has a private tutor at home. Now, I don't want to hear another word about George Eller-shaw, he's best left alone. Besides, the Ellershaws are far above us, my dear. He's only sweet to you because he thinks he's doing his bit in patronising the poor, which we all are to the likes of him. Indeed, I think that's the very reason why Grace and her friends order the odd dress or two from me.' Eliza sighed. She was trying to guide her young niece through the many pitfalls of life, but just how well she was doing it, only time would tell. The last thing she wanted was for Victoria to become too friendly with George Ellershaw, who, in her eyes, was not at all like his sister but showing

14

more of the same traits as his heathen father, the way he flounced around in his own importance.

Eliza sat next to the dwindling fire in her cottage at Pit Lane. Victoria had been put to bed after having a supper of bread and the last of the jam and now Eliza was left on her own with her thoughts and worries and an empty stomach. By the time the rent was paid and the coal bought and Victoria's needs seen to, there was precious money left and she often found herself going without a meal for the sake of her niece. She yawned as she darned the near-threadbare stockings for Victoria to wear the following day. They would have to suffice until she could afford a new pair.

How she wished that her sister, Mary-Anne, would send sufficient provisions for her young daughter, or perhaps return home and take her off her hands. She loved Victoria dearly, but when she had offered to be her guardian until she was sent for she hadn't realised the hardship that it was going to bring to both their lives. The letters and monies sent from Mary-Anne were few and far between, with no mention of Victoria being sent to join her mother. It broke her heart to see Victoria give up hope on ever meeting her mother, let alone starting a new life in New York. It was always the same tale from her sister: John's next job would give him better money, then she would send for her. Or, we're looking for a bigger place to live before we are able to take her off your hands. But the new job with better money never appeared, nor the bigger living quarters, and so Victoria kept Eliza company and it seemed that

15

was how it was going to be until she was grown and able to fend for herself.

Eliza put down her darning and poked the dying embers of the fire before placing the guard around the hearth. Tomorrow was another day and who knew what it might bring. It was no good looking on the dark side of life. They were both well, had a roof over their heads, and were, to some extent, fed. There were a lot who were worse off and she knew it. She picked up the lit tallow candle and made her way to bed.

At least Mary-Anne had a man in her life. Eliza had never glanced twice at one since Tom Thackeray had walked out of hers. Life was hard, but at least she was her own woman and that counted for a lot, she thought, as she changed into her night gown before blowing out the candle to leave her alone with her regrets in the dark of her bedroom.

'Aunt Eliza, Aunt Eliza, look what the postman's brought, it's a letter from Mama!'

Victoria ran in from playing in the small front garden with her stick and hoop and pulled on her aunt's skirts as she brandished the letter.

'Now, isn't that good timing? Your mama must have known that we would receive it on a Saturday and that you would have time to sit with me and read it together. Here, let's open it and we will see what she has to say. Hopefully, she will have sent us some money too.' Eliza dried her hands from washing up and sat down at the kitchen table with Victoria on her knee. 'Careful, Victoria, we don't want to tear any money that might be in it.' Victoria carefully unsealed the letter to reveal a page of paper with Mary-Anne's writing upon it, but no money was forthcoming, no matter how Eliza shook the envelope.

'Never mind, I had hoped she would have sent us something but at least she has written to us.'

Eliza's heart sank, yet another letter with no means of support within it. She was beginning to think something must be wrong in her sister's life that the money she used to send so regularly had dried up with no excuse or reason being given. 'Let's read what she has to say to us together.' Victoria wriggled on her aunt's knee and looked keenly at her mother's words.

Apartment 29
Orchard Street
New York

2nd March 1866

My dear Eliza and my darling Victoria,

I do hope that this letter finds you both well. Both John and I are working long hours; he's working hard for the new rail-road that is making its way through New York and I have just secured a position at a tailor that supplies garments to the theatre. The hours are long but I endure them as I think that every hour worked means I can save some money for my fund to bring you back to me, my darling Victoria. I promise it will not be long, providing that I can secure you a safe passage and home.

New York is thriving now the Civil War is over. New businesses open every day and you would be amazed

17

by the masses of people on the streets. It is a strange world here, completely different to the one in Leeds. New York never sleeps and you can get most things that you want at any time of day or night providing you have the money.

At the moment, people are afeared for the safety of their money as the other week there was a Bank Robbery in broad daylight in Liberty, Missouri. The papers are full of the cowboy gang they are saying is led by a man called Jesse James, pronounced 'Jessie'. I thought that would make you laugh, Victoria. Fancy, a man, an outlaw, with the girl's name Jesse!

Eliza looked at her niece as she giggled at the news and squirmed on her knee.

I miss home, I miss you both. Times may have been hard but maybe I should have stayed. Remember Victoria, that I will always love you no matter what and when I look up at the moon of an evening I know the same moon is looking down upon you. So I send you my love and I make a wish for you.

Eliza, I can never thank you enough for the love you show my daughter and I know that she is in good hands. Until my next letter then my dears, when I hope to be able to send you some money. All my love and kisses, my darlings.

Mary-Anne

Victoria curled up in her aunt's lap and sobbed. 'I wish my mother was here. I wish I could go stay with her.'

'You will one day, my little one, you will, your

18

mother will not let you down,' Eliza whispered as she stroked her niece's long dark hair and hoped that the Lord would forgive her for lying.

Chapter 2

New York

Mary-Anne softly patted her swollen cheek with iced water, trying to contain the swelling under her eye and on her cheekbone. The last thing she wanted was a black eye – just the other month she had received comments from her workmates over marks on her arms that had been made by John holding her too tight.

She breathed in deeply and looked at her reflection in the mirror, pulling a strand of hair over the side of her face to hide the bruising, sighing at the thought of the colours that were bound to develop over the day while she was at work. She held her head in her hands and swore to herself. Somebody was bound to see it and she'd just have to make up an excuse. After all, she worked with actresses, she'd just have to become one herself.

She closed her eyes and fought back the tears. Now she knew how her mother had felt when her stepfather had beaten her. Although John was in no way near as bad as him – he was a good man when he was sober – he did have the same trait of not being able to take his drink, especially after a drop or two of whisky, which he was all too easily plied with by his fellow Irishmen.

He'd not been this way when they had first sailed over from Liverpool. Back then, he had been full of ideas for the future – how they were going to build a new life together, have children of their own. They had tried to put down roots, and had started well when John was working for his brother, but family love soon wore thin, and it was only a matter of months before John walked out of a perfectly decent job and went to work down in New York Harbor. There he had unloaded skins and furs from the boats that had sailed down the mighty Hudson River, and seen to the cargoes of ships from all over the world. All had been well until he'd been caught pilfering bottles of whisky to share with his so-called friends. Nothing in his life seemed to go smoothly. His love of politics and his outspoken views also made his bosses wary of him. Mary-Anne only hoped that he would keep his mouth shut in his new job of navvy for the railway that was to be built through New York.

She stood up quickly as she heard John move in the bed behind her; she didn't want to hear his excuses yet again for his violent behaviour the night before. She didn't want him to beg her to forgive him. His words were empty, and along with his fists they had hurt her too many times before, especially when he raged about her inability to give him a child of his own. Last night, as he had before, he'd raged on about her daughter, Victoria, so much so that now she had been forced to abandon any thoughts of seeing her in the near future, or even sending any money to help support her sister with her upkeep. John begrudged her only child every penny, so she could send nothing home unless she managed to sneak the odd dollar from out of the savings box under their bed.

One of these days John Vasey will go too far, she thought, quickly making her way out of the small one-room apartment and closing the door quietly behind her. No matter how kind and loving he was when not cursed with the liquor, she knew she would leave him one day. She would not stand by a man who let drink get the better of him. Once she had summoned up the courage, she would go back home, by fair means or foul, and return to her daughter Victoria and sister Eliza and hopefully claim some of Edmund Ellershaw's estate for his daughter born out of his uncontrollable wicked ways.

Despite the years that had passed, she still blamed Ellershaw for her downfall, and even her current situation. He should be made to pay for her suffering and his child's upbringing. She should have demanded so when she had the opportunity back in Woodlesford. But for now, she would just have to survive the best she could by using the skills that she had been born with. She focused her thoughts on the day's work ahead in the sewing rooms of Lord and Taylor, repairing and designing outfits for those appearing in the music halls and on the stages of this great city. It was a job she loved and excelled in, it gave her a steady wage and she was treated kindly by the owners. She made her way down to 20th Street and to a world of glitz and glamour; a world millions of miles apart from the harsh realities of her life with John. But it was a world where she could forget her worries and concentrate on sewing spangles and sequins onto her beloved costumes.

Chapter 3

'Oh, my Lord, Victoria, there's Miss Ellershaw coming up our pathway! She must have found something wrong with one of the dresses that I made for her, else why would she be here?' Eliza quickly came away from the window and checked her hair in the mirror, looking around at the sparse room to check all was in its place. 'You go out and play, only in the front garden, mind, don't be going and playing in all the dust on the street with that Betsy from the end of the row.'

Eliza pushed Victoria towards the front door and opened it as soon as she heard the knock from Grace Ellershaw. 'Oh, Miss Ellershaw, what a surprise, please do come in, Victoria was just on her way out to play.'

Victoria squeezed past the unexpected visitor, smelling her sweet perfume.

'Victoria, remember your manners for Miss Ellershaw.'

Victoria stood out on the garden path and turned to look at the well-to-do woman dressed in expensive clothes.

Victoria smiled angelically. 'Sorry, Miss Ellershaw, I was just about to go outside and play.'

Eliza ushered Grace Ellershaw into the front

room, or the parlour, as she called it.

'She's such a sweet child. You have brought her up so well, Eliza. I hope that your sister appreciates it.' Grace glanced around the room before she removed her gloves and stood gazing around her at the sparseness of the small room.

'She does, Miss Ellershaw. She writes quite frequently to us both and promises Victoria that someday soon she will return to her and take her to New York. But until then, Victoria keeps me company and gives me a purpose in life.'

'I'm sure she does, Eliza, but perhaps you would like a life of your own? Is there no man in your life? Or are you like me? Self-sufficient and not about to be told what to do by a husband.' Grace smiled when she saw the worried look on Eliza's face. 'I beg your pardon, it is not for me to probe into your personal life. Perhaps I could tell you the reason for my visit over a cup of tea.'

'I do apologise, it is me who is forgetting my manners. I'll put the kettle on.'

Eliza's stomach churned as she walked into the kitchen and laid the only tea tray she had with the two cups that looked the least chipped. What was Grace Ellershaw doing at her house and why all the questions?

'There's no need for a tray, I'll drink it here.' Eliza jumped and turned to see that Grace had followed her into the kitchen. 'Don't think you have to stand on ceremony just because I have arrived at your door. May I sit?' She made herself comfortable in the Windsor chair next to the fire. 'This is one of my father's houses, isn't it? I must say you keep it spotless, Eliza. He should have no complaints about your tenancy.'

'Thank you, Miss Ellershaw, I'm just glad that he allows us to stay here. After all, these are really pit cottages.' Having allowed the tea to brew, Eliza passed a tea cup to Grace.

'The pit isn't as busy as it used to be, the house would be standing empty if you were not in it. But don't tell him I told you so. He thinks I know nothing of business. Business is for men only and not for the likes of us women, or so he thinks, which brings me nicely to why I am here.' Grace took a sip of her tea. 'My dear grandpapa has agreed to give me some money to set up my own business and I can think of nothing better than putting my money into a high-quality dressmaker. One of quality, with a designer who already has a small but loyal following but who needs assistance in growing her skills. Indeed, I have already secured a premise on Boar Lane in Leeds. It is the ideal position for the more affluent ladies of the district.'

'So you will no longer be needing my skills, Miss Ellershaw? Is that what you have come to tell me?' Eliza could barely control her feelings. Grace Ellershaw and her friends were her best customers; without them, she would not be able to survive.

'Oh, Eliza, ye of little faith. It is the contrary, my dear. I need you to be my designer, to help me run the shop. Who else would I ask? Why, you are quite the talk of my ladies' circle. I'm sure with the right materials and better facilities your work and designs will be worn by all the best-dressed ladies in Leeds. So, my dear, will you join me in my venture? The details I will work out with you once you have agreed.' Grace smiled at the look of disbelief on her dressmaker's face, it would be good to support and help someone who did her best, instead of feeling sorry for her lot in life.

'I don't know what to say! Surely you can't think I'm worthy of all that? I'm just a seamstress that tries to make a living with what she's got.' Eliza could hardly hold back her tears.

'You are much more than that. Given a chance you can make your own way in life and make me some money. So don't think I'm doing this out of kindness, I expect a good return on my investment. However, in return, both you and the beautiful Victoria will gain much, a better home and respect in the community. In fact, if things work out well, perhaps you could become my business partner. Although we would have to keep that from my family. They wouldn't understand, and might make things unnecessarily difficult for us both.' Grace smiled. She was giving Eliza a leg up in life and she knew that she could not say no to her offer. 'To us, Eliza. Let's show Leeds how it is really done.'

Sarah Parker, Eliza and Victoria's next-door neighbour, was living up to her name as a true nosy parker as she beckoned Victoria to come to her. 'Victoria, Victoria, come here, child, I need to speak to you. Now, just you take these to your aunt. They're still warm, I made them this morning and I thought I'd make enough for you both as well as for ourselves. With some dripping on, they will feed you this dinner time.' Sarah Parker thrust two warm barm-baps wrapped up in a red-spotted handkerchief into Victoria's hands. 'Is your aunt all right? Does she know you are out playing on the street by yourself? I think she'll have something to say when she sees the state you're in, what have you been doing to get your apron so dirty? Did my eyes deceive me or was that Grace Ellershaw that's just walked into your house?'

Victoria didn't really want to reply to her nosy neighbour. Although thankful for her gift, she knew it had been a means to find out the latest gossip. 'Miss Ellershaw is here. Aunt Eliza said I had to play in the front while they spoke, but I don't know what about.'

'Never mind, it'll be something or nothing, I'm sure. Aye, child, you look so angelic, even though you are as mucky as my hearth. That curly black hair and dark eyes could win any soul over, it's a pity your mother can't see you. She doesn't know what she's missing watching you grow up, her and her fancy man, she should never have left. Now, go on take them home and don't drop them.'

Sarah Parker watched as Victoria ran up her garden path. She shook her head as she closed the door behind her – she loved the poor little lass. It had been a shame her mother had abandoned her, but at least she was being brought up by her aunt the best she could. It was hard on them both, but Eliza was not short of love for her niece and was doing her best given the circumstances. But what was Grace Ellershaw doing there? That she would have to find out.

'Oh, Victoria, how have you got so dirty in such

a short time? I told you not to play out on the street, and what have you got in that handkerchief?' Eliza looked up from her conversation with Grace Ellershaw as Victoria came running down the hallway with something wrapped in a red-spotted handkerchief in her hands. 'I bet it's next door we have to thank for whatever is within. She'll have seen that we have a visitor and want to know why.'

Victoria nodded her head and passed the precious baps over to her aunt, while she stared silently at their visitor. She smelled so sweet and was dressed so differently to her aunt. Even though she had met her several times before, Victoria was slightly in awe of Miss Ellershaw.

'Come here, and let's wipe your face and hands and take that apron off, else Miss Ellershaw will think you're a filthy street urchin.' Eliza put the handkerchief containing the bread baps onto the table and lifted Victoria onto the wooden draining board of the sink and wiped her niece's face roughly with a tea towel. 'There, that looks better. Miss Ellershaw can see what you look like now.'

'She's beautiful, Eliza, you should be proud of her and your sister should be grateful that she is in safe hands. Hopefully, my offer to you will make both your lives easier and you will not need the charity of neighbours for much longer.' Grace Ellershaw smiled as she looked at the young innocent girl sitting by the sink and staring at her.

'I can't thank you enough for your offer of the position in your new shop, I don't deserve it.' Eliza tried to hold back her tears. It had been so hard bringing Victoria up without her sister's help, and now Grace Ellershaw had decided to back her designs and get her out of the little lean-to that she had tried to run a business from for so long.

'Nonsense, all my friends love your dresses. Besides, Victoria here deserves a better life, which you will be able to give her if I have my way.' Grace leaned over as she stood up and kissed Victoria on her now clean cheek.

'You enjoy your bread while it's warm, little one, and your aunt and I will talk more next week. Don't get up, Eliza, I'll see myself out. I'm sure you have a lot to think about.' Grace smiled as Victoria reached for her bun.

'No, no, please, let me.' Eliza stood Victoria on the stone flags of the kitchen and rushed to open the front door to her benefactor and say goodbye, nearly crying as she closed the door behind her.

'Oh, Victoria, God has sent us an angel today. If we are lucky we'll never have to rely on next door's charity again!' Eliza scooped Victoria up into her arms and sobbed as she held her niece tightly to her.

'I sometimes think my mama is an angel,' Victoria whispered. 'Perhaps she will come back for me one day. Why don't I have a father? Everyone has a father. And what is a fancy man?'

'My darling, Grace Ellershaw has done more for us today than your mother could ever hope to do. But your mother loves you, no matter that she has not kept her promise to return to you as yet. Don't you ever forget that, my darling. And everyone has a father, yours is just a secret, a

28

secret that one day your mother will tell you of, I'm sure. As for a fancy man, it's nothing for you to worry about but I can guess where you've heard the word being said.'

Eliza kissed her innocent ward and wiped away her own tears. She sat back in the Windsor chair next to the fire and watched as Victoria ate her precious barm-bap and vowed that with Grace's help she would always feed the child and school her as well as she could, regardless of her true parentage. It was the start of a new life and she was going to embrace it with arms outstretched.

Chapter 4

Four years later: New York, 1870

Mary-Anne stood at the stern of the steamship RMS *Oceanic* and looked back towards the mighty city of New York. She pulled her fur coat tight and shivered as she watched the ebb of waters flowing past her. She was finally leaving the shores of America to return home to England.

'Are you all right, madam? Is there anything I can help you with?' The steward smiled as he carried out the orders he had been given to make sure that the passengers in the saloon class were well looked after.

'No, I'm fine, thank you.' Mary-Anne dismissed him quickly. She was anything but fine, but she could hardly burden him with her troubles. He wouldn't care, after all. If anyone was to look at her in her fur coat and fine clothes, they'd think she had everything that most people wanted out of life. Little did they know that everything she wore was stolen, along with the money for her passage.

She leaned over the deck railings, looking down into the grey swirling depths, and then turned to watch the bustling crew as they hoisted the sails making ready for open sea, where the steam engine would need to be aided by sail power. She smiled as she heard the jovial voices of the steerage passengers two decks below her. Some would be returning home to their families, while others would be looking for another new start in Liverpool after failing to put down roots in the so-called great new land of America.

America had, at first, been exciting and new but then life had become just as hard as it had been in England and she'd had to live on her wits in the bustling city, just like she had at home. That, along with John's drinking and involvement in politics, had finally convinced her she needed to return home, to be with her daughter, Victoria. The daughter she had not seen since she was a baby, some twelve years ago. Where had those years gone? She'd promised ever since she had left that she would return to bring her daughter to America, but one year had turned to two, three and more, and before she knew it the child was growing up with her sister Eliza tending to her every need.

A cheer went up from the decks below as the great ship passed Bedloe Island. The island was known as the gateway to America. It had been in the newspapers of late as a French intellectual proposed that the island should have a statue representing liberty built upon it as a celebration of independence and the friendship with France since the Civil War. No doubt it would be built, anything could be built or done in America if you had enough money or the right contacts.

She breathed in deeply and closed her eyes. Had it really been twelve years since she and John had left Leeds to start afresh somewhere new? They had both been fleeing from their pasts but little did they know then that their new life would not be full of the dreams that they'd hatched together on their turbulent crossing to a new land. Little did they know that even in America, you had to work just as hard and be even cannier with money and your choices.

She sighed. Poor John. She had loved him once, and could put up with his radical views, but not his fists. During the Civil War that had ripped their new homeland in two, John had just put his head down, knowing that one man on his own could not stop the war. He also had escaped conscription, not wanting to take part in someone else's war while waging his own fight for Ireland in his head. But as depression was starting to build up in the country, he once again had felt the need to stand up for his fellow countryman, as Protestant gangs fought with Catholic gangs in the working-class area that they lived in. Inevitably, he'd end up in a brawl, which he'd then take out on Mary-Anne when he came home, though always to his shame the following morning.

Last week the neighbours had run for the

police to come quickly when they had heard John threatening Mary-Anne and had worried for her life. On their arrival, the police had taken John away, locking him up in the cells to cool down and leaving Mary-Anne alone with her thoughts. It was in despair of her plight, sitting alone in their rooms in the tenement house on Orchard Street after a hard day working at Lord and Taylor on 20th Street, that she had decided to leave the man she had supported for so long and return home. After all, she was worse off than she had ever been at her original home of Woodlesford. She was living in a tiny two-roomed apartment, with all of the rest of the world's unwanted people as neighbours, sewing night and day to just to keep a roof over their heads and to keep John out of trouble. She just had to get away.

Mary-Anne felt her heart flutter as she remembered stealing the clothes that she was now wearing from her employer along with the week's takings that she had been entrusted to bank on her way home. She had enjoyed her work there. It had been exciting working for the stars of Broadway, even though customers could sometimes be temperamental and highly strung and the hours long. She took a sharp breath as a pang of guilt came over her. Mr Lord had been exceptionally kind to her. He had put a lot of trust in her when many would not have given her time of day. However, what was done was done, and there was no turning back, she thought as the winds that were carrying her back to England caressed her face.

She was a tougher, more knowledgeable woman now, and had a burning desire to do better in life.

And then there was the matter of the abusive mine owner Edmund Ellershaw. Twelve years away from his ugly face and lecherous ways had not lessoned her loathing of him – instead it had given her time to dwell on the matter of Victoria's birth. She was now strong enough to confront him and demand some support from the bastard, and that was even more reason for her to return home. To get even with the man who had ruined her and her mother in turn. Now it was his turn to pay. She smiled as a handsome young man that had been watching the departure from America just like her, caught her eye.

'Are you going home or just visiting Liverpool?' Mary-Anne enquired, noticing her fellow passenger's finely made clothes and sleek appearance. He certainly looked wealthy.

'I'm going on business to Liverpool and then on to Leeds. I'm in the wool trade and I'm to visit our British suppliers.' The young man looked at the auburn-haired beauty that stood in front of him and thought her a little forward as she made eyes at him.

'Ah, that is a coincidence, I too am on my way to Leeds. My sister is a top-class dressmaker with a shop on the corner of Boar Lane. You must call in and purchase something for the lady in your life. I can assure you it will be of the best quality.'

'I would indeed, if I had a love in my life. But, unfortunately, my life is too busy for me to have anyone waiting for me at home. They would never be able to expect more of me than a few fleeting moments a week before I moved on to my next trader to visit.' The man smiled at Mary-Anne.

'That is truly a shame, Mr err...' Mary-Anne looked at her fellow passenger and waited for his reply.

'Ashwell. Mark Ashwell, and you are?' Mark Ashwell could not help but notice the rich clothes that adorned the woman's most attractive figure.

'Mary-Anne, Mary-Anne Vasey. I'm travelling to Liverpool and then on to Leeds to appear onstage at the newly opened Thornton's Music Hall.' Mary-Anne held her right hand out to the young man to shake and looked coyly at him. She wished that she had removed the wedding ring from her hand but she could pass herself off as a widow in the music hall as easily as a single woman. The ring was a cheap thing John had once bought her as a promise, but it had proved empty like most of his – he had never made an honest woman of her. And there was safety in pretending to be someone else – she'd blown most of her money on a saloon-class ticket, thinking it a better place to hide in her stolen finery, especially if Mary-Anne Wild would soon be wanted for theft. She'd heard enough theatre talk from her customers over the years to be able to fake an alternative career.

'An actress or a singer, may I enquire? I am honoured to make your acquaintance whichever, Mrs Vasey.' Mark shook her hand gently and looked at her with admiration and excitement.

'Both. I've just left Broadway, where I've been appearing for the last few years and now I'm happy to be playing a new role in Leeds at the new venue there. It might be a bit of a disappointment after the bright lights of Broadway but it fits in nicely with my plans as I aim to visit my sister there. She's the only family I have left after losing my dear husband. But please, let us not stand on ceremony, so please feel free to call me Mary-Anne, all my best friends do. And I am sure we will become very good friends by the time we have reached Liverpool.' Mary-Anne flashed a smile and thought how good it was to be leaving the old Mary-Anne Wild behind in America.

'Well, Mrs Vasey, perhaps you would like to join me in a drink down below and, if you are agreeable, then we could have dinner together later this evening.' Mark held out his hand for her to take.

'Now, Mr Ashwell, you are forgetting, it is Mary-Anne, none of this Mrs Vasey, and a drink would be delightful.' Mary-Anne grinned to herself, knowing that with her new-found friend and his well-padded wallet she would be likely to have a protector on the voyage and a full belly, all for the price of playing on his vanity and ego. Then, once in Liverpool, she would make her excuses and leave, and hopefully never see him again.

'Mary-Anne it is.' Mark held her hand tightly as they walked along the deck and down to the lounge bar below. 'I do believe I am going to enjoy this passage for once.'

'I'm sure you will, Mark, it will be one to remember if nothing else.' Mary-Anne smiled as her new-found friend snapped his fingers for them to be served with a drink as they sat down in the first-class lounge.

'To a smooth passage.' Mark raised his glass of champagne and toasted Mary-Anne, smiling across at her.

'And to new friends.' Mary-Anne took a sip of her wine and looked at him with a smile.

She'd started as she meant to go on, she thought to herself, sitting among the well-to-do people drinking and talking within the palm-filled lounge of the *Oceanic*. This was the life she had hoped for in New York but never had secured – and even if it was just until the ship reached Liverpool she would enjoy it. She would string Mark Ashwell along as best she could for the voyage and then make herself scarce once they docked and make her way home the only way she knew how, by canal barge.

Chapter 5

Levensthorpe Hall, Near Leeds

'Just look at yourself, what a disgrace. To think that I once only had eyes for you. I must have been blind.' William Ellershaw looked at his once beautiful wife, who was crying at the thought of having to attend dinner at Eshald Mansion, and shook his head in disgust. William was worn down by his marriage. He had landed on his feet when he had married Priscilla Eavesham, but he'd little suspected how spoilt she was. She had been ruined by her parents' over-indulgence and he was bearing the brunt of it.

'I can't help it, William. Nothing I do seems to

be right for you, no matter how I try. Please, let me stay at home. I know I would only embarrass you with my presence, you are better off going alone.'

Priscilla sobbed into her handkerchief. She was fully aware of how her husband felt about her these days. He stood tall and proud before her, looking every inch the gentleman, and he clearly hated the simpering wreck that she had become. But she couldn't help the dark thoughts that were growing ever more stronger within her mind.

'Please tell Jessica that I'm sorry, I am a little unwell today, and that I hope to have tea with her as usual next week in Woodlesford.'

She looked up at her dark scowling husband. He could be a cruel man, sharp with his tongue and uncaring when it came to her feelings. Now she wished that she had never married him. His grandfather had only been after her family home and the status that went with it when he had persuaded William to ask for her hand in marriage. For the first year or so, things had been bearable – not good, but he had been kinder then. Only after it had become increasingly likely that she would never be able to give him an heir did things go very bad very quickly and now, years after losing the last child she would ever carry, she hated him as much as he hated her.

'I suppose you want to take that blasted nerve tonic? It is that I believe that is turning you into the witless soul that you have become, but then again you never did have much charm or intelligence. If I'm to progress further in society, perhaps it is best if you no longer join me at these events. I'm always in fear of what you might say or do.' William turned to the window and watched the rain. It was a dark day and it matched his mood well. He was tired of being tied to such a dimwit shrew-like wife, and he needed more in his life.

'I shall, with your permission, retire to my room. I am sorry that I am a disappointment to you, William. Dr Reed says the morphine within the tonic calms my nerves and I do find it beneficial, despite what you say.' Priscilla rose from her seat with as much dignity as she could muster and looked at her husband's back as he stared out the window. 'I take it that I will not see you later? That you will be confining yourself to your quarters?'

Priscilla stood like a delicate doll in front of her husband and waited for his reply. Since her parents had moved out of the hall, William had shown little interest in her and nights where they shared a bed were few and far between. He only came to her as a last resort, when he had not been able to satisfy his sexual appetite with his mistress who she knew he kept in relative luxury in her own home on the other side of Leeds.

'You think right, my dear. What is the use of coming to bed with someone who has long since lost any love or passion for me?'

William noted Priscilla was not shocked by his words. She did not love him any more, he knew that for sure. Had she ever loved him? He doubted that she ever had. She no longer seemed to care that he too mourned their lack of children. He wondered if she realised that he had been forced into their marriage as much as she had.

'Well, at least that means I will not have to put

up with the tortures that you would have me endure. She is welcome to you, William, and I hope you pay her well for her troubles.'

Priscilla held her handkerchief to her mouth and fought back another round of tears as she fled the room. She might not love him but his words still hurt her. Her husband was a cad and she hoped that one day he would rot in hell for what he had done to her and her family.

'Is Priscilla not with you this evening? I was so looking forward to her company,' Jessica Bentley enquired as her father bade William sit next to him at the dinner table.

'Alas, no. She sends her apologies, but I'm afraid she is quite bad with her nerves at the moment and I am quite concerned for her well-being.' William, watching carefully his fellow guests' faces, made an effort to seem every inch the concerned husband.

Timothy Bentley leaned back in his chair. 'The curse of our womenfolk is a nervous disposition. Frail creatures they are. You must take care of her, young William.'

'She says she will meet you for tea next week in Woodlesford, Jessica, and that she is looking forward to catching up on all the news.'

William smiled at Miss Bentley. Perhaps she was the one he should have married. But, for all his strife at home, life with Jessica would not have been as easy as life with Priscilla. Jessica did not suffer fools gladly and she would not have put up with his ways for long.

'I'm glad to hear it.' The servants came in with

soup, and Jessica leant back in her chair as it was placed in front of her. 'Your sister Grace will be joining us as well. We hope to indulge in some of that exquisite Victoria sandwich cake that the tea shop now makes. It truly is quite scrumptious.' Jessica took a sip of her soup.

'I'm surprised Grace has the time to join you, she seems to be always involved in some hare-brained scheme of sorts. I'm sure my father must despair of her sometimes.' William patted his lips with his napkin and pushed his soup aside.

'They are definitely not hare-brained. Why, she and that girl of hers are building up quite a good reputation in their shop in Leeds. They have quite a wealthy clientele, lots of ladies with very good connections. I keep trying to convince Priscilla that she must visit one day and peruse their latest fashions. Eliza is truly a wonder when it comes to following the latest Parisian designs.' Jessica looked at William; he never had the time of day for his sister and yet she was forging a name for herself with just the aid of the money left to her by her grandfather.

'Why she ever got involved with that family, I do not know. Common as muck, they are. Why, I heard that Eliza had a child out of wedlock. She's nothing but a hussy,' William scoffed.

'I think you'll find that the child was her older sister's,' Jessica retorted. 'She left her with Eliza when she emigrated to America. She was supposed to return and take the child back with her, but so far has not fulfilled her promise.'

'Aye, well, whose ever it was, I bet neither one of them could name the father. Wild by name and by nature they are, and their mother not much better from what I heard tell. Can you not remember when the older of the two joined us for tea once? All the social graces of a sailor. She didn't know what to say and how to act and was just hard work.' William laughed.

'If I remember correctly, she caught your eye,' Jessica said with a wicked smile, enjoying his discomfort. 'Poor Priscilla was beside herself that day, thinking that your head had been turned.' Jessica regarded William as she took a long drink from her claret glass. She cared not for William Ellershaw. All the money in the world wouldn't make him a gentleman and she knew how badly he treated her friend Priscilla.

'It's a wise child that knows its own father, that is a fact,' Timothy Bentley interjected, not quite following the undercurrents of conversation between his daughter and his guest. 'Thankfully my dear, there is no doubting that you are mine, we are too similar and your mother up to her death was always faithful to me, of that I'm sure.' Timothy smiled at his daughter. 'Now, William, how's that father of yours? Is the mine doing well? I hear he's got a man working for him by the name of Tom Thackeray. It means a lot to have a good right-hand man, somebody you can trust.'

'I try not to get involved with the pit, sir. I put my time into looking after my mills. Since my grandfather's demise I have very little time for anything else.' William did not want to get involved with a discussion about his father, it was common knowledge that Rose Pit was on the decline because of his bad management. 'But I'm sure my father will have hired well, and that along with this Tom Thackeray will be putting every working hour into the smooth running of the pit.'

'I hear he caught a cold when he bought a pit over near Wakefield. Worked out within six months. A lot of money for nowt, is what I heard.' Timothy looked seriously at his guest while the soup was cleared away.

'As I said, sir, I have little involvement in my father's affairs. I'm afraid we do not have a lot to do with one another at present, but I'm sure he would not have been so foolish.' William tried to look surprised when in fact he knew that his father had been deceived by a rogue who had conned him into believing that he had been buying a pit of quality, while all the time knowing it to be nearly worthless.

'Aye, well, it was only gossip. There's always plenty of that about, as I'm sure you are aware, lad. Now, have you seen my display of oranges on this table? Aren't they magnificent? I've grown them myself, you know, in my orangery. I can grow almost anything in it now I've run heating through it. I'll be keeping your father's pit open by my bill for coal alone – it takes some feeding does the boiler. You must try one for dessert and let me know what you think.'

Timothy Bentley smiled. He knew what he'd heard was right. Edmund Ellershaw was struggling to keep his head above water. No wonder with the lifestyle he had cultivated over the years, what with his women and his drink, as well as pampering his wife and children to the point of stupidity. It was catching up with him now, and it would seem his eldest had washed his hands clean of him, if the disgust on William's face was anything to go by.

'I'm sorry my father questioned you over your father, William, he's concerned more than anything,' Jessica said later, when they were saying their farewells after supper. 'Your father and he used to be such good friends but we have not seen much of your family of late, apart from Grace.'

'It makes no difference to me. My father has always done what he has wanted to do, regardless of what my views are. My mother, bless her soul, goes along with him to keep the peace but even she is finding it hard since Grandfather died and she no longer has him for guidance. She puts all her time into pampering George, who can do no wrong in her eyes. I have learned to be independent of my parents. I find it best.' William took his hat from the servant standing near the door.

'I sometimes think that I am lucky to be the only child, although it can be lonely. And, unlike yourself, I have never found my perfect partner, so I am afraid I will remain an old maid in the eyes of society, when in truth I am happy to look after my dear father, who I love dearly. It suits me as I think myself too outspoken for most men,' Jessica replied. 'Please give my love to Prissy. I'm sorry she did not join us this evening. Is she all right? I thought she looked a little frail of late, the poor dear.'

'Priscilla, I'm afraid, cannot deal with the world at the moment.' He lowered his voice, aware of the servant opening the door to let the guest leave.

'I'm sure you are aware that we will not be blessed with children. It weighs heavily on her that she has been told that she cannot carry a child. She talks of nothing else and feels that she is no longer a woman. I find her state of mind hard to accept, the constant mood changes upset me. Things are not good between us.' William looked at Jessica who had a slight blush on her cheeks. 'I'm sorry – I'm embarrassing you with my home life. Forgive me, I took advantage of a listening ear and I know that you and Priscilla are close.'

'Indeed, we are. She tells me most things and I know she is suffering. She is in need of much sympathy. I cannot imagine the grief of losing so many babies, and their deaths must have affected you both greatly. Please give her my love and I will look forward to seeing her next week. I will always be there for her, William, just as I know you are,' Jessica said as pointedly as she dared with her father in the hall. Both Grace and she knew exactly how Priscilla was hurting, and that the man that stood in front of her did not really care one jot. Instead, he went to his mistress's arms and threw himself into his work, leaving Priscilla to turn inwards upon herself and become more unwell by the day.

'I'll pass on your kind thoughts and thank you once again for a most enjoyable evening. It was a shame Priscilla did not join us. I think we should entertain more often at the Hall, but alas she does not feel up to the stresses that come with entertaining friends.' William put his head down and made for the doorway. 'Goodnight, Jessica. Thank you once again.'

Jessica watched from the door as William mounted his horse and quickly pulled on its bridle, disappearing into the darkness. He would not convey her words to Priscilla, of that she was certain. In fact, she knew that he hardly talked to her at all these days and barely acknowledged her presence on this good earth. While he may not have an heir, he'd got everything else he'd wanted since he had inherited all of his grandfather's wealth and Levensthorpe Hall. Poor Priscilla, she had not realised at the time that she had only been part of a grubby deal that William's grandfather had put together on his behalf. Now, after losing the one hope that might have united them a little, children, they had truly drifted apart and William had taken himself a lover, which poor Priscilla was all too aware of, despite his feeble attempts at discretion. William Ellershaw was to be kept at arm's length, of that she was sure. And his father was even worse from what she had heard. As long as there were men like the Ellershaws, she would not even look at the male of the race.

'Why, my William, you are a late caller. Better late than never though, eh, my darling?' Ruby Bell ran her finger down William's face as he entered the three-bedroom terraced house he paid for. 'Your wife not up for it tonight, then?'

William looked at her in disdain. He was growing tired of the woman he kept for sex and sex alone. He'd found her at the theatre – she was a passable actress but lazy with it and while he still found her attractive there was no love in his heart for her. She was there to keep him away from the prostitutes that distracted him as he walked down by the canal wharf. He didn't want to be tempted by their thick make-up and their breasts nearly falling out of their tight bodices; after all, that was where his father sought his relief. Instead he had taken on a willing mistress and he hoped that behind the closed doors of the well-to-do terrace she kept herself true to him and him alone. He paid her well enough for the privilege.

'Hold your tongue, when you talk of my wife. Remember she is my wife, whereas you are just bought. I have no patience for little-tattle to-night, I have come here for just one thing.'

'Masterful as ever, my dear.' Ruby knew he was getting tired of her and that soon he would stop his visits to her and withdraw all his favours and then she would be back trying to make ends back at the music hall. 'I've got your favourite, William. It's been waiting for you since your last visit, something to relax you.'

Ruby led William upstairs to their bedroom where he made himself comfortable in the cushioned dimly lit room and reached for the pipe of opium that Ruby had placed there for his pleasure. He breathed in deeply and closed his eyes, feeling the effects of the Oriental poppy envelop his senses, calming him and making him ready for the pleasure that Ruby was going to bring him. He laid back and smiled as Ruby, her body now only partly clothed and her long dark hair hanging down over her naked breasts, knelt down and started to undress him. She was good. Her hands knew exactly what to do, how to arouse him and make him feel like the man he knew he was. Gone were the thoughts of Priscilla and the worries of his work as Ruby brought him to a climax the way only she could. He closed his eyes, enjoying the pleasure of Ruby and the opium and felt re-assured that he was William Ellershaw and everything he desired was his for the moment, albeit devoid of anything that could be called love.

Chapter 6

Eliza Wild watched her niece, the pride of her life, put pen to paper as the early morning sun beamed in through the bay-fronted window of their home at Aireville Mansions.

Victoria raised her head and looked at her aunt who had been more mother to her than her own since the day she had been born. 'I find it hard, Aunt Eliza, I don't know what to say some weeks. I wish I could meet her to know what she is like, even what she looks like.'

'One day, she will send for you, she promised, and you know that she loves you, she's always tell-ing you so in her letters.' Eliza ran her hand over her niece's shoulders and sighed. While Mary-Anne's letters to her daughter were always full of good news and promises, she had been more truthful to Eliza. Life in America had not lived up to expectations and Mary-Anne regretted throw-ing her lot in with John Vasey. The rich lifestyle they had both desired never appeared, leaving Eliza to bring up Mary-Anne's daughter alone, and with hardly any payment from her absent mother to do so. Thank the gods that she had managed to better their prospects with help from Grace Ellershaw.

'Am I like her, Aunt Eliza?' Victoria put her pen down. She remembered when she and Eliza had very little, but now her aunt had made a name for herself as a well-respected dressmaker. Her skills meant that the shop on Boar Lane attracted only the best clientele.

Eliza smiled at her niece. 'You are very much like her, you have the same handsome looks and complexion. But I think you also take after your grandmother, God rest her soul, who was sweetness itself. She never had a bad word for anyone.'

'And my father? Did you ever meet my father?' Victoria knew she was born out of wedlock but surely her mother must have mentioned her father and her aunt surely would know of him.

'Victoria, it is best you know nothing of that man. He was wicked and took advantage of your innocent mother, the least said about him the better.'

This wasn't the first time her niece had shown interest in her parentage, but she wasn't going to tell her that her father only lived half a mile away and that his true daughter, Grace, was more of a guardian to her that he would ever be. The less she knew the better.

'I'm sorry, Aunt, it's just that I'm curious.' Victoria hung her head. She would never find out who her father was through her aunt. Perhaps her mother would tell her if they ever were to meet.

'Some things are best left alone. Just be content

that both your mother and I love you a great deal and that we will always do what is right for you.'

Eliza left her niece, who was looking a little dejected, and went to look out of the back door. How could she tell Victoria that she was born because her father had virtually attacked her mother? It would break her heart. She stared outside at the snowdrops, a sure sign that spring was on its way. Her thoughts went back to her old home on Pit Lane. She had always wanted a garden there, instead, there was just the yard and wash house and the lavvy where her poor mother had lost her life. Life had been tough, and when Mary-Anne had left her holding baby Victoria, she didn't know how she was going to live from one day to the next. She had nearly been at breaking point, thinking that she and Victoria would fare better in the workhouse, when Grace Ellershaw had come to her rescue. She remembered nearly feeling sick as Grace had rattled through her plans and then had shown her the premises all filled with the best quality materials and accessories. It was like a dream come true and she had decided, despite her misgivings, she would manage the store. She had named a range of clothes after Grace Ellershaw, and soon Eliza's reputation of combining beautiful design with flawless tailoring meant that customers visited the shop from all over the country.

She took Grace's advice of having a girl to look after young Victoria while she was at work and later, as she started to make money, appointed a tutor to teach her three days a week. The shop had done so well that now she and Victoria lived in comparative luxury. They were still in Woodles-ford, but in a three-bedroomed house in a better area. They even had a maidservant, although today, being a Sunday, meant that she had the day off to visit her parents.

Things indeed had changed for her, but not for her poor sister who was just as penniless as when she first went to America. Mary-Anne had left Eliza with her child and worries, destroyed any hope she'd had of marrying Tom Thackeray and had hardly sent her a penny over the years. But still, she was her sister and she missed her, despite her having left all her troubles on her doorstep. Victoria was growing into a beautiful young woman and her mother wrote when she could afford the postage. That was how it was and Eliza couldn't see it changing until someone or something came into their lives to make it different. No sooner had she thought that then she heard the doorbell.

'I'll get it, Aunt!' Victoria cried.

A voice Eliza vaguely recognised came across the air. It couldn't be, could it?

'Well, this is a bloody swanky place you are living in, sis.' Mary-Anne stepped into the kitchen with Victoria standing aghast behind her. 'Are you glad to see me, or are you going to stand with your mouth wide open until next Christmas?' Mary-Anne dropped her overfilled carpetbag and held her arms open, her eyes filled with tears.

'Mary-Anne! It is you! I can't believe it. Victoria, this is your mother!' Eliza exclaimed. 'I was just thinking, about you–'

'Bloody hell, I thought she was your maid and

pushed her to one side. Let me look at you, girl. Yes, yes, I can see the resemblance, you are definitely my daughter, let me hug you this minute. You don't know how long I have wanted to do this.' Mary-Anne sobbed and hugged the dumbstruck Victoria. 'My daughter, my precious daughter. How beautiful you are. I'm so proud of you and of you, Eliza, for looking after her so well. I can never repay you enough.' Mary-Anne smiled at both of her relatives who were just as tearful. 'Look at us all, you'd have thought somebody had died. Oh, but it's good to see you both, we have so much to catch up upon.' She put her arms around both of them and kissed them on their brows.

'Oh, Mary-Anne, it is so good to see you. Just look at your fancy hair-do, hat, and fur wrap and look at your clothes! You sound different as well, I hardly recognised your voice.' Eliza stood back to regard her sister.

'Well, I'm just the same. Unlike this one here, just look at her. I can't be her mother, she's too beautiful to be mine.' Mary-Anne held out her hand for Victoria to take and smiled at her precious daughter.

Victoria smiled, not knowing what quite to do. 'I'll put the kettle on, shall I?' She went to the kitchen sink and ran the tap as Mary-Anne gasped.

'Well, I never. You've even got piped-in water! What we would have done to have that when we lived in Pit Lane.' Mary-Anne removed her wrap and hat, carefully pulling out the pearl-ended hat pin and placing all on the kitchen table before sitting down and looking around her. 'You've certainly landed on your feet, our Eliza. This house is a bit grand.'

'I've been lucky and have worked long hours to get where I'm at, but never mind me.' Eliza knew her sister wouldn't have returned without good reason. 'What brings you back home after all these years? You've not sent us any notice, unless we have not received your letter yet.'

'I've had enough of living with John.' Mary-Anne sighed and dropped her head. 'He's always taking on other people's problems instead of looking at our lives and how we live. And he's too fond of the drink and isn't afraid of using his fists. We have virtually nothing and I'm not content to live in that squalor. I want more in my life.'

'But your clothes, your hair? You look every inch a lady.'

Victoria pulled up a chair after putting a teapot and cups and saucers upon the table, fascinated by her mother's appearance.

'I stole my clothes from work, along with the takings from their cash box, so that I could make my way home. And my hair, well, I've always been blessed with good hair. I just titivated it up to keep a gentleman traveller interested in me on the passage to Liverpool. He paid for my needs all the way to Leeds, without any payment in kind on my behalf, I must add. I was grateful that I did take his eye, else I might still be in Liverpool, earning my pay behind a bar – or worse – to get me the rest of the way home. I managed to shake him off but it was hard. The poor bugger will be asking for me at the theatre, he thinks I'm an actress there.'

Mary-Anne glanced at her daughter's shocked expression. 'I'm sorry, Victoria, I must be a disappointment to you. I hope you never have to stoop so low.'

'No, Mother. I'm grateful that you are here and that I can now get to know you. I'm sorry that you have had such a terrible journey and had to do what you did to get here.'

Although Victoria knew her life was now one of privilege, she had never forgotten those years when her Aunt Eliza had struggled to make ends meet. A time of being hungry and badly dressed in other people's cast-offs and never knowing if they could pay the rent on Pit Lane. Even at her young age, she knew that life did not deal everyone a fair hand and that sometimes, no matter how you tried to better yourself, you could not change your fortune.

'I'm not proud of it, but I had to come back home while I could, while John couldn't use his charms to keep me by his side.' Mary-Anne sipped her tea. 'He doesn't know I've left him. I just couldn't take it any more. We had no money and lived in worse conditions than we ever did on Pit Lane. Nobody in America has any money except the filthy rich. It's a case of the rich get richer and the poor get poorer. So I made a break for it. I just couldn't live with him. He's turning into another Bill, Eliza.'

'Oh, Mary-Anne, you did right. You must stay with us until you get on your feet. In fact, I could do with an extra pair of hands in our shop on Boar Lane, so don't you worry about a roof over your head and work. I'll make sure you will have both. Grace, I'm sure, will agree.' Eliza held her hands out for Mary-Anne to hold.

'Grace Ellershaw?' Mary-Anne sat back.

'Yes, she owns the shop along with myself, although nobody is supposed to know that. She made me a partner a few years ago. You know she does. I wrote you – did you get my letter? I would have to ask her first.' Eliza smiled.

'I'd prefer that she doesn't know who I am. Not yet. I decided on my way back home to keep the name of Vasey, even though John and I are not rightly married. I still wear his ring that he gave me, although no vicar or priest ever blessed us both, but it is a way of putting my past life behind me. I'm Mary-Anne Vasey, a respectable widow who has lost her husband in the Civil War, if anyone asks. Grace Ellershaw will hardly recognise me, it is that long since she saw me.' Mary-Anne watched the surprise on the faces of her sister and daughter.

Eliza stared at her sister. 'If that's what you want, but I can't see why.'

'You know why, Eliza? Some people don't forget the past and I aim, by hook or by crook, to get someone to pay for the pain I went through. But I will say no more. I'm not about to spoil our re-union with my dark thoughts. It is wonderful to be back home. Victoria, you're such an elegant young lady. I am awestruck that I have such a beautiful, well-spoken daughter. I owe you a great deal, Eliza, and I aim to repay you one day, I really do.'

Mary-Anne yawned.

'You look tired,' Eliza said. 'I bet you've hardly slept. Victoria, show your mother to our spare room. She can unpack her bag and perhaps have a nap before we have luncheon. We've all the time in the world to catch up.'

'Luncheon? When did dinner time turn into luncheon? You've gone posh, our Eliza.' Mary-Anne smiled as she picked up her bag and belongings.

'I'm only trying to better myself, Mary-Anne. We're not in Pit Lane any more.'

'Then I'd better keep that in mind and not let the side down.' Mary-Anne yawned again. 'I am in need of forty winks, the journey has caught up with me. Can I ask that you keep my reappearance a secret for the moment? Grace does not need to be asked to employ me just yet, I have a little money on me for the next week or two.'

'Of course, if that's what you want, Mary-Anne, though I doubt we can keep it a secret for ever.'

Mary-Anne yawned again and sat down heavily on the small brass bed. Victoria put her bag down beside the side of the wardrobe. Mary-Anne reached for her daughter's hand and squeezed it tight.

'I know I haven't been much of a mother to you, Victoria, but I have always loved you, you must know that. I didn't want to desert you. A letter from you would fill me with hope for the future. A future with both of us in it, together.' Mary-Anne's eyes filled with tears.

'I know that you love me, Mother. Your letters and Aunt Eliza have always made that clear. And I love you too, but it is going to take time for us to get to know one another, I think.'

She made for the door and closed it quietly

behind her, standing for a second on the landing before going down to her aunt. What would life be like now? Eliza had always been her mother, and now she had to accept this stranger in to her life.

Mary-Anne lay on top of the padded counterpane on the bed, staring at the walls decorated with flock wallpaper. Eliza had clearly done well for herself. She'd come a lot further than she had, despite the distance she had travelled to get away from her shame to a supposedly better life. Perhaps she should have stayed, Mary-Anne thought as she looked up at the ceiling. However, she had done what she had done, and now it was time to seek some satisfaction in her life and hopefully some standing in the community. Today was the first day of her new life and with a roof over her head and, if she chose to accept it, the promise of employment with her sister, things were already looking more promising.

Chapter 7

Edmund Ellershaw, at his desk in his study, regarded the paperwork that surrounded him and grunted loudly. If only his family knew how much everything cost, then perhaps they wouldn't spend his money like water. He looked at the pile of bills, which were demanding his attention. The bill from the tailor for a new suit that his son George had ordered was on the top and he picked it up, sighing at the frivolous detail and expensive cloth that his youngest son had chosen. He was spoilt, spoilt beyond belief. Why, when he was George's age, he was glad just to be fed, never mind anything else.

He walked over to the sideboard and poured himself a port, his hand shaking as he did so. He didn't feel well from his previous night's exploits down by the docks. Perhaps I should learn not to overdo it so much, he thought as he stood at the window and looked out upon the bleak March morning. After all, I'm not getting any younger. This morning he had caught an unwelcome glimpse of himself in the hallway mirror, and he had thought that he looked as grey as pit dust. To top it off, now he had the shakes as the booze left his body. A medicinal glass of port would revive him, with a bit of luck, and maybe, by some miracle, the bill pile would disappear too. Not for the first time he cursed the fact that his bloody father-in-law had left all his money to his grand-children. How was he going to get his hands on it now? And to make matters worse, George was dependent on him until he was twenty-one, when his grandfather's inheritance would be released to him. That was nearly another six months before he could persuade his youngest son to put his money into the pit. Could he survive until then? Not if bills like the one from the tailors kept coming in. And bloody William was no bet-ter, the upstart. Since he'd married that empty-headed slip of a thing from Levensthorpe Hall and gone into the wool trade he thought himself God's gift. He was nowt, really. Edmund had made his own fortune – and lost it too – but William had been set up for life by his grandfather. He'd never once thought that it was his father who had put him through Cambridge and made him into the man that he was. He should show him more respect and stop making himself out to be something he wasn't. Bloody children, sometimes he wished they'd never been born, then he wouldn't have all this worry. Even his daughter Grace had shown him up going into business with that Wild woman, although he had to give her her due, at least she knew how to make brass. He could always fall back on her with her frills and fancies if need be. He sighed and sat back in his chair. He'd manage somehow. Something always turned up, it wouldn't be the first time he'd been short of a bob or two.

'Edmund, are you hiding in here? It's no good trying to keep a low profile, I know what time you came in at last night and that your clothes smell of cheap perfume and reek of ale. I suppose you've been up to your despicable ways again.' Catherine Ellershaw burst open the study door without knocking to confront her husband. 'Don't you think you are getting too old for cavorting like a man possessed? Quite frankly, I feel sorry for the poor girl that has to put up with you, but at least she saves me from your desires. Though what I feel most upset about is that you make your wanton ways so public. All the servants are sniggering behind my back this morning. They all know what you've been doing.' Catherine scowled at her husband as he held his head in his hands. Catherine looked at the glass of port next to his hand and sighed. 'Hair of the dog, is it? Really, William, it's not even noon yet.'

'Oh, be quiet woman, it's you and yours that make me drink. I've no peace from your wittering and demanding ways. I can't even have an hour's peace in my own home.'

'My father will be turning in his grave at your behaviour. He would never have acted that way. To think I could have had anyone in the county, but it was you I wed.' Catherine stifled a cry.

'Here we go again, "my father" this, "my father" that – and when it comes to wedding anyone else, well, you should have kept your legs closed and then we would both have been free to do what we wanted.' Edmund scowled at his angry wife. 'The old bastard never left you any money though, did he? Not even a brass farthing.'

'Don't forget, he did buy us this house and most of the things in it.' Catherine's eyes flashed in defiance. 'You know why he gave it to our children, he knew you would only spend it on womanising, gambling and drinking. And he was right. It was best our children inherited his money, it sets them up in the world. Just look at our William and Grace, I am so proud of them both.'

Edmund sat back in his chair and looked at her. 'I notice you don't mention bloody George in that list! Just look at this bloody bill he expects me to pay for him looking like a dandy. Ten guineas, woman, you could buy half of bloody Yorkshire for the price of one of his suits. And he doesn't need them; all he does is walk around Woodlesford and Rothwell with his fancy friends. None of them have done a day's work between them. They should do a day down the pit, make them into proper men.' Edmund threw the bill at Catherine and watched as she read it.

'A proper man like you, do you mean? Heaven help us if he turned into anything like you. I'm glad he has pride in his appearance, it means he will attract the right sort of woman when he decides to settle down.' Catherine put the bill back on the desk and turned to leave her husband in his dark mood. 'Lunch will not be ready for another half hour. I hope you don't bring that manner to the table. Leave the bills, my father would not approve of you doing business on a Sunday and as it is you missed chapel. My father used to say no good deal was ever made on a Sunday,' Catherine said as a parting shot.

'Then your father I was a bloody hypocrite – I bet he did many a deal on a Sunday for sure.'

Edmund drained the last drop of port from his glass as he looked at his workload on his desk. He'd have to try and make some sense of the debt that was starting to pile up. He'd see the bank manager next week, but for now, another drink was in order.

Grace Ellershaw smiled across at her brother, deciding to break the awkward silence that had fallen upon Sunday lunch.

'Are you coming with me to see Eliza and Victoria, George? Eliza has invited me for tea, I'm sure she would not mind you attending also?' Grace smiled at her brother, knowing full well what his answer would be.

'That would be delightful, sister. I will indeed.'

George didn't look up, knowing his father would not approve, but their father didn't seem to be listening.

'Mind you are not discussing business, which would never do on a Sunday. Not that they know owt about business.' Edmund glanced at his wife as he helped himself to mashed swede from the tureen that the butler was holding patiently at his elbow.

Catherine glared at him and then smiled at her daughter and son. 'I still find it amazing that someone from Eliza's background has such a good eye for fashion. To think that she used to work in that terrible ramshackle shed and looked so ragged. She has a lot to thank you for, Grace.' Catherine politely bit into her roast beef and watched as Grace smiled.

'She works hard, Mother. Really, it is I who should be thanking her. She is such a good seam-stress, she just needed the backing and some faith in her and then the rest was easy. What she should be really proud of is the way that she has raised her sister's child, Victoria. She is turning into the perfect young lady – intelligent, pretty and so well mannered,' Grace looked across at her brother, knowing that Victoria was his protégé and his indulgence in taking pity on the working class.

'You can't make silk purses out of sows' ears, and that's what that family is. Least you have to do with them the better, especially that young lass, it says something that her own mother abandoned her. Keep it to business and don't go associating yourselves outside of working hours. And you,' he pointed his knife at George for emphasis, 'Keep away from that Victoria, as she's called, she's still a pup and God only knows who her father was.' Edmund had his suspicions that the bastard of a girl was his, but could not very well admit it to his family.

'Father, you are such a snob!' His son replied with a laugh. 'Does it really matter that they have come from nothing? After all, you are a self-made man, so I don't agree with your statement. Eliza and her daughter are good people, and they make both Grace and myself welcome in their home. As for looking at Victoria in that way, she is, as you say, far too young and even if she was of an age, I would not have the inclination to do so.'

'Aye, that's the home that Grace here was daft enough to help her buy. You keep away from that family. Don't get led astray by the aunt or her pretty child. Find another woman who can satisfy your needs. After all, you've spent enough on the clothes that you are swaggering about in. Spend a few pence on a whore, satisfy your needs and then, when it's time for you to wed, you need to find yourself a woman with plenty of money. One that can support you and your expensive tastes so I don't have to!' Edmund stabbed his meat and felt gratified to see the looks of disgust on his children's faces.

'Edmund, really. Can you for once not bring your filthy talk to the table, especially on Sunday? George, do not listen to your father. However, you could do with looking a bit higher in society, I must admit. You will be a man of wealth, shortly, when you come of age, and one day the Rose will be yours and the pit at Wakefield. You are a good catch for the right young lady.' Catherine smiled at her son, who was the apple of her eye.

'I don't aim to die just yet. And if you think that pit at Wakefield is worth owt you are sadly mistaken. The first chance I get to sell that worthless piece of shit the better. I was duped.' Edmund despaired of his family. They knew nothing between them, cosseted in their perfect worlds, with no idea what he was going through.

'Father, I hope that your death is quite a few years away, yet,' Grace said with a smile, 'and I'm sure that you will make some use of the pit at Wakefield. Surely it must have some value?' She had noticed that her father was even more abrupt than usual and wondered if his worries ran deeper than he would admit to his family.

'It is worth nowt to nobody.' Edmund scowled. He had decided to help a friend out of a financial embarrassment with the purchase of his pit at what he thought a reasonable price, believing every word he was told about the pit having good yields of black gold, only to find it was worthless and to end up short of money himself. Damn the lying bastard.

'I'm sorry to hear that, it must be a disappointment.' Grace looked at both of her parents. She felt more sympathy for her mother than her father; it was she who would have to pay in the long run, dealing with her father's anger over being conned into a bad deal.

'Aye, well, I'll have to make the best of it. The Rose is still profitable, so I should be thankful for that.' Edmund wiped his mouth with his napkin and sat back. 'Time you started to contribute to the family coffers, George. Come and spend some time with your father and learn the ways of the pit and how to work it. Get your hands mucky for once.'

'You don't have to, darling,' Catherine re-assured her son. 'I know that you have no interest in mining. You'll find your way in the world just like your older brother. You are more intelligent than your father. A thinker, not a doer.'

'Stop pampering him,' Edmund snapped. 'Let him become a man, will you, Catherine.'

'Father, I'll be honest, I have no interest in the pit. But if you wish me to join you there one day, I will.' George knew his father thought him a wastrel. Perhaps he was correct, because as far as going down the pit, it would be a cold day in hell before he would get him to do that.

Grace knew that there was going to be yet another family argument, and checked the time on the clock on the mantelpiece. 'Will you excuse me? I don't think I will wait for pudding. I'm afraid I have been a bit of a glutton and eaten too much beef. I'll take my walk now.' She rose from the table and glanced at George.

'I'll join you, sister. I must not get too portly, else my tailor will scold me.' George pushed his chair back and joined his sister as they quickly made their way out of the dining room. Their father used their departure as an opportunity to swear once more and argue with his wife about making cuts in the household budget.

'Just listen to them. Father is getting worse and Mother just lets him rant and rail,' Grace whispered, reaching for her mantle and hat from the hall stand.

'Well, she doesn't want to make him worse. She's happy as long as the house is still standing. After all, it's all she's got left of her inheritance, Father has made sure of that.' George pulled on his gloves and picked up his swagger stick. 'I'll visit Eliza and Victoria with you. Despite what father says, they're better company than we'll find here.' George grinned. 'And they're both a lot prettier than dear papa too!'

'You behave yourself, George,' his sister chided gently. 'You don't want to become like Father – you know how the servants gossip about his ... roving eye.'

George smiled at the polite way Grace expressed herself but shook his head vehemently. 'Don't ever liken me to him. I'm ashamed at times to say he is my father, he is so uncouth. And as far as Victoria goes, she's such a sweet little thing, a poppet. I like her company, that's all.' George closed the door behind them both.

'Yes, but he is our father and you'd do well to show him a little more respect, at least to his face. You know your devil-may-care attitude angers him.'

'Well, he should respect us too, especially Mother. He'd have been nothing without her. He tends to forget that.' George sighed. 'In all honesty, I hate the man.'

'Then do something with your life and be independent,' Grace said. 'I've made my own business, surely you can do the same.'

'I will one day, sister, but don't forget I've yet to receive my inheritance. But let us go and visit your working-class friends. I hope there will be cake, as we have both foregone pudding to save any arguments.'

George grinned again and stepped out with his sister on his arm. It was a miserable grey day but he felt warm inside with the thoughts of Eliza and Victoria and their cosy and inviting home and the promise of cake and friendship awaiting them.

Chapter 8

'Oh, Lord, Victoria, I've forgotten we have Grace and perhaps her brother George visiting this afternoon. Now, remember, don't say anything about your mother being here. She doesn't want anybody to know just yet.' Eliza looked around her parlour in horror as she plumped the cushions up and quickly rearranged the flowers. 'Hopefully, she will hear their voices and will stay in her room.'

Victoria sighed. 'I wish I could tell everyone. I've been waiting for her to come home all my life and now that she's here I want to tell the world.'

'You can one day. She has her reasons for keeping her return a secret. Knowing your mother, she must be hatching some sort of a plan. What do you think of her? Is she what you expected?' Eliza saw the slight hesitation on her niece's face.

'She's very beautiful and glamorous but she doesn't half talk funny.' Victoria looked at her aunt, whom she felt more love towards than her true mother.

'That's because she picked up the accent from living over there in America for the past twelve years. She is glamorous, isn't she? She used to always turn heads, did our Mary-Anne.' Eliza looked around her. 'Now why did I give our maid Sunday off? I knew we had visitors.'

'We'll manage. I'll make the tea and I noticed Betty has a cake already made in the pantry. That will make George happy, he's got such a sweet tooth.' Victoria smiled.

'You mean he's sweet on you. Don't think I haven't noticed the way he looks at you.' Eliza looked at her niece's flushed cheeks. 'I don't wish to spoil things for you, but I don't think you should encourage his attention. You are far too young and he should know better. It may be only puppy-love on your part, and I'm sure George is just indulging you because of your age, but your mother hates his father, she will not be happy that his son is so taken with you.'

'I wouldn't say that he's taken with me, Aunt Eliza, he's just very kind and I do find him most interesting. He knows so much and he makes me laugh and I've known him a long time, so we are just friends.'

'Well, his father is definitely not a gentleman, so I'm hoping that George does not take after him. He may have status in the community but he is also known for his many transgressions. The man is a disgrace. Even Grace is ashamed of him. She hears the gossip and knows that most of it is true. I don't think her brother William is much better – poor Priscilla Eavesham should never have married him. When it comes to the Ellershaw family, Grace is the only one to be trusted, believe me.'

Victoria knew her aunt really did dislike her business partner's family and yet she owed so much to Grace. Surely they couldn't be that bad? She made her way to the window and pulled the heavy velvet drapes back to sneak a look out at the street, just in time to see the brother and sister making their way along the path to their door. 'Aunt Eliza, they are here! They are about to ring the doorbell.' Victoria blushed as George tipped his hat to her as he spotted her looking out of the window.

'Now remember to behave yourself, Victoria. Try not to encourage him by being silly.' Eliza brushed down her long skirt and gently patted her blonde plaited bun into place. 'And no giggling. We don't want them to think I'm raising a brainless idiot.' Eliza took a breath before opening the front door. She was annoyed with herself for giving their maid of all work the day off. Grace and George would never stoop so low as to open the door to their guests.

'Grace, George, I am so glad that you could join us for tea. The weather is quite depressing and I have stupidly given our maid the day off to allow her to visit her parents this afternoon, leaving me to open the door to you. Please do come in and join Victoria in the parlour.' Eliza kissed Grace on her cheeks and hesitated before doing the same to George after he took off his top hat and placed it on the hall stand along with his cane.

'These servants, I find, demand more and more time off. I know Mama is always complaining about the days they expect to have off. One Sunday a month is quite sufficient to keep in touch with their families. Otherwise, they are spoilt, and will only expect more.' George looked sternly at Eliza, waiting as his sister untied her bonnet and handed it and her mantle to Eliza. He held out his hand to Grace and led her out of the hallway and into the small parlour.

'George, you are hard.' Grace smiled at her brother. 'What if you saw our dear mama only once a month? You would not be able to be torn from her that long.'

'Maybe not my mother, but in the case of my father, a month would soon fly. In fact, a visit every six months would be too often, given his current ill temper.' George knew that his father and he would never see eye to eye and, quite frankly, he was ashamed of the bluff northerner.

'George, he only does what he thinks is best for you. Now, enough of our family. We are here to enjoy tea and not bring a mood into the house.' Grace walked into the highly decorated parlour and held her hands out to Victoria. 'I swear, Victoria, you get prettier by the minute. Just look at you, in that beautiful green dress, a perfect picture.' Grace kissed Victoria and turned to look at her brother. 'What do you think, George? Is she not a perfect picture?'

'Indeed she is, sister. Miss Wild is a delight to the eye.' George took Victoria's hand, kissed it, then smiled at her with a knowing twinkle in his eye.

Victoria blushed again, trying not to make eye contact with the charming George.

Eliza hesitated in the parlour doorway, and glanced towards the stairs. Mary-Anne, hiding on the landing, was listening to every, word said by the visitors.

'I take it that the dress is one of your aunt's creations, Victoria? She knows just how to make the most of a girl's colouring. I marvel at her skills,' Grace said as Eliza joined her visitors.

'You think too highly of me, Grace. Victoria is a perfect model, anything would suit her.' Eliza looked across at Victoria and smiled. 'Victoria, dear, would you be good enough to make the tea and serve it to us all?'

'Of course, Aunt.' Victoria rose from her seat.

'May I help you, Miss Wild?' George stood up, smiling at the sweet girl whose clear worship of him was amusing.

'I can manage, thank you, George. Everything is laid out, I've just to brew the tea and serve it. But thank you for your offer.' Victoria quickly made her way out of the parlour, thankful to get away from George's teasing, but craving it as well.

Mary-Anne leaned over the banister and caught Victoria's attention as she closed the parlour door behind her. 'Is that Grace Ellershaw that's in there?' she whispered.

'Yes, Mama, and her brother George. Are you coming down to meet them? I'm sure they would like to make your acquaintance.'

'No, no, I don't want to have any part of their lives. George, her brother, you say. He was only young when I left. He sounds like his father, God help him.'

Mary-Anne gathered her thoughts quickly. So, the youngest Ellershaw lad was of marriageable age. He'd be a good catch for someone as long as he wasn't too much like his old man. From what she'd overheard he was friendly with Victoria, something that really should not be encouraged, after all, he was her half-brother. Though perhaps it was a relationship that could be profitable to her daughter, something to encourage – a way, perhaps, of getting back some of the things that Edmund Ellershaw, her daughter's father, owed her. She leaned over the banister once more. 'Victoria,' she whispered.

'Yes, Mama?'

'Young George seems sweet on you. Don't encourage him too much, but a friendship between you both would not go amiss.'

Mary-Anne stepped back from the banister and went to lie on her bed in the spare room, her head full of ideas of how to claim some of the Ellershaw's wealth for herself and Victoria. She had never forgotten how she had felt when she had realised that she was with child, feeling worthless and dirty after being ravished by Edmund Ellershaw. Aye, she would encourage the friendship with George. Victoria was too young to be in any danger of giving her heart or anything else to him, but she'd encourage her to take gladly anything else that he offered her. After all, Victoria was his father's child, part of their home, and the colliery was hers by right; it was only fair that she benefitted from their relationship.

Mary-Anne closed her eyes and thought of what she had left behind in America. Of John, and her employers, who had trusted and loved her. Even though her hatred of Edmund Ellershaw had grown with every year away, she had kept it to

71

herself. Now it was time to put her thoughts into action and make him responsible for his daughter one way or another. She closed her eyes and listened to the light-hearted laughter from the parlour below. To think that her sister was entertaining the bastard's family – that she would never have foreseen. Her eyes grew heavy and her thoughts drifted off as the trauma of the last few weeks' travelling caught up with her, sleep calling her back from her dark thoughts of revenge.

'Ah, a Victoria sandwich cake, named after our glorious Queen and yourself, my dear Miss Wild.' George smiled before biting into the light sponge, trying to catch the crumbs that dropped onto the delicate china plate.

'I must admit, it is a marvellous recipe that our Queen has given her name to. It is now being made in all the houses of distinction. But it is also one that should be affordable to most budgets, so Cook assures me.' Grace Ellershaw ate her slice delicately and smiled at Victoria. 'How are your piano lessons progressing, Victoria? Your aunt tells me that you have a natural ear for music.'

'I am enjoying them greatly, Miss Grace. Mr Wilson tells me I show great promise.' Victoria glanced at her aunt. She hoped that she had not sounded too conceited.

'Perhaps you could entertain us with a tune, Victoria? Something light and soothing, suitable for a Sunday afternoon.' Eliza smiled at her niece, hoping that she would impress her guests with her mastery of the keyboard. Even with their improved circumstances, she had scrimped and saved to afford to buy a second-hand piano for the parlour.

Victoria blushed. 'Oh, Aunt Eliza. I'm sure that Miss Grace and Master George would not want to hear my attempts at a tune.'

'Nonsense, my dear Miss Wild, come, entertain us, and perhaps you will let me join you in a duet. I too have a love of the piano, although I am sure I will not be as proficient as yourself. Or perhaps I could accompany you by singing. Do you have the music for "Home Sweet Home"? I do believe it is loved dearly by our Queen and I know the words by heart.' George walked over to the pile of song sheets that lay on top of the piano.

'We do. Aunt Eliza likes me to play that too. It's by John Howard Payne,' Victoria said excitedly. 'Did you know that, George?'

George smiled indulgently at the little girl as she came over to the piano and they found the piece.

'Here it is, Miss Wild. Why then, you'll play and I'll sing. Are you in agreement, ladies?' George looked triumphant as Victoria sat down and turned to the first page of music.

'Indeed, that would be most entertaining, the perfect Sunday pastime.' Grace crossed her hands and turned to watch the pair perform while Eliza sipped her tea.

George stood tall and proud as Victoria struck the first chord. His voice echoed around Aireville Mansions:

Mid pleasures and palaces though we may roam
Be it ever so humble, there's no place like home.

A charm from the skies seems to hallow us there
Which seek thro' the world, is ne'er met elsewhere
Home! Home!
Sweet, sweet home!
There's no place like home
There's no place like home!
An exile from home splendour dazzles in vain
Oh give me my lowly thatched cottage again
The birds sing gaily that came at my call
And gave me the peace of mind dearer than all
Home, home, sweet, sweet home.
There's no place like home,
* there's no place like home!*

'Wonderful, wonderful, you sounded wonderful together. Didn't the piece suit them well, Eliza? It's as if they were made to perform together.' Grace clapped her hands, her face beaming in admiration.

'Indeed so, Grace.' The young couple would have been ideal suitors once Victoria was of age, if it were not for the fact that Eliza knew they could never be so. 'But the last thing I would want Victoria to do is to work on the stage.' Eliza's voice fell to a whisper. 'Plus I think George is expected to do much more with his life.'

'Oh, I didn't mean on the stage. No, that would never do especially for George. I just meant they are very sweet together. I never expected my brother to have such a knack with children but with your Victoria he does.'

'He's very kind,' Eliza said carefully.

'George has to marry well and carry on the family line, given neither my older brother or I are likely to. He can't marry beneath him.' Grace continued before misreading the look of concern on her friend's face. 'Oh, I'm sorry, Eliza, I don't mean to be rude. It's not that Victoria is not perfectly well educated and she has all the charm any man would be proud of in a wife.' Grace spoke quietly as she watched her brother and Victoria go through the sheet music together. 'You should be pleased that he likes her, and that he spends time with her, she will benefit from his friendship, but he really regards her as his pet. Do you not wish for them both to be happy in one another's company?'

'Indeed I do, but Victoria is only twelve, and she is young and impressionable.' Eliza smiled at her friend and business partner, slightly resentful that she had described Victoria as George's pet.

'Well, let's be content that they are friends for now. Perhaps as Victoria grows older she will realise that friends it will always be with George, and nothing more.' Grace sipped her tea and smiled across at Eliza, who looked less than enthralled in George's interest in Victoria. Did she not know that in the next few months, George would inherit thousands and be one of the wealthiest men in the district? She should be thankful that he even acknowledged Victoria Wild, coming from the differing backgrounds that they did.

Chapter 9

'What are you going to be doing today, Mary-Anne, while I am at work?'

Eliza looked across at her sister while she tucked into the toast that her maid had placed in front of her for breakfast.

'I thought that I'd spend the day with Victoria, get to know her a little better.' Mary-Anne looked up from her plate and smiled at her daughter as she delicately ate her toast.

'I'm afraid Victoria's tutor will be calling just after nine. She takes French and German on a Monday, ready for the day when she is old enough to join the business fully. She will need it to talk to the fashion houses in Paris. At the moment, I'd be lost without Grace's knowledge of the language, so I thought it beneficial for Victoria to learn.' It was at moments like these that Eliza was really conscious of how different her and Mary-Anne's upbringing had been from Victoria's.

'French! We hate the French. Grandfather will be turning in his grave. He wasted his best years fighting against the French and Napoleon. Why does she have to learn their language? They should talk English if they need your clothes, and as for German, well. What can I say?' Mary-Anne couldn't believe what she was hearing. 'Bloody hell, we had a hard enough time getting any schooling in our own language – and you and I were already working at her age! Bloody privileged is what you are, girl! French, well, I've heard it all now.'

'I've ensured she has had the best education I can afford, to prepare for a better life than we ever had a chance of, Mary-Anne. When you left, Victoria was my reason for living, she gave me hope when you abandoned us both to wander off to America with John Vasey. It wasn't easy at times but we made it through – so don't you scoff at my indulgence of bringing her up as a lady.'

Eliza felt her face flush with anger. How could her sister be so ungrateful that she'd ensured her daughter had a good education? She and Mary-Anne had had to live on their wits, hand to mouth, hoping they had enough money to keep them fed. Eliza had never forgotten that. She was determined that Victoria would have the best life possible.

'I'm sorry, I know I owe you a lot. Forgive me, Eliza, it was more amusement at the thought of my daughter speaking languages. What with that and piano lessons, I can see I have a lady in the making.' Mary-Anne glanced at Victoria, who had said nothing as her mother and aunt fought over her.

'She enjoys her piano lessons too. Don't you, Victoria?' Eliza looked at Victoria for reassurance.

'I do. I enjoy music and French, and German. I know that Aunt Eliza has brought me up to be a lady, for which I am grateful. However, I have not forgotten who I am and that our roots are humble.' Victoria tried to hide how hurt she felt at her mother making fun of her education.

'Good, and you should use it all to your advantage. What with that and inheriting your mother's good looks, no wonder that George is so smitten with you. He knows what a beauty you will be once you are fully grown. Take him for what you can, girl, that family owes us a lot.' Mary-Anne noticed the black look on Eliza's face.

'I've told her to keep him at arm's length and not to encourage him. She's too young and he's not for her.' Eliza growled. 'It's best that way.'

'Nonsense, they can be friends. Enjoy one another's company and enjoy his money, if Victoria has any sense.' Mary-Anne grinned across at her daughter and noticed the flush on her cheeks. 'Just make sure he keeps his dick in his pocket.'

'Mary-Anne, there is no need to speak so crudely. Victoria, go into the parlour and make ready for your teacher.' Eliza scowled across at her sister who was sorely testing her patience with her ways.

'Yes, Aunt. Excuse me, Mother, I must prepare for my tutor.' Victoria rose from the table, closing the door upon the frostiness between sisters.

'Really, Mary-Anne, I'm trying to raise her as a lady and you come back with your foul mouth and scheming ways and everything is turned on its head.'

'Scheming ways, is it? Then how did you get Grace Ellershaw's money, then? I suppose she just said one day, "Here, you look like a worthy cause, please run my shop in the centre of Leeds and make a good living for doing nothing." She helped you get this house too, didn't she? You forget, Eliza, it was John and I who made you, when he risked his job, stealing material for you to impress Grace and her followers. While I'm grateful that you have brought Victoria up so well, it is time for her to inherit some of her father's brass, whether you like it or not. Grace may have served you well, but now it is her father's time to pay for his behaviour to myself and our mother. I haven't forgotten the pain of the past and I've not been able to bury myself in all things grand and elegant. Victoria should have some Ellershaw money and I'm going to see that she gets it by fair means or foul.' Mary-Anne put her head in her hands and sighed.

'Leave Victoria out of your schemes – stop encouraging her with George. She'll grow out of her affection for him and I'm sure he's just indulging her. And even if he is interested in her enough to overlook who her mother is, think of who her father is! You know they cannot be together when she is of age. They cannot fall in love, they are brother and sister!' Eliza stood up from her chair and went to look out of the window, not liking her sister's dark plans.

'I will tell her before it is too late. She need not know until we have secured some of his fortune. For all George's education and fine ways he will probably have his father's traits, which he will soon make Victoria aware of. Let her see just how much she can receive from him as her so-called friend.' Mary-Anne stood beside her sister and placed her hand on Eliza's arm. 'Trust me: like you I only want the best for her and this way she will get part of what her father owes her.'

'It is a dangerous game you play, Mary-Anne

79

Wild. Hearts will be broken, one of which may be yours if you lose the love of your daughter through your lust for money and vengeance.' Eliza looked at her sister. 'I've tried to forget the past but it is always in the back of my mind, reminding me of how much we both went through with the death of our mother. For that and that alone, I will go along with your hare-brained scheme but if you hurt that girl...'

'I promise I won't,' her sister assured her, hugging her deeply. Eliza sighed, realising that for all her years away, Mary-Anne had not changed.

'It's good to have you home, but I'd forgotten how crafty and cunning you were. I can't say I missed the way you plot and scheme, though maybe my life has been a little dull without you in it.'

'Dull? We must do something about that, but I'm acting only through desperation. Mentioning which, I will take a walk into Leeds and see Aunt Patsy and Uncle Mick. I suppose they still live in that terrible yard. Does Ma Fletcher still do the market up Briggate? I'll show my face to her as well.'

'I don't know where Aunty Patsy lives now. I washed my hands of her after you left. We ... we had words.' Eliza sighed. 'I still think she was partly responsible for our mother's death and she would have got rid of Victoria if you had let her.'

Mary-Anne gasped. 'How could you do that? She was always there for us both.'

'She was, but did you write to her after you ran off to America? I bet not. Especially after she was so keen for you to leave Victoria on the workhouse steps. So don't you lecture me! She did offer to help with Victoria when she was first born, but then Pounders Court got flooded when a drain burst and that was when Mick and she disappeared back to Ireland with no by-your-leave, and I've not heard of them since. As for Ma Fletcher, you won't find her in Briggate. Her husband died the other year and she is infirm, living in her home at Hyde Park Corner. You know where I mean, don't you, just off Headingley Lane in the better part of Leeds? You wouldn't think she could afford to live there, she never seemed to have a penny to her name. It just shows that looks can be deceiving.'

'I know where you mean. That's a bit of a walk, right over on the outskirts of Leeds, but it doesn't surprise me that the old girl is worth a bob or two, she always did watch every penny. I'll hunt her down first, she may have kept in touch with Aunt Patsy. You shouldn't be so hard on Patsy, you know, she only did what she thought was best. She's had a hard life like our mother. And Ma would not have wanted us to wash our hands of her or Mick. Blood is thicker than water, you should remember that when you are mixing with your new-found friends. You've changed, Eliza. Family was always precious to you.' Mary-Anne watched her sister's face cloud over.

'I've had to, to survive,' Eliza snapped. 'And family is precious to me. Everything I've done, I've done for Victoria – to ensure that she and I had a better life and I don't think I've done too badly. Better than you, Mary-Anne. You are back where you started. We would all be penniless and

81

homeless if it weren't for me.'

'At least I've seen the world, not just stayed here and sold my soul to the Ellershaws,' Mary-Anne snapped back.

'What choice did I have if I was to do right by Victoria? Besides, we have raised ourselves out of the gutter and are now quite respectable, don't you be doing anything to put us back there.' Eliza glared at her sister. Just who was she to pass judgement on how she had led her life?

'I'll not endanger your new life, so you needn't worry. But I will seek what is rightly mine and Victoria's, and make sure you are done right by too for looking after my girl all these years. Now, let us not squabble any more. The shop awaits you, and I will walk as we used to do, down the canalside into Leeds. I'll call in and visit your grand empire once I've visited Ma Fletcher. I did stand outside your impressive shop on my way here and was amazed at the display and to see the name of Ellershaw and Wild over the doorway. Will Grace be working with you there today? I don't want her to know of my presence here just yet. And I don't mean to sound ungrateful of how you've brought up my daughter. She is perfect in every way, and it is all thanks to you.' Mary-Anne put her hand on her sister's arm. 'I do love you, Eliza, and I'm sorry I left you with all my troubles. I aim to put that right now I am back home.'

'Just don't do anything rash, Mary-Anne. Victoria and I have a good life now. I still remember all our hurt caused by Edmund Ellershaw, and I hate him as much as you do. But I fear you'll not get much satisfaction from him – I've heard tell he's in debt. Grace seems to worry about him all the time, and George doesn't seem to have much time for him. I'm not expecting Grace to be in the shop today. She's doing the accounts at home. She insists that she keeps the books, but she mostly acts as a silent partner and leaves the everyday running of the shop to me. So you should have no fears of meeting her when you visit.' Eliza walked with her sister to the hallway as the maid bustled into the room to clear the breakfast table.

'When it comes to the Ellershaws, it is time for us to get what is ours now, sister, without hurting Victoria, of course, or Grace. She has always been good to both of us, which I never will forget.' Mary-Anne smiled. 'Now get yourself prepared for work and I will go on my way into Leeds, a journey I have done many a time in my mind as I walked the windy streets of New York. It was a cold, unwelcoming place if you had no brass. Nowhere wants you if you have no money. I should have stayed and been a mother to Victoria, instead of burdening you with her.' Mary-Anne reached for her shawl from the hall stand, checking her looks in the hall mirror.

'She was no burden, she made me fight for our survival and made me strong. We would still be living on Pit Lane if it had not been for Victoria's needs and the faith Grace Ellershaw had in me.' Eliza watched as her sister opened the front door. 'I'll see you later, dear sister. Despite everything, I'm glad that you are home safe and sound.'

Mary-Anne kissed her sister on her cheek and stepped out into the morning sunshine. 'I love you, Eliza, and I will be seeing you shortly.'

Eliza watched her sister walk down the cobbled street of Aireville Mansions. Her return had re-kindled old memories of bad times and their hatred for Edmund Ellershaw. Was Mary-Anne right? Was it was time he paid for what he had done? From what Grace had let slip, he was no longer the man he once was. She sensed Mary-Anne would not be steered away from her plans. The easiest thing to do would be to assist her, as long as Victoria and her happiness was not jeo-pardised. Whatever happened, Victoria had to be protected from the truth.

Mary-Anne made her way down the canalside, wishing that she had borrowed a heavier shawl from Eliza as she shivered in the frosty late March morning. How she had missed this part of the world. She smiled as she remembered all the times Eliza and she had walked down this very towpath, chattering and hoping that Ma Fletcher had some good buys awaiting them, and sharing dreams. Those dreams had disappeared just like the frost on the delicate spiderwebs that adorned the canalside disappeared when the sun rose to its full height. Eliza had done well enough for herself, now it was her turn to make her fortune and repay her debt to her sister by setting a trap just like the hard-working spider.

Chapter 10

Mary-Anne made her way past the loading bays on the quayside of the canal. Little had altered in the twelve years she had been away. Barges and Tom Puddings were being unloaded as the canal and dock workers went about their jobs. Prostitutes tried their luck for passing trade, giving cheek back when their advances were spurned by respectable men.

She was grinning at one of the barge handlers who was staring at her as she made her way along the dockside, when she stopped in her tracks. Coming out of one of the whorehouses along the canal was a man that she had not wanted to see that morning. She knew instantly it was him. He had the same build and he still wore the same style of coat he had worn over twelve years ago, and the type of establishment he was vacating told her that her eyes did not deceive her. Twelve years of worry and hatred welled up inside of her as she watched him walking towards her. Edmund Ellershaw was still up to his old tricks! Mary-Anne felt sick. His head was down and he was looking at his pocket watch, so he had not seen her yet. Should she take flight or should she confront him? Instinct told her she should do the former, but she knew when he lifted his head up and spotted her that she was going to have to take courage and say what she had needed to say for over twelve years.

'So, you recognise me, do you?' Mary-Anne looked at the ageing mine owner. The years had not been kind to him.

'No. Why? Should I?' Edmund recognised Mary-Anne straight away – he would always remember her – but he wasn't going to give her the satisfaction of knowing that he did.

'You know damn well why you should! I'm Mary-Anne Wild,' she said with quiet determination, 'I'm the mother of your daughter, a daughter that has never seen a penny from you. Well, I will make it my job to ensure that some of the Ellershaw money will be hers.' Mary-Anne felt her legs go weak as she watched Edmund Ellershaw's face turn purple with rage.

'Leave me be, you common whore. Take your tall tales back to the brothel where you belong! I don't know you and I don't owe you a penny.' Edmund knocked her out of his way. 'I'll call the Peelers if you are not careful.'

The dock workers were watching the argument between them, and a prostitute from the whorehouse shouted, 'Give her some money you dirty old bastard. I bet you owe her it.'

Mary-Anne looked at his back as he walked away from her. Now was not the time or place to tackle him further. He would call the police and she couldn't afford for them to be involved. There was still a chance the crimes she committed in order to escape New York would catch up with her. 'You will pay one way or another, I'll make sure of that,' she yelled as she watched him making his way out of the canal basin.

Mary-Anne stood for a second to calm herself

86

down and regain her dignity. If nothing else, it would have given him a shock to have seen her and for him to know that her business with him was not yet finished. She wasn't about to let him get off his dirty deeds lightly. He'd be held accountable for his repulsive actions one way or another, she'd see to that.

She smiled at the prostitute who'd wished her luck before walking along The Calls. The newly built Corn Exchange with its round domed top stood proud and glistening white in the spring sunshine. So, she thought, it had finally been built for all the grain traders, they would welcome somewhere grand for them to do business. She decided to forget her run-in with Edmund Ellershaw and enjoy her day in Leeds, a town that she had missed so much.

She made her way along Lower Briggate, smiling as she watched pedlars and stall holders going about their trade. She had missed the banter and the Yorkshire accents that she had known all her life. She stood for a minute in the place where Ma Fletcher once had her stall. Where the old woman had once traded was an organ grinder and his monkey, the monkey making people laugh with its trick. It was dressed in a little natty jacket and clapping its hands as people placed coins in the cap that it had been trained to carry around the admiring crowds. It chattered as the old man played his tunes, putting its cap back on its head and going to sit back on its owner's shoulder once he had finished. It was a novelty, something to brighten a cold winter's day; a monkey was a rarity on the streets of Leeds, unlike along the docksides of Liverpool where sailors often had them on their shoulders as companions and pets on their long sea-faring journeys.

The smell of roasting chestnuts filled the air as she passed a brazier, red with glowing embers and made her mouth water, even though Eliza had fed her well at breakfast time. At the top of Briggate, she dodged past workmen as they toiled on the new shopping arcade. Thornton's Arcade, the posters on the hoardings proclaimed, named after the hostelry owner at the White Swan and theatre. She smiled, remembering lying to the salesman about her acting and singing abilities. The poor devil had been so easy to deceive. The hoardings promised lots of individual small shops along the glass-covered arcade connecting Briggate and Lands Lane. No doubt that it would attract the more genteel shopper – a stroll under glass without getting wet would be of great appeal to the more refined. No care had been given to the families that had once inhabited the rat run of squalid housing that the arcade was replacing and Mary-Anne couldn't help but wonder where they were now. Leeds was definitely thriving, but the poor would be brushed to one side, forgotten about by the great and the mighty.

She turned along The Headrow, quickly making her way out to the quieter part of Leeds, past the grassland known as Woodhouse Moor which hid the reservoir. Then she turned onto Hyde Park Road, where the middle class of Leeds lived, and where, just as in London, people of Leeds were allowed to gather and voice their concerns, whether it be with the government or just life itself.

Mary-Anne found the house where Ma Fletcher lived, according to Eliza. It was a double-fronted terraced house built in Yorkshire stone with iron railings enclosing the small piece of garden in front of it. She had been impressed with Eliza's new home but this was something else entirely, although it had clearly seen better days. The lintel above the door read 1769, and the windows were made of small panes of glass that looked in need of cleaning. Behind them, the curtains were pulled.

Mary-Anne walked up the stone-slabbed path and knocked hard on the claret-coloured door that was cracked and peeling. She waited, and when nobody came to open the door to her, she knocked again. Recalling that Eliza had told her Ma Fletcher was infirm, she opened the door slightly and let light into the dismal room.

From behind a high back chair, a voice yelled, 'Piss off. I'll let my dog on you. He's a vicious devil, likes to bite shins, so he does,' Ma Fletcher shouted. 'And I've got a cudgel and I'm not afraid of using it.'

'Mrs Fletcher, it's me, Mary-Anne Wild. I've come to see you.' Mary-Anne stood in the doorway and let her eyes get used to the gloom that filled the darkened room. There was a strange smell too.

'Nay, it can't be. She buggered off to America with an Irishman. You don't sound owt like her. Now bugger off.'

'It is, it is me, I'm back. I've come home and am staying with Eliza.' Mary-Anne walked gingerly over to the chair where she knew Ma Fletcher was sat, expecting a vicious dog to be set on her at any moment. She stood at the side of the old woman with a cat curled up on her knee and smiled. 'It's all right. You can call that wild dog on your knee to heel, he'll not be needed today.'

'Aye, lass, it is you, I thought it was them buggers from out of Woodhouse Street. They come in and plague me for entertainment, knowing there is nowt I can do to stop them. Aye, you are a sight for sore eyes, Mary-Anne. I thought I'd never see you again, lass.'

'I'm surprised you can see me in this gloom. Do you not want the curtains opened? It's not a bad day out there.' Mary-Anne was shaken to see the frail old lady. Age had clearly caught up with the robust woman that once stood in the market on Briggate.

'Aye, you can do that, seeing you are visiting. I don't bother pulling them much, it's such an effort to stand on these old legs of mine and folk only gawp in when they are drawn, thinking nobody lives here. I'm in a bit of state, lass; the cold and rain over the years have given me pain in these old limbs of mine, it's nowt getting old.' Ma Fletcher screwed her eyes tight as light filled the room, and dust from the heavy velvet curtains danced in the beams of light.

Mary-Anne pulled up a chair next to the old woman. 'You've not even got your fire lit. You must be frozen.' Mary-Anne reached for the old woman's hand and felt the cold in her bones as the cat on her knee spat at her, protecting its mistress.

'Mr Tibbs here keeps me warm and I've plenty of blankets and shawls.' Ma Fletcher stroked the

90

bad-tempered cat on her knee, which looked in as sorry a state as its mistress. 'Now, what brings you back to us? Had enough of wandering? I could have told you that there's only land, sea and sky wherever you go and that no matter how far you travel, your demons will always be there with you, reminding you why you are running from the past.' Mary-Anne was still a beautiful woman, Ma Fletcher thought. Age had only benefited her, and although by the looks of the clothes on her back she was doing well, she didn't miss her rough chapped hands that told the real tale.

'Things didn't work out, so I decided to come home. America isn't all it is cracked up to be.' Mary-Anne bent down and raked the cinders in the hearth, setting the fire with kindling from a nearby basket and gently adding coal lump by lump as the light from the match that she struck took hold of the kindling, bringing instant warmth and light to the room.

'And your man, did he wed you? Was he all you thought he'd be? You must have loved him to leave that bairn behind, or was it that you were running from?' Ma Fletcher scrutinised Mary-Anne's face as she stood up and looked down at her. 'I hear she's growing into a pretty little thing, and that Eliza has made sure she wants for noth-ing. You have a lot to thank her for. Not many sisters would have done such a good job.'

'We lived as a married couple but we never got around to getting wed. I'm known now as Mary-Anne Vasey, I'm so used to using his name. I do still wear his ring, look.' Mary-Anne showed Ma Fletcher the thin band of gold that John had once lovingly given her on Liverpool docks. She knew that if it had been worth anything, John would have pawned it. 'I did love him, Ma, but he wasn't a worker. Too busy looking after other folk and fighting their corner, as well as me when he'd had a few drinks. As for Victoria, Eliza puts me to shame, she's been more of a mother to Eliza than I could ever be. Plus she's done well for herself.'

'And you've come home with nowt, despite the fancy clothes that you are dressed in.' Ma Fletcher could see through the glamour. 'Back to square one and, to make matters worse, your sister is in business with that Ellershaw lass. Now that will cause you hurt, if what I heard is true.' Ma Fletcher held her wizened hands out for Mary-Anne to hold.

'You hear too much, old woman.' Mary-Anne regarded the woman that had known her since she had taken her very first steps. She took the wrinkled hands in hers and noticed the kindness that shone in Ma Fletcher's eyes. 'I've just met Edmund Ellershaw down by the canal, but though I tried to confront him, I thought twice about causing a scene with him. How I long for him to recognise Victoria as his daughter.'

'Aye, I always thought that child of yours is Edmund Ellershaw's. He always was a bastard. He came from nowt and he is nowt. If he hadn't married that snooty wife of his he'd still be in the gutter, where he belongs. He ought to pay for his wanton ways.' Ma Fletcher pulled a face, dropped Mary-Anne's hands and pushed her cat from off her knee. 'So what are you going to do about it? It's time folk knew what he is truly like, him and his eldest son too, because he's not much better. He has a mistress, from what I hear, and treats his wife like an idiot.'

'You seem to know a lot for someone who is housebound. I hoped that William would not follow in his father's footsteps but it sounds like the hope was false. Poor Priscilla. She always was empty-headed and I knew he only married her for her position in society. I doubt he ever loved her. He once tried to take advantage of me, just after he'd announced his marriage plans. Like father, like son. That marriage was doomed to failure from the start.'

'He might be like his father, but he's got more brass than him, lass. If he's had eyes for you in the past, he most definitely will now. You've grown into a bonnier woman than you ever were. If you want to claim back something that Edmund Ellershaw owes you, make yourself known to William again. The father's pissed away his fortune – you'll get nowt there but more heartache. William might be the key. He'd have to be blind not to take notice of you, lass, and as Mary-Anne Vasey, he doesn't have to acknowledge you as the timid young Mary-Anne Wild that once tempted him before marriage. Tell him you've come back from the Americas wealthy, he doesn't need to know the truth until you wed him.'

'I don't think I could put up with his hands on me. I'd only think of his father doing the same and I ran away from all that.' It seemed that the cunning old woman hated the Ellershaws as much as her.

'Think of his brass, lass. Now, where are you

living at? With Eliza, I suppose? You'll need a roof of your own over your head if you are to carry out your plan. Why don't you come and live with me? All I ask is that you tend to my few needs. You can come and go as you please, I've enough brass to feed us both. It'll be better than being dependent on Eliza. I know you deserve a bit of luck in your life, so let me offer you my home to stay in for now. It's not a bad place – I know it looks like a hovel but it was grand once, just needs a good clean and a bit of care. Plenty of nice china and glass around the place, I love my pots. Now, what do you think to my idea? He's not a bad-looking man, that William. He owns half of Leeds these days. Did you know that his grandfather left most of his mills to him? Seems to me that's the way to go, my lass. Don't aim your bow and arrow at the father, aim it at his son, and make this old woman happy at the same time.'

Mary-Anne looked around the large neglected house. It was crammed with good china and glass all of which were in need of washing, dusting and putting tidy. Could she manage to look after her? Did she really want to be bound to the old woman, despite her generous offer?

'The Guild Ball will be held at the Guild Hall. You need to get yourself invited, make yourself known to William. Dress up and flaunt your beauty – that's what he likes. You have more brains than he will have ever known in his wife, he'll like that. Go on, lass, let's take him for what he's worth.' Ma Fletcher grinned, showing her rotten teeth to Mary-Anne.

'I couldn't. I aim to get even with his father, not

William, and I couldn't take advantage of your generosity. Why would you offer me your home to live in? It's of no consequence to you what I do with my life.'

'I have my own reasons to want to see Edmund Ellershaw suffer. One day, perhaps, I'll tell you. But for now don't look a gift horse in the mouth, Mary-Anne, because that's what I am, a gift! Besides, you and me we go way back, and you're down on your luck and could do with a helping hand.'

Mary-Anne sighed and looked around her. 'We will always be at the bottom of life's pile. There's not a lot we can do about it.'

'That's where you are wrong, lass. Look at me in this old place – bet you never thought I had two pennies to rub together. And look at your Eliza, she's crawling her way up life's ladder. But you can do just the same and I'll back you, just to get some satisfaction in my last years of life. People still tell me things – I can find out what you need to know to get revenge on the Ellershaws. This is the best chance you will ever get. Come and live with me, make eyes at his son, and cause that bastard Edmund some heartache for a change. Go on, go and have a look around the house, choose a bedroom to sleep in. I know it's a bit of a state but you will soon have it back to its past glory. I won't ask a lot of you, just a bit of company on a long evening and something to eat when we are both hungry. I'll not ask where you are going and who you are seeing, just as long as that Ellershaw family pay for the hurt they have caused us both. That'll be payment enough.' Ma

95

Fletcher closed her eyes and pulled her shawl around her, only to open her eyes again and give Mary-Anne her first orders. 'Go on, have a look around and then take that brass on the dresser and go to the Packhorse Inn on Woodhouse Lane. Benjamin Jubb, the landlord there, usually sends his lad with a bowl of broth for my dinner. Well, we will need two today, and you might as well get to know old Jubb, there isn't much he doesn't know about what folk are up to around here. He's been a good help since my old man passed away but only because he thinks he will have first dibs on my house after I've gone. He doesn't do owt for nowt, that one.'

Mary-Anne got up from her chair and added a few more lumps of coal to the fire. 'I'll take a look around and go for dinner and then I'll let you know what I think.'

The old woman had closed her eyes. Mary-Anne decided not to say anything more until dinner had been brought to her. Ma Fletcher was determined for her to stay, but did she really want to?

Mary-Anne walked from room to room in the large rambling house. Despite the dark, she could see with growing amazement that it was packed with the best quality furniture and pottery, the likes of which she had never seen before. The old woman was clearly worth a small fortune. Mary-Anne wandered around, opening the heavy draped curtains to let the light in. Layers of dust were on everything, but once washed and cleaned the house would reveal its true wealth. Mary-Anne sighed and looked out of the first bedroom window at the cobbled street below, a hundred thoughts running through her mind. Should she take up the offer of Ma Fletcher and come to live with her? Was she right to tell her to hunt down William, rather than seeking her revenge directly on Edmund Ellershaw? Her visit to the old woman had shown her a new path to get even with the Ellershaws, and now she was confused. Mary-Anne pulled her skirts up and tripped downstairs. Ma Fletcher was asleep in her chair, so she quietly took the few coppers on the dresser for her dinner.

She left the house and walked down to the end of Headingley Lane, making her way to the Packhorse Inn. She looked up at the squat square building with wooden shutters at its windows and a board in the centre of the upstairs windows depicting pack horses and their owners. Mary-Anne had never been inside before, but she knew that in years past it had had a reputation for its rough and ready drinkers. She hesitated for a second, then pushed open the heavy oak door and blinked as her eyes adjusted to the light within it. In the corner was a group of men playing dominoes and leaning on the bar were two women, their bodices cut low, revealing their best assets.

'Well, what can I do for you?' The landlord took in Mary-Anne's fine clothes, grinning as he did so at the two rough-looking women.

'Mrs Fletcher has sent me for her dinner. Can I have an extra bowl as I'll be eating with her today.'

'So she's been good enough to save my lad's legs today? Got you doing her dirty work for her, has she, the old crone? Tell her I'm still waiting for an answer to my offer for that house of hers and its contents, she'll not get a fairer offer and I'd look after her and all, make sure she wasn't on her own and had company.' Benjamin Jubb reached for two soup bowls and made his way to the open fire where a huge black pot was suspended over the fire's flames. The smell of simmering bones and veg filled the air and Mary-Anne watched in horror as he rubbed the edges of the soup bowl with the dirtiest cloth she had ever seen after he slopped the ladled soup over the sides.

'She don't want to be staying there on her own,' the landlord continued. 'You never know what could happen one dark night and then where would she be? Dead and nobody knowing anything was wrong. Best she sells to me and to be put where she belongs.'

Jubb passed the bowls to Mary-Anne and held out his hand for the money in payment.

'You mean you want to take advantage of her and rob her blind? Put her in the workhouse so that you can claim all? Well, you needn't worry about her any more. This will be the last broth we will be having from you. I'll be looking after Mrs Fletcher from now on as I'll be staying with her.' Mary-Anne placed the coppers into the scowling landlord's hand. 'I'll pass on your regards to her. Good day.' She balanced the two bowls of broth and pushed the inn's door open with her hip.

'You'll not last long, she's a cantankerous old bag. You'll see. She's had me running after her like an idiot, she owes me,' Benjamin Jubb yelled after her as she made her way down the street. 'The old bag will be begging for me to buy that house of hers when you've left her, and leave you will.'

Mary-Anne made her way to Ma Fletcher's, where she put the broth down on the table and pulled off her shawl.

'So you're back. What's that rogue Jubb got to say for himself? Is he still after my house? I might have lost my legs but I've not lost my marbles. A pitiful offer he made, and I know what he'd do with me once I'd signed my home away. There's some bread in the pantry and spoons are in the kitchen table drawer.' Ma Fletcher looked up at Mary-Anne. 'Happen he's helped make your mind up for you.'

'I don't think he's a good man, you want to be careful.' Mary-Anne put some more coal on the fire and then placed a little table between Ma Fletcher and her chair before putting the broth and bread on the table in front of them. 'I don't like the way he spoke to me. I always thought that the Packhorse was a rough place, but I know it is now.'

Ma Fletcher sipped her broth slowly with trembling hands, dunking her bread in and slurping it up. 'I know the likes of Jubb. You've got to use him as much as he uses you. Have you decided then, are you coming to live with me? You can bring your lass if you want to.'

'It's the best offer I've had since I came back. I don't want to be under my sister's feet, her world has changed since I left. I'll leave Victoria at Aireville Mansions as well. Eliza has been more of a mother to her than I've ever been. Besides, I'm going to be busy for the next few weeks, making sure your home is back up to scratch and then I'll look at making my acquaintance once again with William Ellershaw, because as you say he is the one with the money. It will give Edmund something to worry about. Along with Eliza and Victoria being friendly with Grace and his youngest son, he'll think his world is going to the dogs.'

'Yes, I heard tell your Victoria was sweet on George. You want to watch that.'

'She's too young for him to be a bother,' Mary-Anne reassured her. 'Besides, he seems to treat her like a pet monkey more than anything. Whereas William and I, well, that is a different matter.' Mary-Anne looked up from her broth and grinned.

'Good lass. I knew you'd see the sense in it. You take the bedroom at the front, it's the best one. It'll need airing but it gets all the morning sun.' Ma Fletcher sat back and sighed. 'I sleep down here these days so you don't have to worry about taking my room. And between us, we'll sort out the Ellershaws. That bloody Judd can whistle for my house, I'll be looked after now.'

'Well, if he's anything like his broth, he hasn't much substance. It tastes more like washing-up water than beef broth. I'll move in tomorrow but right this minute I'm going to get away. I was going to call in and see Aunt Patsy and Uncle Mick but Eliza told me that they have gone to Ireland.'

'Aye, they moved, lass. Mick had enough of the gossips and the filth. The Borough Council is about to pull them slums down, they've had enough of the complaints made about the stench coming up the sewers from Pounders Court.' Ma

100

Fletcher looked at the sadness that clouded Mary-Anne's face. 'She'll be better over in Ireland, the grass is always green over there and Mick will look after her.'

Mary-Anne sighed. 'Uncle Mick is a good enough bloke but he can't look after himself, let alone Aunt Patsy. I thought she would at least have given Eliza their address before they left or let her know when they had got settled.'

'Had a row, did they? Aye, well, there is nothing stranger than families, you should know that. I'll see you in the morning, then. Just bank the fire up and then it will nearly last me the rest of the day.' Ma Fletcher pointed at the coal scuttle and Mary-Anne put a good helping of coal on the fire. 'You'll not regret your decision. We are like peas in a pod, me and you. Play your cards right, lass, and maybe I'll leave you something in my will. Though if you play that that William Ellershaw right, you might not need it. And don't you feel sorry for that wife of his, he's already made her half-mad. She was too weak for him, not like you. You know what you want now. America might not have been good to you but it certainly has toughened you up. Now, make sure you go and get it, you know what is yours and I will stand by you no matter what.' Ma Fletcher sat back in her chair and watched as Mary-Anne took the bowls away and moved the small table back to its place. 'It's time to make folk take notice and realise that the Ellershaws are nothing but a bad stench in the air.'

Mary-Anne said her goodbyes to Ma Fletcher and closed the door behind her. She was curious to learn why Ma hated the family as much as she did, but she could wait for the answer. In the meantime, that hate would unite them in a common purpose and drive them onwards to change both their lives.

Chapter 11

Mary-Anne stood outside the doorway of her sister's shop and looked at the window display. The windows were filled with the finest of clothes, displayed beautifully on mannequins that must have cost a small fortune to buy. Hats with feathers and flowers of all colours adorned their heads, while matching velvet gloves were on their wooden hands. It truly was the most tempting shop window for the fashionable ladies of Leeds. Eliza had come a long way from the dirty little lean-to that used to be their workplace in Woodlesford, the only legacy their father had left them.

This grand place was owned by Grace Ellershaw, with Eliza's name over the doorway announcing that she was the designer and seamstress and also acknowledging that she now owned a small part of the business, but Eliza had not progressed all that far, Mary-Anne thought, apart from becoming known for her designs and getting a regular income from Grace Ellershaw. After all, Grace was still in charge.

Mary-Anne checked her reflection in the shop's window and plucked up the courage to enter the wonderful emporium.

'Good afternoon, madam, may I be of assistance?' A pretty blonde-haired girl pounced, smiling politely as she looked her latest customer up and down, deciding what the tall, beautiful auburn-haired woman in front of her could be tempted to buy.

'I'd like to see Miss Wild, if I may?'

'Certainly, madam, but she might be busy. Would you like to make an appointment or if you have a specific request I might be able to help you?' A dry smile came over her face, a smile that Mary-Anne suspected she'd used plenty of times in order to deter customers.

'It is of a personal nature that I need to see Eliza – Miss Wild. She knows that I am calling in on her this afternoon.' The young girl's smile faltered but she urged her to follow her through the shop. Mary-Anne walked tall, her long black coat and laced-up high-heel boots giving her the graceful look of a much younger woman as she climbed the stairs to Eliza's inner sanctum. Below her on the shop floor were ladies looking through the latest materials, adornments and perfumes, helped by numerous staff that had all been trained on how to pamper the most difficult of customers.

Her guide knocked on the oak door of Eliza's fitting room and office, 'There's a lady here to see you, ma'am. She says you are expecting her.' The young girl stepped to one side and let Mary-Anne sweep past her.

'Mary-Anne, you came! Well, what do you think? Go on, tell me. It's a lot different from when we worked together.'

Mary-Anne sat herself in a chair and grinned at

103

her sister. The shop girl, realising that the visitor was expected, made herself scarce. 'Bloody hell, Eliza, talk about grand! I didn't think I was going to get to see you, with the guard dog in place looking after you.'

'That's just Lizzie. She makes sure I'm not disturbed by some of the empty-headed women with nothing else better to do than saying they have spoken to me and had a personal fitting even though they don't intend buying anything. But what do you think of the shop, isn't it everything we ever dreamed of?' Eliza looked at her sister who was clearly taking note of all the materials, lace and cotton stacked on the shelves of the upstairs office.

'Well, you've certainly landed on your feet. I'm beginning to wonder why I disappeared to America when I could perhaps have been part of all this.' Mary-Anne gave her sister a smile, hiding her true feelings about her living in Grace Ellershaw's pocket.

'It's taken time and patience to get as well known and as well respected as this, and I couldn't have done any of it without Grace. Without her I'd be back in the gutter.'

'If I hadn't just left Ma Fletcher's I would be well and truly jealous, but as it stands, I've found a backer of my own. We've both got to make the best of what we have got and I aim to do that, now I have the old girl on my side.' Mary-Anne grinned at her sister.

'Why, what are you on about, Mary-Anne? I know that look on your face, you are scheming again!'

'Me? I'd never do anything like that. Ma Fletcher, bless her, has said as long as I look after her I can have the run of her home. So, I'm moving in with her in the morning.'

'What about Victoria, is she to go with you?' Eliza's face couldn't help but betray her emotions. 'Have you thought about her?'

'When it comes to Victoria, I think she will be better staying with you. She's been brought up more of a lady than I could ever have raised her. She'd be broken-hearted to leave you.' Mary-Anne smiled at her sister's obvious relief.

'But why is Ma Fletcher being so kind? She never used to be. And why should she offer all that on a plate to you? We are nothing to her.'

'She's desperate for someone to care for her and ... let's just say we have a lot in common. Besides, I've got plans that won't involve Victoria and I don't want her being under my feet.'

'You've not changed, have you? Always thinking of yourself. In fact, I think you are worse. You flit into Victoria's life, expecting her to treat you with love and kindness, and then, days later, you desert her. The poor girl will not know how to feel. How am I to explain that you are leaving her behind again?'

'It's because of Victoria that I am doing this. I need something behind me if I am ever to be able to support her and be a proper mother to her. Ma Fletcher is giving me that chance and I'm going to take it. Everyone might remember her as an old, dirty market trader, but her house alone is worth a small fortune and her support will enable me to make myself known once more to William

Ellershaw. William was once attracted to me, perhaps he will be again and from what I hear, he is the one with money and power. I'll admit I was wrong to encourage Victoria's friendship with George Ellershaw. I looked at his fondness for Victoria as a way to seek revenge. But now I have realised that I couldn't abide my sweet Victoria ending up broken-hearted. When the right time comes, I will tell her who her true father is and why she cannot be anything more than friends with George.' Mary-Anne folded her hands and looked at her sister.

'You can't do that to yourself. William Ellershaw is married. He moves in high society, even Grace has very little to do with him now he has inherited most of his grandfather's mills. Everyone knows that he's almost as bad as his father – Grace suspects he has a mistress for his pleasure. Don't even think of going near him, Mary-Anne. Just look after Ma Fletcher, keep your head down and make the most of your life. And if you must tell Victoria who her father is, tell her sooner rather than later. She already idolises George and I can see a heartache afoot.'

'But don't you see it is William who is the weak one in the Ellershaw family? That empty-headed Priscilla should never have been his wife. It was his grandfather who made him marry her. I remember when he had eyes for me and, well, perhaps he still has.' Mary-Anne grinned. 'And now he has money, a lot of money, and it would cause no end of pain to his bastard of a father if he was to court me.'

'Oh, Mary-Anne, you weave a web full of hurt

and deceit. I think your years away from home have made you brood over things that you should accept and move on from.'

Mary-Anne stood up. 'Easy for you to say when it wasn't you he took advantage of. And have you forgotten what our mother endured at Edmund Ellershaw's hands? How I found her dying in the privy because of him? Perhaps all of these fine trappings have helped you to forget.'

'I've forgotten none of that. Like you, I can never forgive him.' Eliza looked up at her sister. 'But I'm my own woman now. I don't need to feel bitter.'

'You are Grace Ellershaw's pet, just like Victoria is George's, and well you know it! Don't forget that you lost Tom Thackeray too. He was the love of your life, still is, I presume, seeing you have never married. Does he still live round here? Did he ever marry? Is his mother alive?'

Eliza fought back tears. 'I am not Grace's pet, she respects me. No, Tom didn't marry, and his mother died quite recently, I heard. He still works at the Rose Pit, he's the manager there. He's quite a voice in the local community often giving talks about social reform and bad working practices. I think if he had his way, The Rose would be an altogether different pit.' Eliza blew her nose into her handkerchief and managed a weak smile.

'Well, if you're moving on, you aim your sights at Tom Thackeray and I'll make William Ellershaw my business. Together, we might yet end up rich.'

Mary-Anne stopped talking as the office door opened.

'Oh! I'm sorry, I didn't realise that you had a customer with you, Eliza.' Grace Ellershaw hesitated in the doorway as she took in the well-dressed woman deep in conversation with her business partner.

'Please, don't apologise, it is I who is taking up my sister's precious time and I should really be on my way.' Mary-Anne smiled at Grace Ellershaw. She had hardly changed since the day she had set sail for America, a few grey hairs around her temple being the only sign of the passing years.

'Your sister! Yes, of course, I can see now, it's Mary-Anne, isn't it? Goodness, it's been a long time. When did you return? Eliza never told me of your arrival.' Grace shot Eliza a questioning look and then turned to look at Mary-Anne more closely.

'I only arrived a short time ago and I am just catching up with my sister before moving into my new home on Hyde Park Corner. I've been lucky enough to purchase a residency there.' Mary-Anne smiled.

'It sounds as if America has been kind to you and you look so youthful and elegant. It would be a delight for us to be of assistance to you if you were in need of our services as dressmakers, Miss Wild.'

'Please, it is Mary-Anne, Mary-Anne Vasey, nowadays. I married while I was over in America.' Mary-Anne looked Grace up and down and then smiled at her sister, hoping that she would not contradict what she was about to say. 'I'm afraid I came back without giving Eliza any warning of my arrival. You see, my husband died suddenly and I just felt the need to come back to my family.'

'Oh, my condolences, Mrs Vasey, it must be a terrible loss for you. Especially seeing that you are still so young.' Grace Ellershaw patted Mary-Anne's hand gently. 'If there is anything I can do, please let me know.'

'Thank you, Miss Ellershaw, but I think you have done enough for our family. I am impressed at the business that you have set up with my sister. She has come a long way from the little shack that we both had in Woodlesford. We both have.'

'I couldn't have done it without Eliza. I might have had the money, but she had the skills, determination and excellent fashion sense. This business is as much hers as mine. I just keep the books in order, which is why I am here. I seem to have misplaced my order entry book. I believe it might be in my desk.' Grace walked over to the desk next to the window that overlooked Boar Lane and pulled open a drawer, taking out a large invoice book covered with marble effect paper. 'Yes, I thought as much, I'd forget my head if it was not screwed on.' She tucked it under her arm and smiled at Mary-Anne and Eliza. 'Now, I'll leave you both alone, you must have a lot to catch up on. Good day to you both. Eliza, I will see you in the morning.'

'Yes, Grace, we need to discuss the new line in corsetry. The representative has just dropped us some new samples in.'

Grace smiled as Eliza inclined her head and left the room.

After Grace had departed, Eliza threw a

questioning look in her sister's direction. 'What was that all about?'

'Don't you start lecturing me, our Eliza. I've got to get myself known to the Ellershaw family and make them think that I've gone up in the world.'

'You told her John was dead! How could you do that? You are tempting fate and bringing bad luck upon your head. That was just sinful!' Eliza scowled at her sister.

'I need to make William aware that I am a footloose and fancy-free widow and that I am in no need of his support. Your friend Grace is bound to tell him. They were once so very close, I'm sure that she will not hesitate for one minute in relaying my reappearance.'

'You are a wicked woman, Mary-Anne Wild, and yes, that is your true name I'm using. I will not use poor John Vasey's name, just in case he reappears like a ghost from America. This will not end in a good way if you lie about the ones you love.'

'But I don't love him any more. I told you how he treated me. I need better things in my life and I'm going to get them,' Mary-Anne said firmly.

'Then God have mercy on us all because although it is good to have you home, I can't help but think you've bought more trouble to my door. Just don't hurt Victoria, she is the innocent one in all this and don't you forget it.'

Chapter 12

'Oh, Prissy, you don't look at all well. Are you eating?' Jessica Bentley could not hide the concern on her face as her oldest and closest friends sat down next to her in the tea shop that they frequented once a month on Woodlesford's high street.

'Yes, I'm eating, I'm just having difficulty sleeping, especially if I don't take my tonic. I sometimes wonder if what the doctor gives me helps me. I've tried not to be so dependent on his tinctures but I just can't manage without them. Life seems to be so hard, the days are so long. William is always at work and when he isn't, he either hides in the study with a drink or can be so demanding of me that I dread him coming to bed at night.' Prissy held her handkerchief to her mouth and quelled a sob. 'I'm sorry, I shouldn't talk about such personal things, but I have no one else to turn to.'

'Men can be such beasts, which is why I've never married. William is an uncaring cad, even Grace will back me up with that, when she joins us shortly. As you know, she does not have a good word for him at the moment, but she does share the same concerns as me over you. You wouldn't think that she and William are brother and sister they are so unlike and yet they used to be so close. I doubt that it's William's wealth and business have turned him into an ogre. Grace is such a lovely woman, while I'm afraid your husband is such an uncaring beast.' Jessica stopped her conversation as the shop girl placed an elaborate plate of cakes and fancies upon the table in front of them both, and poured the tea.

'Oh, is Grace joining us today? I'd rather hoped we would be by ourselves. She looks at me with such pity. She knows what exactly I have to endure with William. It's only because he has so many mills to keep his eye on, and he worries about his employees and property. He even works late into the night, in order to keep his business successful.' Priscilla bowed her head and tried not to make eye contact with Jessica, who she knew had no time for her husband.

'He still should show you more care, Prissy, there is no excuse for his lack of diligence towards you.' Jessica looked at Prissy over the top of her tea cup.

Priscilla whispered to Jessica not to discuss her fragile state of mind as the shop door opened and Grace walked in.

'Afternoon, ladies. I trust we are all well?' Grace passed her mantle to the shop girl and sat down in her usual chair, smiling at both her friends.

'Afternoon, Grace. Is Sarah not with you?' Jessica asked.

'No, she sends her apologies. She has had to go down to London with her husband. His father has been taken gravely ill, so it was only right that Freddie was by his bedside.' Grace pulled up her chair. 'If the worst happens, she thinks that they may have to move down to London, to take over the estate. Poor her, she hates her mother-in-law. She wraps Freddie around her little finger and he doesn't stand up to her. So, how are you two? What tasty morsels of gossip have you got for me?'

'Life is quiet. Father is busy at the brewery. That is, when his head is not turned by his new love of plants in the orangery.' Jessica reached for a cake.

'I've nothing new, it seems an age since I went anywhere.' Prissy sipped her tea.

'You look tired, Prissy. Are you keeping well? Or is it that intolerable brother of mine giving you worry?' Grace looked at her close friend in concern, she was so frail.

'I will never change William, so no, it is not him. It is just that I am having trouble sleeping, as I've just told Jessica. But please, I don't wish to talk about it. I'm fine. Nothing for you to be concerned about.' Priscilla gave a wan smile.

'Well, I've some news.' Grace reached for a highly decorated fancy and cut it into two, enjoying the faces of her friends that were full of anticipation of what she was about to say. She delicately ate her first mouthful.

'Go on, you are obviously dying to tell us,' Jessica said.

'Do you remember Eliza's sister? Well, Mary-Anne Wild is back from America. Although she is no longer Mary-Anne Wild, she is now Mary-Anne Vasey.'

'Who?' Jessica asked.

'Eliza my seamstress's sister? You surely remember? She used to work with her sister when we first found Eliza in that ramshackle hut across the street, next to the butcher's.' Grace pointed out of the tea-shop's window to where the hut once stood. 'We had tea with her once in this very establishment?'

'Oh, yes, I remember. She was very attractive. Long auburn hair. Has she come back for her daughter? After all, Victoria is hers, isn't she?' Prissy leaned forward. As long as it distracted attention from her, any news was welcome.

'She's bought a house up on Speakers' Corner. She's also a widow, her husband has died, and he must have left her quite comfortably off by the sounds of it – given the house and the way she dresses.'

'Is she still as beautiful?' Jessica enquired.

Grace sighed. 'I think even more so. Age seems to suit her.'

'Some women are so lucky. I have to try so hard to keep my looks.' Prissy hung her head.

'Nonsense, you are just as beautiful. It's my brother that gives you sleepless nights and makes you look so pale and drawn. We all know that.'

'Is her daughter to live with her?' Jessica enquired.

'I really don't know. I only spoke to her briefly when she was visiting Eliza at work. I hope not – it would break Eliza's heart if she lost her. George also enjoys Victoria's company, he treats her like his little pet. If she was to live with her mother it would be more awkward for him to see her.'

'He's still friends with her then? Does he not have anything better to do in his life? Surely he should be looking at more suitable girls of marriageable age by now?' Prissy smiled.

'Friends, yes, very much so. Although my father would be furious if he ever found out he still visits. He dislikes the Wild family, no matter that Eliza has made me, his daughter, a small fortune and a name for herself. He always has hated them and I don't quite know why.'

'Well, I think we should welcome Mary-Anne, especially if she is as wealthy as you think she is. Both sisters are to be complimented on raising themselves from out of the gutter. It just shows what women can do, with or without the help of menfolk.' Jessica smiled at Grace, knowing full well that neither of them would ever marry. Independence was their freedom, and they were more than grateful when they saw the lives Sarah and Priscilla had to endure, married to their husbands of so-called status.

'And what did you do today, dear wife? Yet another day of sleeping and idling the hours away?'

William Ellershaw poured himself a brandy and sat down in his chair next to the roaring fire as he glared at Prissy doing her cross-stitch.

'I had tea with your sister and Jessica Bentley, actually. A very enjoyable afternoon it was as well. I sometimes think I should make myself go out more often, it does my spirits good.' Prissy wondered why she was honoured with his presence. Work must not need him and he must be in no mood for his gentleman's club or his mistress else he would not be here.

'And what did those two witches have to say? Did they fill your head with their worthless gossip and ideas? No wonder no man will look at

115

either of them, they are both miserable old maids.' William swilled his brandy down.

'We had much to discuss. Sarah has had to follow her husband to London and Grace also said that Eliza Wild's sister has returned from America.' Priscilla looked up from her needlework and noticed William taking notice in what she had said for once.

'Eliza Wild's sister. Am I supposed to know her?' William enquired.

'I think so, you once brought her to tea with you. You should recall Mary-Anne Wild, although now she is called Mary-Anne Vasey. She took your eye, if I remember rightly. Anyway, she's back from America, a wealthy widow and living in Leeds near Speakers' Corner. Grace was full of it. Jessica said we should welcome her into society, even though she is of lowly birth. I don't see why we should – all the money in the world won't give her the breeding that is expected in our circles.'

'She was nothing more than a tart, if I remember correctly. Isn't it her illegitimate daughter that Eliza Wild looks after? Both sisters are as common as muck. I don't know why my sister got involved with that family. Just for once I agree with my father: Grace should have had nothing to do with them. They are not our sort. Thank God that she had the sense not to make her a partner in her shop, I know she talked about it at one time.' William snorted. 'I think Father and our solicitor persuaded her against it.'

Priscilla smiled. 'I quite admire them. From what I understand, they are both so independent.'

'Well you would, because you are as empty-headed as my sister. Women should know their place, it is a man's world and they would do well to remember that.' William finished his drink and slammed down the empty glass on the small teak table by his side. 'If that's the best conversation that you can have, I'm going to my bed. You'll be glad to know I'm leaving you alone tonight.'

William rose from his seat and made his way up the curving stairs of Levensthorpe Hall. Prissy started crying, but she was thankful that she would not have to satisfy her husband with his perverted ways that night.

In the silence of his room, William lay on his bed and thought about Mary-Anne Wild. He had never forgotten the beautiful girl who had slipped through his fingers. Now she was back, he could find her and see if she still took his interest. Especially if she was now a woman of substance, which would be the icing on the cake. He'd visit his sister at home and get to find out more about Mary-Anne Vasey. Was she still as beautiful? More to the point, would she be interested in him, now he had everything a woman desired? Perhaps he should start looking at getting rid of Ruby Bell. He had grown tired of her and Mary-Anne would fit her place perfectly.

Chapter 13

Eliza looked across the breakfast table at Victoria. Her niece was strangely quiet, engrossed in her own thoughts. It had been hard to judge what had gone through her head when her mother had told her that she was leaving her yet again to lead her own life. She had shown no emotion when told and now had little to say to Eliza. Above their heads, the floorboards creaked as Mary-Anne tidied her room and packed her few belongings before going into Leeds and her new life with Ma Fletcher.

'Are you all right, Victoria? Not too upset about your mother leaving us, to live in Leeds?' Eliza decided to break the silence and confront the problem of Mary-Anne's leaving, head on. 'At least she won't be too far away this time,' Eliza added, trying to make light of the situation.

'Why shouldn't I be all right? She's just someone who has come into my life for a few fleeting moments and is now moving on. Neither her nor I have formed any attachment because we don't know one another and never will. I'm not wanted by her and to be quite honest, I'm grateful for that. Because what I've seen of her, I'm not keen on. She's so brash and common. Besides, you are my true mother. It is you I owe my existence to, you have always shown me love and care.' Victoria fought back the tears as she heard her mother close her bedroom door and come down the stairs.

'Well, that's me packed. Let's face it, I didn't have a lot.' Mary-Anne looked at her daughter and her sister and felt there was tension in the room. 'You know I'm not deserting you, don't you, Victoria? Not again. I'm only living in Leeds for the moment and once I'm able to stand on my own two feet, I want you to come and live with me. Share our time together, the way mother and daughter should do. I can't give you the things that your aunt Eliza has, not yet, so it is for the best that you stay with her.' Mary-Anne kissed her daughter on her cheek but the gesture was not returned.

'I've told Victoria that you will visit us frequently and that she is free to visit you at the house at Speakers' Corner any time she wishes. It's not as if there are hundreds of miles of ocean between us, this time you are only four miles away.' Eliza saw the hurt on Mary-Anne's face as she felt her daughter's coldness towards her.

'Of course I will, and you will come to see that I am leaving in the belief that I hope to set us up in life with my work looking after Ma Fletcher.' Mary-Anne ran her hand over Victoria's shoulder and smiled.

Victoria withdrew from her mother's touch. 'I don't care what you do. Why should I worry, you've never worried about me.' Victoria threw her napkin down on the table and pushed her chair back, crying as she ran out of the dining room past her aunt and mother upstairs to her bedroom.

'Victoria, you are wrong, I do love you. It's

because of you and the hope of a better life that I'm doing this.' Mary-Anne stood at the bottom of the stairs and shouted up to her daughter.

'Leave her be, Mary-Anne, she's upset. She thinks you are leaving her again. Just as she was getting to know you.'

'But I'm not. I'm going to be there for her now no matter what and I'm going to make sure she gets what she deserves, if I possibly can.' Mary-Anne looked up at the top of the stairs and tried to decide whether to climb them and hug her daughter as she heard her sobbing in her room.

'Just go, she'll be fine. I'll see to her. I'll suggest she visit me at work this afternoon. I will arrange a carriage to pick her up, and she can choose a new dress from our new range. That should cheer her up.' Eliza picked up her sister's carpetbag and handed it to her. 'Don't worry, she will come around once she knows you have no intention of leaving her life completely. Now go. Ma Fletcher will be expecting you.' Eliza smiled. 'She does love you, she just feels hurt.'

Mary-Anne sighed. 'What would I do without you, Eliza? This is my one chance to make things more even for us all. I hope one day Victoria will realise that.'

'Shush. Stop worrying and know that we both love you. Now, leave Victoria to me. She will be fine, believe me. If I've time we will come and see you at the beginning of next week, once you've tidied up your new home and settled in.'

Eliza kissed her sister as she said goodbye to her on the doorstep of Aireville Mansions. She watched her as she made her way down the street, her carpetbag in her hand and her stolen fur wrapped around her neck.

In the window above, the net curtain moved as Victoria watched her mother leaving her once more. She wiped her tears away and vowed that she would not let her hurt her again. Aunt Eliza was more of a mother than her true mother would ever be.

Mary-Anne made her way down the canalside with a heavy heart. She loved her daughter dearly and had only left her in the care of Eliza because she knew she would be happier there until she sorted her life out. She could understand the hurt she was feeling but she'd be there for her when needed, she was never again going to be far from her side. If the plan she had in her head came to fruition, Victoria would be a wealthy young woman someday. Then she'd realise just how much her mother loved her. She only hoped that her plan would work and eventually she would be a woman of note and worthy of being Victoria's mother.

The miles into Leeds soon disappeared as she worried and thought about her life and that of her daughter, and in a short space of time she was walking along Woodhouse Lane and then into Speakers' Corner with Ma Fletcher's house looking straight at her. Mary-Anne dropped her carpetbag down beside her feet and stopped to look at the square squat house that was to be her home. No wonder Benjamin Jubb was after it, it was a well-built house that was worthy of coveting.

She took a deep breath and crossed the road,

stopping briefly to look at the poster pasted on a stables' doorway giving notice of the next meeting of speakers on the corner. She gazed down the list of people. There, halfway down the list, was a name she was familiar with. Tom Thackeray was to be the main speaker on Sunday 9 April speaking upon 'The Dangers Within Our Mines'. Now that was a talk she was going to have to listen to, and while she was there, she'd try to speak to Tom. Poor Tom, whom she suspected had been left as broken-hearted as Eliza, though he had sided with his mother rather than the girl he loved. Perhaps it was time she tried to put things right between him and Eliza. After all, it was never too late to find true love, and Eliza needed a man in her life. If Mary-Anne could help Eliza find happiness, it might be a way to pay her back for all the sacrifices she had had to make for Victoria.

'So you didn't think better of it and decide to leave that old bitch to rot in her own filth?'

Ma Fletcher looked up at Mary-Anne as she hung her fur up on the coat stand and placed her carpetbag on the bottom of the stairs to take up with her once she had laid the fire and boiled the kettle.

'Why, did you think I would? Did you think I'd go back on my word and not take the best chance of my life to better myself and get even with the Ellershaws? If you did, you don't know me very well. Besides, you need me. Look at you – no fire, dust everywhere, and I bet you haven't eaten yet. Do you sleep over there in that corner? It looks like the sheets on that day bed have not been washed for months, but then again you could do with a lick of soap and water too by the looks of it.' Cleanliness was definitely not next to godliness in Ma Fletcher's world.

'You cheeky bitch! Don't forget, I can change my mind and send you back to live with your Eliza. I'll not be beholden to anyone. Don't forget this is my home, you respect what I say, madam.' Despite her words, Ma Fletcher grinned. Mary-Anne would soon have the house spick and span and her well fed in payment for the roof over her head and help in getting justice done against the Ellershaws.

'Aye, I know, but let's make a start by getting you and your bedding washed. There's a good breeze blowing today. I'll get the sheets pegged out and let them blow in the wind.' Mary-Anne laid the fire with kindling sticks and coals, setting light to them and then placed the kettle to boil on the black crook that hung from the chimney breast. 'That fleabag on your knee could do with a bath and all.'

'You don't touch my Mr Tibbs. He's fine and I'll suffice with a good wash. If you go out the back door there's a good size garden and a washhouse with a boiler, there should be everything you need in the lean-to. It's a while since I've been out there. There's plenty of clean bedding in the bedding box upstairs on the landing. You'll need to air your bed if you are to stay here tonight.' Ma Fletcher called out to Mary-Anne as she went into the kitchen. 'We could do with some bread, cheese and butter when you've time. Best you go this morning, you don't want what's leftover when folk has had the best.'

'Not a lot to do today, then!' Mary-Anne grinned. 'It'll keep me out of mischief.'

'You kept out of mischief? That'll be a first. Now go and get that bread, I've had nothing to eat this morning. I'll watch the kettle, me and Mr Tibbs.' Ma Fletcher stroked her cat, who purred in satisfaction at her love. 'You'll find what money you want in a tin box under my bed.' Ma Fletcher pointed to the crumpled filthy covers that made her bed up in the corner of the kitchen.

Mary-Anne pulled the covers up from the sofa which acted as a bed and nearly was sick by the stench that hit her.

'How many unemptied piss pots are under here?' Mary-Anne gasped as she pulled two chamber pots full to the brim out from under the bed.

'Could be two or three. That lad of Jubb's wouldn't empty them, the lazy little bastard. I offered him threepence and all.'

Mary-Anne, her hand over her mouth in a futile attempt to quell the stench, went out into the street and emptied both down the main sewer, coming back to retrieve a further two and leaving the front door open to dissipate the smell.

'Now you've done that it'll get better. There's nothing worse than smelling someone else's shit and piss. Take an extra bit of money from the cash box and treat yourself to something you fancy.' Ma Fletcher caught the look on Mary-Anne's face when she opened the cash box and took a few coins out of it for what they needed.

'Aye, I'm not short of a bob or two. You've made the right decision, despite the state I'm in.'

'I'll empty those chamber pots every day. It's a wonder you haven't gone down with something. How did you put up with the smell?' Mary-Anne held the money in her hand. 'I'll get some bleach and soap, get rid of the stench. It wasn't until I disturbed the pots that I realised what the funny smell was in here.'

'I'm sorry, lass, it'll get better. I'm thankful that you've decided to help me out. But don't forget it's a two-way bargain, and I'll see you right.' Ma Fletcher felt a slight embarrassment over her situation but knew Mary-Anne had no option but to fulfill her promise if she wanted to get what she had set her head on. She'd no option but to take the rough with the smooth.

Mary-Anne hooked a straw basket over her arm and pulled a shawl that she had found hung behind the kitchen door around her shoulders and left Ma Fletcher taking forty winks next to the fire with Mr Tibbs guarding her on her knee. She closed the front door quietly and walked briskly down the Headrow and onto Briggate to buy what they needed from the market. There was nothing to eat in the house, so she had helped herself to more money out of the cash box to buy what they needed for the next two days. Then at least she could get to grips with cleaning the house and not have to keep going out for supplies. Her first stop was at the butcher's stall, she knew him of old and trusted his meat.

Mary-Anne pushed her way through the row of customers waiting for their orders. 'Half a pound of mutton and some tripe, enough for two.' She asked a spotty-faced lad who was eager to serve her. 'And I'll have some of that pig's brawn. It'll be good in a sandwich.' She fumbled for her money and placed the change and the meat into the bottom of her basket before making her way to the bakery, which, by the looks of the shop window, had nearly sold out of fresh bread.

She was just about to step into the shop when she caught a fleeting glance of someone she knew all too well. John! John Vasey, she was sure it was him. She knew that cut of the coat, those broad shoulders and that long dark hair. She caught her breath. Surely it couldn't be him? She'd left him locked up in the cells in New York, he'd not think of following her back home. It couldn't be him, he hadn't any money to get himself back over the water. She looked down Briggate, her eyes scanning the crowd and her heart pounding fast, but she could not see him.

'Are you coming into this shop? Or are you just going to block the doorway?' The baker barked at her.

'I'm sorry, I thought I saw somebody I know.' Mary-Anne looked around her, worried that any moment John Vasey might discover her.

'Well, what do you want? My time's more precious than it is to you gossiping women.'

'A household loaf and it had better not be filled with rubbish like plaster powder, because I'll know.' Mary-Anne quickly recovered her wits and bit back at the baker.

'There's nowt wrong with my bread, it's made with the finest flour. That'll be threepence, I take it that'll be all you'll be needing.' The baker passed over the heavy large loaf and thought twice about pushing his customer any more, knowing full well that the flour in his loaf had been mixed with alum to make him more money.

'Threepence! At least Dick Turpin had the decency to wear a mask.' Mary-Anne counted the pennies out and put her loaf in her basket.

Turning her back on him, she walked to the stall that sold cheese and butter and looked over at the vegetables on the next table. The sooner she made her way out of the market the better. She had no intention of confronting John Vasey. It had been him, of that she was sure. She weaved her way through the busy shoppers, trying to hide in the crowd as she quickly made her way back to the safety of Speakers' Corner. He would never find her there, he'd never think of her living in that part of Leeds. Hopefully, he would give up his search for her and return to his life in America. The last thing she wanted him was for him to show his ugly face and spoil her plans.

'Aye, that smells good.' Ma Fletcher yawned and looked over at the simmering pot of mutton stew on the side of the Yorkshire range. 'Even Mr Tibbs is dribbling. There'll be some broth left over for you, don't worry. I'll leave you some on my plate.' She tickled the cat under his chin. 'You look more like the old Mary-Anne that I used to know. Tha's still a bonny woman, even with those skirts on. William Ellershaw doesn't deserve you, so you don't feel guilty when you catch him and take him for what you can get.'

'If I get the chance. I still don't know how to make him realise I'm back, although I have made myself known to his sister. Thank God, she didn't see me dressed like this.' Mary-Anne had a scrubbing brush in her hand and soda suds running down her arms after scrubbing under Ma Fletcher's bed. She looked down at her sack-cloth apron and the tatty old clothes that she'd found in the downstairs spare room, clothes left from the Fletchers' earlier life as rag-and-bone dealers.

The day had gone fast since her return from the market and now it was nearly supper time, and time to peel Ma Fletcher out of the clothes she was wearing and encourage her to wear the clean ones that she had brought down out of her bedroom drawers. They were hanging over the clothes rack, along with a clean nightdress, for her to wear that evening. Her makeshift bed was newly made up with clean bedding, the dirty linen having been soaked and boiled in soda crystals and hung up in the relatively clean air out in the backyard. Scrubbing the main room's floor was the last job of the day, and Mary-Anne was thankful for that. The room was so filthy that she had itched with the fear of lice when she had changed the bedding. Tomorrow she would wash the curtains and make a start in the kitchen and scullery. But after helping Ma Fletcher wash and change, she was away to her bed. She finally washed her scrubbing brush off in the mop bucket and went to pour the dirty water out down the red earthenware sink in the scullery, returning with a flannel, soap, and a warm bowl of water, smiling at Ma Fletcher as she placed it on the table next to her.

'Right, missis, now it's your turn. Do you want me to help or can you manage yourself?' Mary-

Anne asked the old woman, whose pride in her appearance had disappeared along with her ability to walk with ease.

'I'm not mucky, you know. I don't know why I should have to do this.' Ma Fletcher scowled and pushed her cat off her knee.

'You'll feel better. Just how long have you been in those clothes? You look as if you've been sleeping in them.' Mary-Anne put her arm around the old woman for support and helped her to her feet. 'That's it, let's take off this skirt and petticoat and then your bodices, and then you can wash in private while I take these to be washed.' Mary-Anne tried not to breathe in as Ma Fletcher's many layers of clothes were discarded, leaving a frail wizened body of a woman with just her greying mop cap left on her tangled hair.

'You've locked the door, haven't you? What if someone was to come in and find me in this state?' Ma Fletcher said as she lowered herself naked into her chair and started to wash.

'Yes, it's bolted, no one's going to come in.' Mary-Anne held the clothes out at arm's length and dumped them in the out-house before returning to make sure Ma Fletcher was all right. 'There you are. I'll get some scissors and let's wash and tidy your hair while we are at it.'

'Not my hair, Mary-Anne, I'll be to bury if you wash it tonight. It's only spring, I usually wait until at least June. When the weather is warm.' Ma Fletcher's face was a picture of fear.

'Nonsense. Here I'll put some more coal on the fire, get a good blaze going while you eat your stew, and it will dry in no time.' She added some coal to the fire and walked over to the kitchen mirror where the scissors were hung and watched the old woman pull a face and try to dry herself in the firelight.

'Go on do your worst, before I bloody freeze to death. At least let me cover myself with a blanket.' Ma Fletcher couldn't blame her lodger for wanting her to look better, she knew she had smelt a bit ripe, but she'd not been naked in front of anyone before and longed to keep her modesty.

'I won't be long, I promise.' Mary-Anne removed the grubby mop cap and gently combed her long straggly hair. 'I'll take about this much off and then will wash it.' Mary-Anne showed approximately three inches between her thumb and finger and then proceeded to cut as the old woman swore under her breath.

'You'll do what you like, so it's pointless to complain. You are a bloody bully, Mary-Anne Wild. And to think I was daft enough to ask you to stay with me.'

'It's Mary-Anne Vasey, and by the time I've finished with you, you'll look better than you've ever done. It'll be William Ellershaw coming to court you.'

'Now I know you are a bloody liar, girl. Besides, I'm like you, I'd have his money but I wouldn't have that bastard in my bed. Too much like his father, you remember that.'

Mary-Anne sighed as she tidied the woman up. She wasn't worried about William Ellershaw. At the moment, it was the sighting of John Vasey that she was concerned with. How had he managed to afford to follow her and would he find her?

Chapter 14

'I don't know why you turned the carriage away yesterday if you are wishing to join me at work today?' Eliza sighed at the surly expression of Victoria's face which she had worn since her mother had left them.

'I didn't feel like viewing your new collection yesterday, and besides, George has sent a message with his footman. He is to meet me in Morley's in the Rose and Crown Yard for tea for a treat at three, so I can do both today.'

'The Rose and Crown Yard? My dear, that is no place for you to be seen, it is so seedy and grubby. Can he not think of a better place to take you to? Perhaps that little tea shop on Park Lane? That is the place to be seen.' Eliza thought of only protecting Victoria and Morley's was right next door to Bink's Hotel, which sold alcoholic refreshments day and night.

'Morley's is extremely fashionable. Besides, I wouldn't think that would worry you. After all, you and my mother will have been in worse. Sometimes you can be such a hypocrite,' Victoria spat.

'Victoria, I'll ignore that only because I know you are feeling upset with your mother. If you are to have tea with George Ellershaw, remember to be a proper young lady and be careful. I don't agree with him showing you so much interest.' Eliza prayed that Victoria's anger with her mother would not spill out in her attentions towards George.

'We are just good friends, Aunt Eliza, that is all. Unlike you and Mother, I can reserve my feelings.'

Victoria's comments were caustic to Eliza's ears. Never before had her niece spoken to her like that. She'd overlook it this time, but if her attitude continued, words would have to be had.

Victoria gazed at herself in the long-length mirrors that hung on the fitting-room walls of her aunt's workroom. She took in the cut of the dress her aunt had designed and held the latest material from Paris next to her. 'But this material catches the light so beautifully.' Victoria smiled at her reflection and then turned to her aunt with the sample of shimmering purple taffeta in her hand. 'Why do I have to have something so babyish to wear? I'm almost grown.'

'You're just a girl, Victoria. Purple is too old for you and it doesn't really suit your colouring. How about the green? Look, it shines too and it is far more suitable. You have your mother's complexion and she would definitely choose the green.'

'Then I definitely would like the purple, it is so vibrant.' Victoria turned and stared at her aunt. 'I can wear it to the Guild Ball. I'm old enough now.' In the reflection of the mirror, Victoria noticed her aunt's annoyance with her stubbornness.

'I still think the green would be better, but I suppose you are old enough to wear the purple and carry it off.' Eliza sighed. 'But you are far too young for the Guild Ball, young lady.'

'George said Grace wasn't much older than me

when she started attending parties.' Victoria said with a scowl.

'Really? Well, it would be nice to have you by my side.' Her aunt couldn't help but smile as she reached into her desk drawer. 'As luck would have it, a pair of invitations arrived at my desk yesterday. They always send me two in the hope that I will bring a partner with me, which I never do. The organisers hate having a woman walk in on her own. I suppose there would be no harm in you going just for an hour – no more, mind – just for you to get a taste of higher society.' Eliza took the purple taffeta from Victoria and put it to one side to work on later.

'You would let me go with you to the ball, to the Guild Hall? I didn't think for a minute you'd agree!' Victoria said excitedly.

'Providing your mood improves. I don't like this sulky side of you, which seems to have taken over you since your mother left. You will eventually realise that she did it for your good. She will be there for you once she has made a home for herself. And as for George, you would be better spending less time with him. We owe Grace Eller-shaw a great deal, but I don't want us to be beholden to any of the men of that family, they are known to be uncaring and selfish.' Eliza didn't want her niece's heart to be broken, but at the same time she had to keep her parentage a secret.

'George is not one bit uncaring or selfish. I think you are wrong there, dear Aunt.' Victoria picked up a hat from a nearby stand and tried it on, smiling to herself as she admired the ribbons and flowers that adorned it, and thinking of how lucky she was to be attending the largest ball in Leeds at her age.

'Just be careful, Victoria, you don't know him well.'

One of Eliza's staff knocked on the fitting room doors. She went quiet when she saw the man standing behind the shop girl.

'Excuse me, ma'am, I'm sorry to interrupt but this gentleman is quite insistent that he speaks to you.' Milly bobbed and curtsied and made way for the uninvited guest as he entered the fitting room.

'John, is it you? My, you are a sight for sore eyes!' Eliza gasped and held her hand out to shake. 'What brings you here? Is Mary-Anne with you?'

Victoria looked questioningly at her aunt. Was this John Vasey, her mother's lover? And why was her aunt acting as if she had no knowledge of her mother?'

'It's good to see you, Eliza. For sure, it's been a long time and I've missed you. But, no, Mary-Anne is not with me, I was hoping that you'd tell me she was here, with you. We've both got ourselves into a bit of bother and I thought the first thing that she would do would be to return home.'

'Bother? What's up? You are both all right, aren't you? What's gone wrong for you to return from America?'

'Nothing for you to worry your head about. I got locked up for being a stupid bloody idiot and Mary-Anne must have finally got fed up with me and decided to do something equally as stupid in an attempt, I thought, to get herself back home. I must have thought wrong. Damn it, where is that bloody woman? Don't say I've come all this way to have left her back in America. I'd do anything to see her bonny face and tell her I'm a stupid Irishman and that I'm sorry for being so stubborn.' John finally noticed Victoria. 'This must be Victoria, it can't be anybody else. Sure, you are the image of your mother. She'd be so proud of you and she'd tell you how much she loves you if she was here.'

Victoria smiled and held her hand out for John to shake. 'It's a pleasure to meet you, Mr Vasey.' Victoria lingered with her handshake and wanted to tell him where her mother was but hesitated as she saw her aunt give her a warning glance. But if she told him, he'd take her mother back to America with him and life would be back to normal. She wouldn't have to be ashamed of her mother and feel obliged to love her.

'Listen to you, a real lady in the making. Mary-Anne would be so proud of you. You've done well, Eliza, Victoria is everything that her mother ever wished her to be. And just look at you, in a shop in the centre of Leeds. You've certainly come a long way since I last saw you.'

'Yes, fortune has smiled on me and Victoria. But you've got me worried about Mary-Anne. Where can she be? Where are you staying so that I can get in touch with you if she shows her face?'

'I'm in lodgings down by the docks. It's rife with rats and lice but it will do for the time being. I aim to return to New York shortly if I can't find Mary-Anne.' John went to leave, but turned back at the door. 'I'd thank you kindly if you could tell me if she shows her face. I love that woman. But I won't

135

take any more of your time. I'm on my way to see Mick and Patsy and catch up over a gill.'

'You'll have a long way to walk. I understand that they've moved back to Ireland. Pounders Court is to be demolished.' Eliza could see the disappointment on John's face.

'It seems everybody has moved on. The sooner I get back to America the better, there's nothing here in Leeds for me. At least there I have a decent job, a roof over my head and friends around me. But it won't be the same without the woman I love. I thank you for your help, Eliza, and may the good Lord look after you both.' John bowed his head and made his way out of the fitting room and down the stairs and out of the shop.

Victoria watched him through the window as he crossed the bustling Boar Lane. She saw him pull his collar up against the cold wind and weave his way through the crowds.

'Why didn't you tell him my mother is here? He sounds broken-hearted.'

Eliza stood next to Victoria. 'Because your mother has had enough of him. The sooner he goes back to America the better. She's been with him twelve years and is no better off than when she left with him. In fact, she's worse off.'

'But he loves her.'

'Love doesn't pay the bills, Victoria, the sooner you realise that the better. And some men can charm you with words but they're just empty promises.' Eliza put her arm around her niece. 'It's better you find an honest man with money, if there's any such thing.'

'Is John Vasey my father, Aunt?' Victoria waited

for her aunt to answer the question that had been a thorn in her side all her young life.

'No, my dear Victoria. Your father is a man of much more standing than that of John Vasey. That is, and always will be the problem. Now, don't ask any more of me, your mother will tell you when she is ready. You are loved dearly by your mother and me, and you are better off without your father, believe me.' Eliza kissed her niece on the cheek and they both watched John Vasey disappear into the crowds. One day Victoria would have to know who her true father was and she just hoped it would not break her heart.

Victoria sat across from George Ellershaw, feeling uneasy as he watched her every move. She'd told her aunt that she would not be in need of a chaperone as she was accompanied by George and he was to be trusted. However, it was the first time she had been alone with him and while she usually enjoyed his teasing and attention she now felt uncomfortable with him being so direct. Still, she was determined to be the good girl her aunt had raised her to be.

'It's a delightful tearoom, George, I would never have guessed to have come here. How did you hear about Morley's?' Victoria decided to make polite conversation and keep him from staring at her.

'My mother has tea with her cronies here. So I knew it would be suitable.' George smiled across at the girl.

'It is full of very wealthy people, which is strange as it is situated in a rather disreputable area. My aunt was quite beside herself worrying that I would not be safe here.' Victoria sipped her tea and looked around her at the bustling tearoom filled with the great and the good of Leeds. But could see why they were drawn there – the cake that she had just eaten was divine and the people she could see and hear seemed to be besotted with how the lower classes acted and how, if they had their way, they could reform them. The tea shop was a window on how the poor of Leeds lived, yet in the warmth and safety of upper-class society. It was a do-gooder's paradise, and, without getting her hands dirty, the perfect place for George's mother to say that she felt for the working classes and perhaps give a few pence to them to ease her conscience.

'My mother says I should be thankful for the position that I have been born into. But these folk that are lost souls and all the worse for a drink are just idle in my eyes. They deserve the lifestyle they live. Why, they too could eat cake if they didn't waste their money on drink. I mean, just look at that man who has just come out of Binks Hotel. He can hardly stand because he is so inebriated.' George pointed out across the Rose and Crown Yard and scoffed at the dark-haired man who was leaning against the wall of the Binks Hotel, trying to light his pipe.

Victoria recognised the man instantly as John Vasey and watched as he slumped down upon the cobbled yard with his head in his hands, in drunken despair of losing his one love in his life, Victoria's mother.

'I know that man, I think I shall help him.'

138

Victoria pushed her chair back from the table and before George could stop her she made her way out of the shop to John Vasey's side.

'Mr Vasey, are you all right? Do you need a hand?' Victoria bent down and looked at the broken Irish man.

'Are you an angel? Has my Mary-Anne sent me an angel to look after me?' John Vasey looked up at the young fresh face and grinned. 'Sorry, sweetheart, I'm worse for the drink. I know who you are, you are Victoria and you probably need your mother as much as I do.' John Vasey slurred his words and then started to prop himself up against the lime-washed wall of the hotel. He grinned and put his hand on Victoria's shoulder.

'Mr Vasey, I think I can help. I know where she is. She's living up near Speakers' Corner with an old beggar woman. She is in Leeds, go and find her and take her back with you, back to America.' The sooner her mother was out of her life the better. How could she let the likes of George Ellershaw ever meet her? She was a thief, foul-mouthed and common. 'Here, take this penny and sober yourself up.' Victoria placed a penny in his hand and pretended to take care of him as the ladies of society and George watched her. 'Please don't tell my mother that I told you where she is. I am only telling you because I can see you are hurting so.'

'Bless you, you don't know what this means to me, I love that woman. God bless you, miss.' John Vasey decided a hug was in order as he held her close, his ale-laden breath making her cringe.

'Yes, well, I've told you now but I'd prefer that you don't tell my mother how you came to her.

139

I'll go back to my tea, you take care of yourself.'
Victoria watched John Vasey stumble off down
the cobbled yard then went back into the tea
shop, aware of the customers muttering about
what she had just done.

George looked in disbelief at his tea partner.
'You shouldn't have done that. Were you trying to
impress me? He could have attacked you. Besides,
he will only go back to the public house and buy
himself another drink.'

'You could have come with me. But I know
him. He's harmless. He's just looking for his
wife.' Victoria took a sip of her tea.

'Oh no, he might have soiled my new jacket, the
dirty ruffian. In future, Victoria, try not to be so
impulsive, it has made you the talk of the tea
shop.' George looked most upset. 'You should act
less like a child.'

'I'm sorry, George.' Victoria began to realise
what type of boy George was. He was a fop and a
shallow mother's boy, worse than that, he was a
snob. 'But I am a child.' She raised her voice a
little. 'I'm only twelve, after all, and now I'm going
to enjoy one of these lovely cakes.' She helped
herself to the prettiest of the fancies, relieved that
she would soon be home with her aunt and hopeful that her intervention with John Vasey would
mean that her mother would soon be out of her
life for good.

Chapter 15

Edmund Ellershaw sat on the edge of the bed, pulled his braces up over his shirt and reached for his waistcoat from off the bedpost, giving a quick glance to the woman that lay there, undisturbed by her lover leaving her. He pulled his waistcoat on and buttoned it up, putting his fob watch in the breast pocket before looking down at his portly belly and sighing. He felt into his pocket and placed what change he had on the bedside table, though he did wonder if he could get away with not paying for his night of so-called pleasure. But if he didn't pay her, word would soon get about Leeds not to give him the time of day in the brothels.

As it was, he was dreading the gossip that was already circulating about him. He'd never had this trouble before. He could always perform, perform so well that many a woman could hardly walk after a night with him. But now, something was wrong. His dick just wouldn't go hard for him, and even when it did he couldn't manage it for long, becoming short of breath and exhausted. Perhaps losing a pound or two would not hurt. After all, he wasn't getting much younger. The spirit was willing but the flesh definitely was not.

He pulled his jacket on, looked again at the pile of change he'd left for the whore that had not kept her scorn to herself at him not reaching his maximum potential and took two of the coins from the pile. She shouldn't have grinned so much when she realised it was going to be easy money, the bitch, he thought as he put them back in his jacket pocket. He left her still asleep in bed in one of his favourite haunts, the gentlemen's club.

Tom Thackeray stood at the head of Rose Pit as he listened to the complaints from the latest shift to come up from the shafts.

'I tell you, Tom, that those new props are not strong enough. The wood's not worth owt. I wouldn't build a shithouse with that stuff,' Bill Parker said. His face was blackened by coal and his eyes were sore from rubbing the dust out of them. 'The lads said they were sure they heard them creaking the other day, they just can't hold the weight.'

'I'll have a word with Ellershaw when he turns up. He's got them from a new supplier. He was saying that he was more than happy with them, so he'll not be pleased.' Tom Thackeray knew that Bill's concerns were justified. He'd looked at the wooden props before they had been taken down the pit, and although they did look strong the wood was softer than usual, no doubt a saving on Ellershaw's side. He was as tight as a duck's arse, but lately it had gone too far. Men's lives were being put at risk through his money-saving schemes. Perhaps if he didn't spend so much at his so-called gentlemen's club he'd have more brass in his pocket.

'Aye, well do, before there's an accident. Besides, the men can't concentrate on the coalface,

142

they are too busy listening to every groan and creak coming from those props. So if he thinks he's saving brass with his shite props, he isn't.' Bill spat a mouthful of coal dust out and walked away. He'd said his bit, now it was up to Tom and Ellershaw to sort it.

Tom watched as the next shift went down in the cage and looked up at the pithead wheel turning. 'Please let them men be safe,' he whispered to himself. At least until he'd tackled Edmund Ellershaw about it and got him to replace the props with wood from their original supplier. Those props should never have put in place. It was men's lives they were protecting, and that of their families, but all that seemed to matter to Ellershaw was profit.

Tom looked around the yard and pit head. If this mine was his, he'd run it a lot different, it would be safer and secure. You got out of your men what you put into them. Edmund Ellershaw gave nowt to his men, so he got nowt back.

'Isn't it nice to have William join us for a meal tonight? Catherine Ellershaw passed the terrine of green beans to William and looked around the table at her family all sat down together for once. 'It is such a pity Priscilla could not have joined you, William. Is she still not herself? The girl is so frail, I do worry about her. You must look after her, you owe her and your late grandfather a great deal.'

'No, she sends her apologies, Mama. She did not feel like company tonight as she has a headache.' William glanced across at his sister who he feared would have something to say about the absence of his wife by his side.

'She did seem a bit down last week.' Grace looked pointedly at her brother. 'Perhaps you should make her attend events more often, William. You can get to a point of not wanting to see people if you stay at home too long. I'm sure if you encouraged her, and showed her a bit of attention, her spirits would improve.'

'I only wish your father would listen to your advice as well, Grace.' Catherine glanced at her husband. 'Where were you last night? At that infernal gentlemen's club? What keeps you there until dawn? No sooner do you arrive back from there, than off you go to your beloved mine. I may as well never have married you, from what I see of you.'

'I'd some business to do at my club. And how do you think we can eat like this if I don't go to the pit?'

Edmund sliced his beef with vigour while thinking about what Tom Thackeray had said to him earlier in the day. The cheeky bastard had confronted him over the strength of the props and beams. Who did he think he was? It wasn't his pit and he'd never own one if he wasted money like that. He looked up to see George grinning, knowing full well what his father had been up to until the early hours. 'And you can wipe that smile from your face. You need to get your arse into some work, stop hiding behind your mother's apron strings and stop dreaming over that Wild lass.' Edmund wiped his chin and scowled. 'Aye, that's right, I heard you'd taken that little girl for tea at Morley's. Old Brown's wife had seen you there and he nearly broke his neck to tell me last night. You want nowt with her, she's a child and rubbish to boot. From what I hear she showed herself up by giving some money to a drunk she took pity on.' Edmund turned his attention to Grace. 'And you are paying that Eliza too much if her daughter can give money to someone lying in the gutter. Some bloody family I have.' Edmund sneered at his family. He was disgusted at their self-righteous behaviour.

'This is exactly why I don't come to dinner very often.' William pushed his chair back, stood, and threw his napkin onto the table. 'It always ends with an argument and my father cursing everybody. You should really look at yourself, Father, and realise that you yourself are not perfect, in fact, far from it, with your dissolute habits.'

'Sit down, William. I don't want you to go, we hardly ever see you. Your father is just tired. You know how hard he works and he's not getting any younger.' Catherine Ellershaw pulled on her son's arm.

William ignored the plea. 'Works hard at whoring in that club of his. Don't deny you know what he gets up to there, Mother, because we all know it.' William's eyes flashed as he looked at his father.

'Excuse me, I don't need to hear this.' Grace left the table, fighting back the tears though she looked in sympathy at her mother before leaving the room.

Edmund grunted. 'And I suppose you are not to be found in your mistress's bed over at the other side of town? Aye, I know about you and

145

all. There's nowt I don't know about this family, so don't look at me with such disdain.'

Edmund sat back in his chair and watched George leave his dinner uneaten, going to join his sister in the parlour.

William bent down and kissed his mother on her cheek. 'I'm sorry, Mother. I'm not staying here to be insulted and I'm sorry if I have upset you. You deserve better than my father and myself, we all must be a huge disappointment to you.' William glared at his father and walked out of the room, slamming the front door of Highfield House behind him.

Catherine tried to control her tears. 'Well, another family meal spoilt by you, Edmund Ellershaw. My father was right, I never should have married you. You came from the gutter and you'll end up back there, the way you behave. But you won't take me and mine with you, we are better than that.'

'Just be quiet, woman, you know nowt,' Edmund growled. 'It was time they heard the truth. They sit around this table like thieving crows, picking me clean of any money they can get out of me, and showing no respect. They and those they associate with can go to hell, as far as I'm concerned, especially that Eliza Wild and the brat she has raised as her own. Bloodsuckers, that's all they are. They will bleed Grace and George dry if they have their way. As for our William, he always has thought himself better than the rest of us. Well, I don't want to see his face again in this house, he's not welcome. Now, you hear what I say, you wash your hands of him.' Edmund pushed his empty plate back. 'I've had enough of today, I'm away to my bed. I'll sleep in the spare room tonight because no doubt you'll not be showing me any affection tonight.'

Edmund got up from the table and belched loudly, leaving Catherine looking at the dinner table in disarray. What had she done to deserve such a family? She'd always been brought up to respect her elders, and there had been William, spouting forth about his father's sins at the dinner table. If she could, she'd leave, but she had nowhere to go to. Edmund had spent all her money and Grace and George needed her. At least Grace had done something with her life and she could be proud of her. Catherine hung her head only to raise it when the butler came to clear the table. 'Thank you, Jenkins, I'm afraid none of us were very hungry.' The butler, full of tact, just smiled. At least someone has manners, she thought as she left the table to face the night on her own.

'Father, Father, wake up. Can you not hear there's trouble at the pit? I can hear the hooter being sounded, it carries on the wind.' Grace shook her father awake and then turned to pull the heavy drapes back and open the window for him to hear the commotion outside.

'Tell Banks to saddle my horse. I'll have to get there quickly. That bloody Tom Thackeray will not know what to do.'

Grace left the room to do his bidding, and Edmund held his head in his hands. He knew exactly what was wrong. He'd been told in no uncertain terms yesterday that the props were not strong

147

enough but he'd chosen to ignore Tom's warnings. Bloody hell, this is all I need, he thought as he went downstairs, still buttoning up as he made his way past his wife who was flapping around him, and strode out into the late spring morning. He caught his breath once he was up and saddled in his horse. His heart beat fast and the blood surged through his veins as he urged his horse forward to the Rose Pit.

Tom Thackeray watched as the men from below in the smoke-filled mine were hoisted up in the metal cage that served as an intermediary between the dark world of the pit face and the world on top. Tom was thankful that the wheel and cage were still working; at least he could get the men out.

He had arrived just as the night shift came up from their long night of picking the black gold from the coalface, blinking in the sharp spring light as they left the cage that brought them back to the real world. Then the day's workforce, shaking their work colleagues' hands as they went down, had returned to the dark underworld they knew so well.

It was a few minutes after that they had heard, from far down in the bowels of the earth, a terrible rumble. Dust and smoke rose up through the mineshaft, which told everybody of the disaster that had unfolded below the earth. The fight was now on to save lives and tend to the injured as the cage lifted the miners to safety. Sweat ran off the cage operators' faces and worry and despair soon filled the pit yard as they waited for the news from below. The wives of the miners huddled together at the pit gates, shawls wrapped around them, waiting for news of their menfolk and hoping to see the faces of their loved ones appear from out of the cage.

Tom swore under his breath. This should not have happened, it was Ellershaw's doing. He should have closed the pit yesterday when he had told him the props were weak. None of this would have happened if he hadn't put profit before lives. Tom rolled up his sleeves and took hold of Bill Parker as he clambered out of the cage filled with wounded men.

'It's not as bad as it looks. None of the day shift had got to the coalface when the ceiling down there gave way. I don't think we've lost anybody,' Bill Parker shouted across the din of the moaning men and the noise of the cage being lowered back down to the men still trapped at the bottom of the shaft. 'But if you'd done something earlier, there needn't have been any of this.' Bill gestured at the men being helped with broken arms and legs and those in shock, thankful that they were above ground and breathing fresh air. 'Both you and Ellershaw are bloody useless. You think nowt of us, we are dispensable, there's always some poor bugger willing to take our place if we die or get maimed. Look at the bastard, he's only just getting his arse here. It's his doing, him and his bloody cheap wood, he should be hung, drawn and quartered.' Edmund Ellershaw was pushing his horse through the crowds of women at the pit gate. Bill Parker turned away abruptly to help a miner with a broken leg away from the hordes around the pit head.

149

'Thackeray, what the hell's going on here?' Edmund Ellershaw strode over to Tom and surveyed the mayhem that came with a pitfall.

'The props have given way on level two. The men had not quite reached the pit head, so Bill Parker has said he doesn't think we have any fatalities, just a lot of injuries.'

'This is all I bloody needed. It'll put us back weeks, and it'll bankrupt me.' Edmund swore.

'Perhaps if the props, like I said yesterday, had been replaced, we would not have been facing this disaster. Some of your best men are coming out injured, but if Bill is right at least no one will have a funeral this day. That is something to be thankful for.'

'Perhaps if you were a better manager and did a better job it wouldn't have happened either. You had every chance to inspect those woods before they were put in, so we are as much to blame as one another. So don't be so condescending, Thackeray. These injured men are just as much your doing as mine, and don't you forget that when you're trying to earn your next crust. Because as of now, you are not working for me. Get your stuff and bugger off. Don't show your face to me again and don't expect this week's wages because there won't be any for the likes of you.'

Edmund Ellershaw knew that Tom would not stand by him if there was to be an inquest into the pit disaster. It was better that he should get rid of the would-be troublemaker before he was to speak the truth.

'I couldn't stay another minute longer anyway. You'd kill all of your men for sake of a few guineas. It's like working for Old Nick himself. Keep your pit and your money, my day will come shortly.'

Tom Thackeray stalked away from Edmund Ellershaw. Bankruptcy was too good for him. No, a man like Ellershaw would be better off dead and buried. One day he would have his own pit, and he would be a better employer than Edmund Ellershaw could ever be. He picked up his belongings and pushed his way through the wailing wives. His days at the Rose were over for now, but he knew that wasn't the last time he'd stand in the pit's yard. The only difference was that the next time he stood there he planned to own it.

Chapter 16

William sat at his desk on the third floor of Aire Valley woollen mill and thought about his father's lecture to his family. He was nothing but a bloody hypocrite. How many whores had he slept with in his life and how many people had he used to get what he wanted? The old bastard.

He was in no mood for work. He leaned back in his chair. On the wall across from him hung a picture of his mother's father, his grandfather, who had once owned the mill, his severe image the very picture of sobriety. Yet another hypocrite, William thought to himself. Everyone knew how he had taken advantage of many of his workers. But at least he had kept a secret, and not flaunted his sexual appetite, unlike his father whose reputation was no better than that of a pig in a gutter. Damn the man. How could someone with his foul manners, language and lascivious behaviour have the gall to tell him what to do?

William rose from his seat and opened his office door that led out to a balcony and stairs that overlooked the carding room. The machines below him cleaned and combed the rough woollen fleeces, the noise from them making it nearly impossible to speak to your fellow worker, and the air was filled with the smell of lanolin and grease that was being extracted from the fleeces. He watched the mill workers go about their jobs. He reached for his pocket watch. Another thirty minutes and then the mill hooter would blow to release the workers from their daily toil, and the machines would fall silent until they arrived at work at six the next morning. Unlike him, most of his employees would going back to homes where they were loved and welcomed. All he returned to was a big house, beautiful but heartless, with a wife more lunatic than sane. He had nowhere to go to seek love and affection, apart from if he paid for it with Ruby Bell, as his father had so sordidly pointed out.

A flash of auburn hair caught his eye as one of his workers adjusted her mob cap, quickly putting it back on again in fear of entrapping her long hair in the machinery. The flash of auburn reminded him of what Priscilla had told him: Mary-Anne Wild was back. And now she had money and a new name, perhaps he should visit her, she had always taken his eye. She had been

152

more beautiful than any of the women of distinction in the area. How stupid he had been, abusing his position, thinking that she would give herself to him. Just because he had thought she should have been impressed at him even looking at her. Besides, it was a good job that he was rejected by her as she must have been carrying the child that her sister had been left rearing. He could have been named as the father if he she had succumbed to his advances. Now that would have given his father something to growl about, with his unjust hatred of the Wild family.

In fact, William mused, nothing would hurt his father more than if he re-kindled a relationship with Mary-Anne Vasey. If that was not reason enough to knock on her door, nothing was. He'd pay her a visit and make himself known to her, despite her rebuke of him all those years ago. He smiled to himself. All he could wish for now was for George to come clean about his own inclinations, and then his father would well and truly upset. But George would not be so stupid as to tell him the truth. He was such a strutting peacock and, if William was not mistaken, more interested in the male of the species than any fair lady. Although he was trying hard to hide it, as his father would more than certainly disinherit him without a second thought – not that his father would have much to leave anyone at this rate. William smiled. 'Father, dear, you don't know anything about your family,' he whispered to himself as he closed his office door behind him.

Mary-Anne sat down, exhausted but satisfied.

153

'Well, we've had a bit of a day,' she told Ma Fletcher, 'but will sleep better tonight in a proper bed.'

She took a mouthful of her supper of bread and dripping and smiled at the old woman. She was such determined old bugger but behind the hard exterior beat a heart of gold.

'Aye, I must thank you for that. I should have got someone to bring that bed from the spare room down before I went off my legs, it will be a lot better than sleeping on that day bed. And the curtain across the room means you don't have to look at my backside as you set the fire.' Ma Fletcher grinned and bit into her bread and dripping.

'You know you could have been more private if you'd put your bed in the front parlour, because I don't think we will ever use it.' Mary-Anne looked across at the curtained off part of the large room that the both of them lived in for most of the day and then took a drink of her tea.

'Nay, it would mean lighting the fire through there, money spent and work that we could do without. It's a good job you've done so far, lass, my old home is beginning to shine again. I could never have done it without you.' Ma Fletcher looked around her at her newly washed ornaments and the scrubbed clean floor. It was a partnership that was working well but they had yet to put their main plan into place.

'I'm grateful for a roof over my head and some privacy. Eliza has made a new life for herself and Victoria and I'd only be in the way. Victoria, I fear, is a little disappointed in me. I'm not what she had hoped to find, I can tell by the disapproving look on her face. It is best that I leave her with my sister until she gets used to me. I must admit, I thought she would have called to visit us by now.' Mary-Anne played with the piece of crust that she had left and stared into the fire.

'She'll be along soon. Give her time. Eliza will talk her around.' Ma Fletcher noticed Mary-Anne's hurt expression and felt sorry for her. 'I'll away to my bed now, it'll be a real luxury. Some nights I thought I'd end up on the floor, balancing on that old sofa. But I couldn't do anything else until you arrived.'

'Come on, take my hand and let's get you to your bed.' Mary-Anne walked over to Ma Fletcher and held her arm out for her to take.

'It's no fun getting old, lass, you'd be better off putting me out of my misery.' Leaning on Mary-Anne, Ma Fletcher shuffled her way to sit on her bed. Mary-Anne peeled the many layers of clothes from her and helped her pull her nightdress on over her head.

'You'll be all right, I'm here now.' Mary-Anne lifted her legs into bed and tucked the clean sheets and blankets up around her.

'Aye, but for how long? You'll soon have men running after you. If you can't snare William Ellershaw, somebody will be soon sniffing at your door.'

'Don't worry about things that haven't happened yet. I'm here and that's all that matters. You enjoy a good night's sleep and tomorrow we will take in our stride.'

The old woman closed her eyes, and Mary-Anne pulled the newly erected curtain behind her, leaving Ma Fletcher to sleep and hopefully forget her worries.

She sat next to the fire and took up a pair of scissors and needle and cotton to alter a dress she had found upstairs. She knew she could make it look stunning if she spent some time on altering and mending the delicate fabric. She soon became engrossed in her mending but was disturbed by a soft knock on the door of her home. The clock on the tall sandstone mantelpiece said it was ten o'clock. Who on earth would be calling on her at that time of night? She placed her sewing down on the arm of her chair and hoped that the knocking had not disturbed Ma Fletcher. She opened the door a crack.

'Hello, Mary-Anne. So I've finally tracked you down.' John Vasey's familiar voice filled her with fear. He stepped forward and wedged his foot.

'John! What are you doing here? How did you get here? I thought you were still in jail!' Mary-Anne exclaimed.

'I bet you did. You couldn't get away from me fast enough could you, my lovely wee bonny girl. I've pawned everything we owned to find you, that's how much I love you, woman.' John pushed the door open and slammed it closed behind him as he pushed Mary-Anne into the room.

'I'd had enough. I was sick and tired of listening to you fighting everybody else's corner but ours, and the drink was getting the better of you. I'm not a woman that will keep taking a beating. I saw my mother take too many so I left you when I saw my chance. I can't live like that any more, John. I need stability in my life and I owe more to my daughter than what I've been giving her.'

'I'm sorry the drink has got the better of me. But you broke my heart when you left. And it is for the likes of you and us that I make a stand for the downtrodden of the world; someone needs a voice that everyone can hear. I love you, Mary-Anne, I'll always love you. Come back with me to where you belong. Victoria can join us, we'll manage somehow. We can go anywhere, even back to New York, although your boss sent the police around when he realised what you had done.' John took Mary-Anne by her arms and looked into her tear-filled eyes. 'For sure, I can't live without you. If you won't come with me, then I'll have nothing in the world. I love you, woman, do I have to spell it out?'

'I'm sorry, John, I didn't mean to hurt you. But you've hurt me once too often. I've had enough of my life in America, it's no better than the one I left here, and at least here I'm near to my daughter and you know how much she means to me.' Mary-Anne looked away, not wanting to see the hurt in John's eyes. He was sober now but after a drink or two his tune would be different.

'And me, do you not love me any more? I thought we lived for one another. I risked everything for you. You've stolen money from your employers and I was thrown out of our apartment. To be sure, you've left me with nothing, Mary-Anne, except the hope that you'll give me a chance to mend my ways.'

'Then all hope is dead, John. I don't love you any more and I won't be returning back to New York with you.' Mary-Anne stood her ground.

157

'I've had enough. I'm back where I belong, with my family, and I have a good home here. I hope to gain a secure future for both Victoria and myself without you.' Mary-Anne breathed in deeply. She had loved John once and hadn't wanted to hurt him further. Why had he followed her and how had he found out where she was living? She trusted Eliza not to tell him about her new home with Ma Fletcher.

'Please, Mary-Anne, I can't face life without you. It is you that gives me strength and purpose.' John pleaded. 'There's a ship I can earn our passage on from Liverpool on Friday, so I'll be away by Wednesday, which gives you two days to change your mind. I'm lodging down by the docks, you'll find me down there. Please return with me, Mary-Anne. One day I'll give you a house like this and more besides, if that's what you want. And Victoria is such a grand little lass, she takes after you. If it hadn't been for her I'd never have found you.'

'Victoria! You've met my Victoria?' Mary-Anne exclaimed.

'Aye, it was her who told me where I could find you and she gave me a copper or two. She's a grand little lady, your Eliza has brought her up well. She must want us to stay together, either that or she felt sorry for me when I said I was here to take you back to America because I couldn't live without you.' John smiled at the woman he loved.

'Well, she thought wrong. Now get on your way and don't hold any hope of me returning with you because my life is here now. After all, we're not even married, so that just shows how much you love me, John Vasey. You've had twelve years to make me an honest woman. I'm about to change my life and this time for the better.' Mary-Anne went to the door and opened it wide, letting the night air in and making the flames flicker in the oil lamps.

'I'll always love you, Mary-Anne.' John put his hand on her arm. 'I can't face life without you.'

'Aye, well, you'll soon get over me. Go on, take care of yourself and find somebody better than me. You deserve a better woman than me.' Mary-Anne watched him put his cap on his head, pull his collar up against the cold and walk out into the dark night. She turned and wiped tears away from her cheeks. A cloak of sadness fell over her; she had loved John Vasey once, but now she needed more from life.

From behind the curtain, Ma Fletcher's voice came. 'That man loves you, Mary-Anne. He's come halfway round the world to find you.'

Mary-Anne sniffed. 'Well, I don't love him any more. He'll never give me what I want and need.'

'Brass isn't everything, lass. I hope you know what you are doing, else more hurt will follow,' Ma Fletcher said softly.

'I don't care, he'll be waiting a long time to hear from me again. The sooner he gets himself home the sooner we can both get on with our lives.'

Mary-Anne had no intentions of returning to John Vasey, not now, not ever.

Chapter 17

It was the early morning, and mist swirled around a group of dock workers. They were all staring at the body that had just been pulled out of the cut. It had taken three or four men to drag the body of the man out of the dirty waters and now they sat exhausted on the cobbled bank. A crowd had already gathered, and was leering at the body. It was their source of entertainment for the day, something to talk about over the supper table and for the truth to be embroidered upon as they fantasised on how his death had come about.

One of the dock workers knelt down at the side of the fully dressed broad-shouldered man. 'Bloody hell, he's taken some fishing out.' He rifled through the drowned man's sodden pockets but found no evidence of his name and address. 'Anyone here knows him?' He looked, around at the men and women staring at the corpse. The crowd shook their heads and mumbled to one another as the local Peeler pushed himself through them and stood over the dead body.

'Right now, you lot, get yourself home. There's nothing more to see here.' The Peeler summoned the two young Peelers that had followed him with a stretcher. All three struggled as they lifted up the body and were just about to carry it away when the woman who ran the boarding house ran to them holding a scrap of paper and a dirty knotted handkerchief full of possessions.

'Here, officer, I know who he is, the poor bugger. He's been lodging with me, he came over from the Americas looking for his wife. He was drunk again the other night because she had told him to bugger off back without him. The silly fool must have fallen into the cut. He gave his name as John Vasey. Here, he'd obviously known she wasn't going to go back with him because he'd written this letter, it's got her address on it.' The old crone handed John's letter over to the first Peeler and watched as he read it and opened the handkerchief to reveal a pocket watch, a bible with a pressed flower in it and a few coins.

'Are you sure that is all he left behind?' the Peeler asked the old woman.

'Now, sir, I wouldn't steal from the dead. I need my soul to go to heaven, so I do.' The old woman turned her back on the body and the Peelers. She sighed. Sometimes, no matter how honest you were, you'd never be believed that when you'd helped yourself to the gold sovereign within, it was to pay for his board, with perhaps a bit left over. After all, his wife didn't deserve it and he wouldn't be wanting it any more.

'Old woman, did he owe you anything?' the Peeler shouted after her.

She stopped in her tracks and smiled. 'That he did. He'd been with me for nearly a week and only paid for the first two days.'

'Here then, take these few pence, it's not as if he'll be needing them where he's gone to.' The Peeler shoved the few coins in her grubby hands. 'You have an extra bed to let tonight,' he said as he and his colleagues walked away with the corpse of John Vasey.

'Who the devil is knocking on the door at this time of the morning? I'm not even decent yet!' Ma Fletcher, still in her nightdress, said as she ate her dishful of porridge next to the newly lighted fire. 'It'll be your man coming to plead for you again. Tell him to be on his way and not to bother us again, the poor bugger.'

Mary-Anne wiped her hands on her apron and glanced out of the room's panelled window. 'Bugger, it's a Peeler. They must have had news from America about me being here, but I don't know how! You know nothing, you just took me in because you needed my help and I needed somewhere to live.' Mary-Anne warned Ma Fletcher as she opened the door to the unwelcome visitor.

'Mrs Vasey?' The Peeler took off his helmet.

'Yes. What do you want with me at this time of the morning?' Why had the officer called her Mrs Vasey?

'I think you had better let me in, Mrs Vasey, and you may need to sit down. I'm afraid I've some bad news.' The officer bent his head and pushed his way inside. 'And you are?' He asked Ma Fletcher.

'I own this place. Mary-Anne lives here with me and looks after me. Now, what are you about?' Ma Fletcher hated the Peelers. They had always been on her back when dealing with the market.

'He says he's got bad news, Ma. Tell me it's not my Victoria or my sister. They are both all right, aren't they?' Mary-Anne shook, watching the officer as he drew the note and handkerchief out of his pocket.

'As far as I know, Mrs Vasey. I'm afraid it is your husband, John. I'm sorry to say that he lost his life sometime late last night after falling into the canal. The landlady said that he'd been drinking. He was fished out of the cut just below Crown Point Bridge. He left you this letter where he had been staying, that's how we have tracked you down.' The Peeler passed Mary-Anne the letter and the handkerchief and watched her eyes fill with tears as she slumped into a chair. 'His body is being held in the morgue. There are no suspicious circumstances, the letter tells us what state of mind he was in. I'm sorry for your loss. Is it true that you were estranged from Mr Vasey?'

Mary-Anne couldn't stop her hands from trembling. 'We were never married. I took his name but we were never wed. That was why I had returned home, that and the fact that I was missing my daughter.'

'Your daughter?' The Peeler looked at her.

'Yes, she's been living with my sister Eliza Wild. She runs the dress and haberdashery shop on Boar Lane. Grace Ellershaw is the main owner.'

'I know it well. My wife would very much like me to earn more pay so that she could shop there.' The Peeler looked embarrassed at mentioning his home life to a woman who had just lost her man. 'I'm so sorry for your loss, miss. He must have been feeling low in spirits, and turned to the drink a little too much.' He glanced at Ma Fletcher who sat silently next to the fire, a shawl hastily wrapped around her nightdress. These seemed like decent people and he was sorry to bring sorrow to their door. 'We will hold his body in the mortuary for seven days and then give him a pauper's burial, unless you want to claim the body, miss?'

'I've not much money, I don't know if I can afford to bury him,' Mary-Anne sobbed.

Ma Fletcher said in a severe voice, 'You'll do right by him, Mary-Anne. You'll give him as decent a grave as you can, seeing he's died in disgrace in the good Lord's eyes. I'll give you the money to bury the lost soul.' Ma Fletcher's hand shook as she held her handkerchief to her nose. 'We'll do right by him, officer, he's not a pauper, and he was a good man. Too caring, if anything.' Ma Fletcher sighed. She'd warned Mary-Anne that her flippant ways towards John Vasey would bring no good and now this was the outcome. 'He was a Catholic. We'll see if the priest will accept him and take him off your hands as soon as possible.'

Mary-Anne hung her head. She wanted to be alone in her grief and to read the last words of John, the man that she did once love.

'I'll leave it to you, then. I take it you'll arrange everything?' The officer looked at Mary-Anne and then Ma Fletcher.

'Aye, lad, we will sort it. Thank you for coming out with the news, albeit bad.' Ma Fletcher watched Mary-Anne show the Peeler out, and, as he gave his sympathies to her once again, she noticed her wipe a tear away as she shut the door behind him.

'Well, that's the end of him, lass. There's no

going back to Yank land now. You've made your bed so you must lie on it. Let's hope that your plans for William Ellershaw come to something, else he's lost his life for nowt.' Ma Fletcher's words might have been harsh, but her voice was tinged with sympathy.

Mary-Anne sobbed. 'I didn't think he cared that much for me. Why, why did he turn to the drink, Ma? He could have a good life, he was clever and kind when not drinking. He could have found somebody else.'

'You'll might find out when you read his letter, lass. I'll get dressed while you read it and then we'll have to sort him a funeral.' Ma Fletcher got up from her seat and made her way to the privacy of her curtained room, leaving Mary-Anne sat reading the last words of John Vasey.

My dearest Mary-Anne,

By the time you read this letter, I will be on my way back to Liverpool. I have realised that you have no intentions of joining me, no matter how much I tell you I love you. I'm sorry that I have caused you pain and have disappointed you, however I know I have only myself to blame. I don't know if I have the strength to live without you, I'm a broken man, Mary-Anne. Everything and everybody I have ever loved, I have lost. Life holds no more joy for me but I will have to learn to live without you by my side.
My heart will always be yours.
Take care, my love.
John

Mary-Anne wept, then reached for the handker-chief that held the few humble possessions that John had left behind him. He had told her that he had pawned the few things they owned to get to her. But possessions had meant nothing to her when she had first loved him. When had she be-come so hard-hearted? Was the pursuit of wealth and all its trappings really worth the heartache it seemed to bring? She held John's pocket watch in her hand and remembered her stubborn Irishman who had once filled her life with hope and love.

Mary-Anne stood in the gloom of the churchyard of St Mary's. It was dark, lit only with the grave-diggers' lamps as they filled in John's grave. No one else had attended the graveside, not even the priest to bless his body as he was lowered below into the earth. The priest had muttered that he was concerned that John's death might have well been suicide and not an accident when told of his death, and suicide was a most unforgivable sin in the eyes of the Catholic Church. Because of that, John's body was being buried at the fall of the night on the north side of the churchyard in a place es-pecially saved for the unbaptised, the suicides, the criminal and insane of society. She looked around her at the dark tree branches hanging over the churchyard and at the small tower of the church that John had always attended along with the rest of the Irish immigrant community of Leeds when he had first lived there. She sighed. What a waste of a life, to die like that. Guilt had racked her body since the news of his death and now her heart hurt as she looked down upon his grave.

'Right, we are off now, missus. We reckon nowt to being here after dark, especially about these unholy souls that are buried in this part.' The gravediggers looked at her for a second and then disappeared into the fading light, leaving Mary-Anne standing over the fresh grave with a small spray of forget-me-nots in her hands, which she bent down and placed on the unmarked grave.

'Forgive me, John. I did once love you. But I wanted more, something that you could not give me. Perhaps now we will both be happy. I hope that you will be reunited in heaven with your family, no matter what the priest says. You were a good man at heart. God bless.'

Mary-Anne wiped away her tears as she turned her back on the grave and made her way back to Ma Fletcher's and her new life. She would never forget John Vasey, and guilt would always settle over her when she thought of her mild-mannered Irishman.

Chapter 18

Mary-Anne stepped out along the flowering banks of the canal's towpath on her way to visit Victoria. Since John's death and his burial, she had put her heartache into cleaning Ma Fletcher's house, which was now spotless. All the pottery had been washed, along with bedding and cur-tains, the floors were swept, and the house looked suitable for the Queen herself. Ma Fletcher also now looked more like the woman she used to be and was more than satisfied with her bargain with Mary-Anne. She enjoyed waking up to the fire lit and the kettle singing on the hearth every morning.

Now, it was time for Mary-Anne to get to know her daughter better, to assure her that even though John Vasey had turned up looking for her, that she never had any intention of returning to America with him. At one time, she would have followed him even to the ends of the earth, but she realised now he had been too much of an idealist and that he should have known that he would never be able to change the world on his own. That had been part of the problem – he had expected everybody to be perfect, but, unfortunately, neither the world nor the people within it would ever be.

She crossed over the bridge that she had stood on a long time ago. She had been at her lowest ebb – unmarried and undone, pregnant with Victoria – and she had almost thrown herself in. A cold shiver went down her spine as she stopped to look down into the dark, filthy waters of the canal. She herself had nearly ended up in the cut and, as she tried block out thoughts of John fighting for his life, a feeling of desperation flowed over her. She owed a lot to John Vasey. He had saved her life that day when he had stopped her from doing herself harm. Why couldn't she have been there for him in his hour of need? Poor John, he might not have always been kind to her, but there were times when she could have treated him better.

She thought about everything she needed to do to make Edmund Ellershaw pay for his treatment of both her and her mother. It was all for Victoria's sake, and she must not lose sight of that, no matter what. She gathered herself together and walked quickly along the towpath, nodding her head in greeting to the barge hands as their horses pulled the heavy barges filled with coal. Coal that might have come from the Rose Pit and should rightly be part of Victoria's inheritance, she thought, as she climbed the path away from the canalside and followed the road into Woodlesford.

'Mother! I wasn't expecting you.' Victoria rose from her chair and placed her embroidery down on the small walnut table next to the window, where she had been sitting. The maid that had answered the door, curtsied, and left mother and child together.

Mary-Anne looked at the surprise on her daughter's face. 'Did you think I'd have disappeared with John Vasey, seeing you were good enough to tell him where I live?' Despite Mary-Anne's intention to mend bridges with her young daughter, she couldn't help the tinge of anger that seeped into her words. 'I thought I made it clear that I did not want to be found by him. Or did you want him to find me? Perhaps for me to return to America with him and then your life could return back to normal?' Mary-Anne sat down in the chair across from her daughter, removing the hat pin from her small green velvet hat and placing it on the table next to Victoria's embroidery.

'No, Mother, I didn't do it for that reason, you are wrong.' Victoria dropped her head, realising that even though she had not known her mother long, her mother knew her well enough to realise that she had told John on purpose. 'I told him because he was in such a state. He was heartbroken, I had to tell him. And when Aunt Eliza saw the news of his death in the paper, she knew that you'd be upset, and she was waiting to hear from you.'

'Well, my dear, I wish you had said nothing and then he might still be alive today and making his way back to America. As it is, I buried him on Monday. I'm afraid it was as they printed, that he drowned himself in the canal. I couldn't face Eliza and you before his funeral, it has caused me so much pain.' Mary-Anne bowed her head and then lifted it up to look at her daughter, realising she felt guilty enough over John without laying blame at her daughter's feet. 'I don't mean to be hard on you. It's not your fault, Victoria, but it is mine. It seems everything I touch ends up broken and destroyed. But I aim to amend that. This is to be a new chapter in my life and I am not going to let you down. I'm going to make you proud of your mother, just like you are of Aunt Eliza. You are my most precious girl. And although I might be a bit rough around the edges, it is only because I have had to fight for everything I've ever held precious to me.'

'Oh, Mother, poor John Vasey, I knew he looked heartbroken. George scoffed at me taking pity on him, but he looked so lost.' Victoria held her tears back for the man that she hardly knew, feeling slightly guilty that perhaps if she had not given the address of her mother, he may still be alive. 'I'm sorry if you think that I have shown you any disrespect, I don't mean to. I must admit, I'm finding it hard as Aunt Eliza has always been there for me and I feel that I no longer know what to feel now you are here in the flesh.'

Most of the time, Victoria felt no love towards her mother. She had wanted to meet her for so long, but now that she had, she didn't feel the connection to her that she had expected. Her love was for her Aunt Eliza, not the woman that sat across from her, and who seemed to think that she should be welcomed with open arms.

'It will take time, Victoria, for us to get to know one another. We will take it slow, share our time together when we can. You remind me of myself at your age: you are stubborn and know your own mind. Which is sometimes a good thing. Now, you said you were with George Ellershaw when you spoke to John? I do wish that he would keep his distance from you.' Mary-Anne noticed a blush rise to her daughter's cheeks.

'I don't know why he takes so much interest in me. Aunt Eliza says that he regards me as his pet. I did think he was wonderful once, but no longer – he thinks too much of himself. Aunt Eliza has told me to keep him at arm's length and that's what I do.' Victoria, embarrassed by her confession, looked out of the window.

'When I first arrived, I thought that his affections towards you were to be encouraged. Now I think it is best that you should not see so much of him. The men of his family are to be avoided, their morals are not of the highest standard as I'm sure your aunt may have told you.'

Mary-Anne smiled at her daughter. Time would bind them together and she aimed to spend a lot of time with her daughter now she was back home.

'Now, what are you about today? Embroidery? Do you enjoy sewing? Eliza will be hoping that you will join her in the shop one day, I suppose. Myself, I hope for you to set your sights higher, marry a man high up in society. You have all the skills, education and manners to secure one, in good time, of course.'

'Aunt Eliza wants the same thing, in fact, she is making me a new ball gown to introduce me to society at the Guild Ball. She says it is the place to be seen, although I am only allowed to stay an hour as I am really too young.' Victoria looked coyly at her mother.

'Quite right, but do you have tickets for the ball? They are sent out only to the few that the Guild think worthy of attending.'

'Oh, yes, Aunt Eliza has been invited for the last few years, however this year she said we can both attend.'

'Do you think I could ask for you to show me your invitation? I've heard so much about the ball, it is such an honour for you both to be asked to attend.'

'Of course, Mother. Aunt Eliza will have them on the top of her desk, I'll go and get them for you from the room next door.' Victoria smiled at the excitement on her mother's face and left the room to retrieve the coveted tickets.

While Mary-Anne waited for her daughter to return, she looked around her sister's parlour. While the furnishings were plush and expensive, and while Mary-Anne had seen the high esteem Eliza was held in by her staff and customers, the true sign of having come up in the world was an invitation to attend the Guild Ball, and Eliza had been invited. Her sister's life now was a million miles away from Pit Lane and buying the second-hand rags from Ma Fletcher's stall, where they both had started out.

'Here, Mother, aren't they a delight? The lettering is always in gold, they look so expensive.' Victoria passed the gold embossed cards over to Mary-Anne and sat across from her, watching her reading every word.

'Well, I never thought I'd hold one of these in my hands. Your aunt should be proud of herself, and yes, you go and enjoy yourself while you're too young to get into trouble. You are about to start the best years of your life, but believe me, those years are fleeting. Especially when you are married and have responsibilities.' Mary-Anne held the cards with care in her hands. She noted that the invitations did not show the recipient's name upon them. She tried not to let her excitement show on her face when she passed the cards back to Victoria, instead she swallowed hard as if to suppress a cough but then started to splutter and cough harder.

'Mother, are you all right? Would you like a drink of water?' Victoria stood up and placed the invitations safely upon the marble fireplace.

'Thank you, my dear. I don't quite know what

173

is wrong with me. Perhaps the air in this room is a little too dry for me. After all, you do have a blazing fire lit and it is quite a fine day.' Mary-Anne smiled when Victoria left the room and gratefully took a sip of water from the glass her daughter handed her when she returned.

'Would you like me to open the window for you, in order to let some fresh air into the room?'

'Don't worry, my dear.' Mary-Anne rose from her chair. 'I'm going to have to go now. I can't leave Ma Fletcher too long, she has become rather dependent on me. Now, will you come and have tea with me at my home? Or should we meet in a tearoom and then we could visit your aunt and you can show me this dress that you are going to stun society in?'

'I'll come to your home, Mother. Aunt Eliza has told me so much about Ma Fletcher and the days that you used to buy clothes from her. I'd like to meet her, I think.' Victoria hesitated, thinking about the tales of how rough and ready Aunt Eliza had told her Ma Fletcher was and wondered if she should have agreed to visit her.

'Ma Fletcher's bark is worse than her bite. I think you'll be pleasantly surprised by her home. I couldn't believe that she had such a lovely house and it is sparkling like a new penny now, thanks to my elbow grease. Do come, I would like for her to meet you.' Mary-Anne placed her hat upon her head as she passed the hallway mirror, securing it with the pearl-handled hatpin, and smiled at her reflection. 'Perhaps Monday next week?'

'I will then, Mother. Monday, next week, and then we can still go and see Aunt Eliza in the store. My dress should be finished by then and I can try it on for you.' Victoria opened the front door for her mother, who kissed her on both cheeks and made her way down the scrubbed-clean sandstone steps.

'Until next week then, Victoria. I'll look forward to seeing you. You know where Speakers' Corner is, don't you?' Mary-Anne pulled the iron garden gate open and waited for a reply.

'Yes, Mother, I know Speakers' Corner. I'll ask my aunt if I can bring a cake.' She watched as her mother bustled down the street, her auburn hair shining from beneath her jaunty hat and her skirts billowing in the soft spring breeze. Her aunt was right: Mary-Anne had the looks while her aunt had the brains. Victoria's only hope was that she had been blessed with both – and as for inheriting any of her father's traits, she would never know. As she turned to close the door she remembered poor John Vasey. Perhaps she was partly responsible for his death as her mother said.

'You are a terribly wicked woman, Mary-Anne Vasey. How could you steal from your own daughter? Your sister will soon put one and one together when she cottons on to when it went missing.' Ma Fletcher looked at Mary-Anne's precious prize, stolen from under her daughter's own nose.

'I couldn't resist. Besides, our Eliza will be able to get another invitation. She's obviously thought a lot of in the society she keeps.' Mary-Anne smiled as she looked at the gilt-edged card. This was her way into the Guild Ball and the chance to flaunt herself in front of William Ellershaw.

'And there was me thinking that your visit to see your Victoria was to win her around. She's not going to think a lot of you when she discovers you've stolen the invitation to her first ball.' Ma Fletcher shook her head. Sometimes the lass had no sense.

'She'll never know. Eliza won't tell her, she's got more sense than to do that. Besides, there'll be plenty of time for balls when Victoria is grown up.' Mary-Anne placed the invitation safely in the top drawer of the chest that held Ma Fletcher's valued documents. 'Now, what am I going to wear? Should I ask our Eliza to make me something or is that pushing our love of one another a bit too far?'

'Brazen, that's what you are. If you've any sense you'll not even think of it. But if you must, go and look in that far room upstairs, the one with the locked trunks. You'll find the keys to them in those drawers. I'm sure there will be something in one of them that'll take your fancy. You might have to alter and titivate it to your style and fitting, but that's no hardship for you. You were always a fair seamstress even if your sister was more handy with her designs. The clothes up in those trunks came from Rothwell Hall, my old man had an understanding with the butler there. A few pence and he got all Lady Armstrong's cast-offs. Some of those dresses will be worth a small fortune – you'll look the part in one of them.' Ma Fletcher sat back in her chair and watched a smile on Mary-Anne's face grow into a grin.

'What would I do without you, Ma? You are my

saviour.' Mary-Anne opened the top drawer and searched for the keys to the trunks, finding them behind numerous paid bills and other documents that hadn't been sorted for years. She smiled as she made her way across the stone-flagged floor and up the creaking oak stairs to the top bedrooms.

'I suppose I'll have to wait for my supper?' Ma Fletcher yelled up after her, but never got a reply as she heard the floorboards above her head creak with Mary-Anne's weight walking over them. She'd have to wait at least an hour, she thought as she closed her eyes and imagined Mary-Anne's delight on finding the expensive garments that had been put away for safe keeping and a future purpose. That purpose was now here and Mary-Anne would be one of the best-dressed women in Leeds, if they both had their way.

Mary-Anne walked into the back bedroom that she had cleared and cleaned. She had wondered at the time what was inside the two locked trunks that she had struggled to move when she had swept the floor clear of dust and cobwebs. It was early evening, and she pulled back the curtains to let more light into the darkening bedroom. The clothes inside must be precious, she thought, fumbling with the locks in eagerness to see what lay within.

When she opened the lid, she was not disappointed as layers of the most expensive clothes lay inside, waiting to be worn and shown off to their best advantage. Green silks, blue taffeta, red velvets all embellished with the best Nottingham lace and finest ribbons. Mary-Anne couldn't believe it as she pulled all the dresses out, laying them out on the oak boards of the bedroom floor before opening the second trunk. It was filled with fine day clothes, plainer in colour but very well made and timeless in design. Mary-Anne sat among the clothes and luggage holding a long, red velvet dress to her waist. This was the one. If she was going to play the scarlet lady, she might as well be dressed the part when she made her entrance at the Guild Ball. She gazed around her in disbelief of the amount of clothes spread about her and the sheer beauty of them.

Just before she rose to her feet, she noticed right at the bottom of one of the trunks a pair of baby's booties and a silver rattle wrapped up lovingly in tissue paper. They seemed at odds with the elegant ball gowns and finery. What were they doing there? Ma Fletcher had no children, yet there they were carefully preserved along with the rest of the clothes. She'd ask Ma Fletcher whose they were when she went back downstairs, but for now, she must go and see herself in her wardrobe mirror. She ran into her bedroom, holding the red dress to her and pulling out the long exotic skirt to its full width, and admired herself in her wardrobe mirror. How could anyone not admire me in this dress, she thought. William Ellershaw would have to be blind and stupid not to notice her, and she knew he was neither. This was the dress: a tuck here and a tuck there and it would be perfect.

Mary-Anne sat beside Ma Fletcher's bed, waiting until she had finished her hot milk before going

to sleep. The baby clothes had
her mind since she had found the
'Ma, when I was going throug
came across a rattle and some boot
dered whose they were. The little l
lovely.'

The old woman's eyes filled with te_ _and pain. 'I'd nearly forgotten about them being there. They are the only things I have left of my bonny lad, Charlie. My bonny lad that was killed, murdered by the bastard Ellershaw. I've never told you this before, but Edmund Ellershaw ran his horse over my only son when he was playing in the street. He could see him as clear as day but he still galloped his horse right into him, shouting, "Get out of my way, you vermin" and then laughed as my little boy was stamped on and tangled around his horse's hooves. Left him for dead, he did. Charlie weren't even four but he didn't give a damn. Ellershaw tried to make things right and calm the gossip about him by giving me a sovereign, but I wouldn't take it. When it came up under the magistrate's court, the big wigs took his side, they didn't dare do any other, saying I was an uncaring mother, letting my child play in the street at such a young age. He is the scum of the earth – a cold-hearted bastard – and before I depart this mortal coil, I hope to see him rot in hell.' Ma Fletcher stifled a sob. 'We have a lot in common when it comes to Edmund Ellershaw. He took my child away from me and he gave you one you didn't want. I can never forgive him. I still awake of a night, screaming as I did when I ran out of the house to see my lad lying like a rag doll, dead in

t. And he, with his posh friends in high s, was never held accountable for his actions. e lied when he said my lad ran out straight in front of him. The bastard.' Ma Fletcher sat back in her bed, wiped tears from her eyes and sniffed hard.

'I didn't know that you had lost a child, and under such terrible circumstances, I'm so sorry for you.' Mary-Anne put her arms around the old woman. 'How could he gallop his horse over a child?'

'Life is cheap to him. How many people have been maimed or killed in his pits? Your father among them. And William's father-in-law is no better, the children that were harmed and left limbless because of his woollen mills must number in the hundreds. Life is nothing to those sort of men; money and profit is everything.' Ma Fletcher breathed in deeply and leaned back in her bed to sleep. 'Now, lass, leave me be, this old woman's ready to sleep. At least I forget my troubles when I'm in the land of nod.'

Mary-Anne kissed Ma on her forehead and watched her furrowed brow become smooth in sleep. So, that was why she had taken pity on Mary-Anne's plight. They were both victims of that uncaring bastard Edmund Ellershaw.

Chapter 19

William Ellershaw blended into the shadows of the ginnel that led off Speakers' Corner. This was the most convenient spot for him to watch the comings and goings of Mary-Anne Vasey. He'd spied on the house for an evening or two, waiting to see if she had any gentlemen callers in her new home or if she was all alone in the house. Up to now, he'd seen nobody, so, taking a long draw on his cigar, he decided to make himself known to Mrs Vasey. From what he could see, she was still as beautiful; even more so now she was so elegantly dressed. God, he'd been a fool not to treat her with a bit more care. She'd always had more brains than his simple wife and he should have known that. He'd regretted her slipping through his fingers from the minute he had married Priscilla but all was not yet lost. Perhaps her going to America and him building himself up in business had to happen before he realised what he wanted in life.

He threw down his cigar and stamped the glowing embers out with his foot before walking across the cobbled road. He hesitated for a second before opening the garden gate and knocking on the door, and his stomach churned as he waited for a reply. What was wrong with him? She was only a woman, a woman who had been penniless a few years ago. Perhaps if he had had his way with her then, he would have forgotten her by now. Standing on the step, he felt like an errant schoolboy, worrying over how to explain his calling on her at this late hour.

Mary-Anne sat contentedly, altering the red velvet dress she had set her heart on wearing for the Guild Ball. She smiled to herself as she added a tight tuck to the bodice. She was intent on showing her curves off to one and all. She might not be wealthy, but her figure and her looks had always helped her when it came to turning heads.

From behind the curtains, Ma Fletcher snored like a stuffed pig. While Ma had been a surprising benefactor to Mary-Anne, since she'd reappeared in her life, Ma had steadily improved. She was no longer the lost soul who depended on Benjamin Jubb and the likes to keep her fed. As long as Ma kept her part of the deal, Mary-Anne would be happy. After all, what more could she want for? She was fed, warm, with a roof over her head and had all the fine clothes she needed. It was up to her which way her life went from now on.

She went back to concentrating on her alterations, only to be interrupted by a knock on the door. The knock was so loud it stopped Ma Fletcher from snoring and Mary-Anne heard her turn over in her bed and mumble something to herself. She placed her mending down by her side and went to see who it was calling so late.

She slid back the bolt and opened the door to find a tall gentleman, finely dressed with a cape and top hat with a walking cane in his hand, his back was turned to her as if he wasn't expecting her to open the door to his knock.

'Yes, may I help you?' The stranger turned to face her and she caught sight of his features in the dim gaslight.

'I do apologise, I know I'm calling late, but Grace told me you had returned to Leeds, and since I was in the area I thought that I would call and make myself known to you once again.' William saw the shocked expression on Mary-Anne's face, he looked down at his shoes and tapped his cane. Now that he was face to face with his quarry, he felt a little embarrassed at calling on her at such an hour. He'd also lied about who had told him of Mary-Anne's arrival back to Leeds, but in the circumstances, it didn't seem right to mention his wife. 'I'm sorry, I can leave if you wish, I'd totally understand.'

'No, not at all, it is just a shock to see you. For a second or two, I didn't recognise you. After all, it has been nearly thirteen years since we last met.' William had aged. There was a sprinkling of grey in the hair she could see beneath the hat and he'd grown a moustache. But the high cheekbones were still there, giving him a debonair look.

'Yes, that is why I'm here. I felt the need to apologise for my fearful conduct during our last meeting. I fear I was young and arrogant and should have known better.' William looked into Mary-Anne's eyes and he remembered the look of fear in them as she had told him no uncertain manner that his advances to her had not been welcome. 'Anyway, it is late. Perhaps, if you have it in your heart to trust me, we could meet at a politer time and have tea together?'

Mary-Anne couldn't quite believe that the man she'd planned to catch was standing on her doorstep. He'd come to her without any need to plot and scheme.

'Would you care to join me for tea now? The kettle is near to the boil. It's not that late and I don't retire until after eleven as a rule.' Mary-Anne wondered for a fleeting moment whether she had done the right thing, however Ma Fletcher was there as a witness, and would to raise the alarm if she needed rescuing.

'Are you sure? I don't want to impose.'

'No, please, do come in. You have taken the trouble to find me and apologise for the pasts misgivings. Let us start afresh and perhaps become friends. After all, your sister and mine are in business together, and your brother George is very sweet to my Victoria. We should be friends. After all, we are both more mature now and we can put our past misunderstandings behind us.' Mary-Anne smiled at William as she guided him into the drawing room.

'I thank you for your kindness and understanding. As you say, we may as well be related, Grace thinks so highly of your sister. As for George, I didn't realise that he was friends with your daughter. I don't have much to do with my younger brother, we are different in many ways.' William looked around him. 'You have a beautiful home. America must have been good to you. Grace told me that you are a widow, so perhaps I should re-phrase that and say that you have succeeded in wealth but perhaps not happiness, as the death of your husband must have been a

184

shock, as you are very young to be a widow.'

Mary-Anne remembered that she had told Grace that her husband was dead and felt a pang of guilt, wondering if she had brought on the death of John Vasey with her wishful thinking. In the last day or two, she had realised that for all their problems she had loved him and that her life was sadder without him in it.

'Yes, I lost my husband, nothing could be done for him. Please do sit down and I will make us both a cup of tea.' Mary-Anne did not want to dwell on the subject for fear that she would show the emotion that she had been feeling over the John's death.

'I'm sorry, I've upset you. Please don't bother with the tea, I won't stay. But would you meet me for luncheon? Say next Tuesday? I've some business to do in the centre of Leeds but Whitelocks Luncheon Bar, just off Briggate, is not out of my way and it serves some wonderful food.'

'Yes, that would be lovely. I'll look forward to it.' Mary-Anne couldn't believe how polite and agreeable William had become.

'Until Tuesday, then.' As Mary-Anne led William back through the house to the front door, he glimpsed the pulled curtain in the main room but did not comment on it.

'Thank you. I will look forward to our meeting on Tuesday. Goodnight.' Mary-Anne stood on the doorstep and watched William make his way into the dark night. Closing the door, she leaned against it for a moment, thinking of what she should do next.

'Bloody hell, lass. If I could bottle what them

men see in you, I'd make a bloody fortune. He's played right into your hands and you didn't have to lift a finger,' Ma Fletcher shouted from behind her curtain.

'He's changed, he's changed a lot. He's quite a gentleman.' Mary-Anne pulled the curtain back to see her landlady lying in her bed, wide awake and clearly enjoying her late-night eavesdropping.

'Nay, he hasn't, lass. A leopard never changes its spots. He'll still be the bastard he always was. You take heed and look out for yourself. Dinner at the Luncheon Bar. That'll cost him a pretty penny, you fill your boots and get what you can out of him.' Ma Fletcher plumped her pillow up and closed her eyes.

'That I will do, Ma, don't you worry.' Mary-Anne smiled and left her benefactor to sleep.

Monday morning found Mary-Anne in a quiet state of panic as she waited for Victoria to visit her. Ma Fletcher was up, washed and dressed in one of her better dresses, and had been asked to watch her Ps and Qs when speaking to Victoria.

'She's no but your lass. She might share our good Queen's name but that doesn't mean I should curtsey and pull my forelock,' Ma Fletcher moaned as Mary-Anne fussed around her.

'No, but our Eliza has brought her up proper and I want her to know that we can have manners too.' Mary-Anne twitched the net curtains aside, looking down the cobbled street to see if she could see her daughter.

'Well, pinching her ball ticket won't have helped you, let's face it.' Ma Fletcher huffed and sat back in her chair with the cat on her knee.

'She might not have realised it is missing. Now, shush, she's here. Remember: we have manners.'

Mary-Anne breathed in deeply and smiled as she answered the door before her daughter even knocked on it.

'Victoria, I saw you coming. Do come in, my darling. Ma Fletcher is waiting to see you and I have baked a cake. I do hope that you like caraway seed cake, it does have a certain taste, it is one of those that you either love or hate.' Mary-Anne felt as if she was being inspected by her young daughter as she kissed her on the cheek and stepped into Ma Fletcher's.

'Caraway seed cake will be wonderful, Mother. But, you really should not have gone to the bother of making a cake.' Victoria looked across at Ma Fletcher in her usual chair next to the fire and spotted the mangy cat that was upon her knee. 'Good morning, I'm Victoria, Mrs Fletcher. Now I don't know who this is?' Victoria bent down and tickled the scraggy cat under his chin. He purred, enjoying the attention that he was being given.

'This is Mr Tibbs. He seems to have taken a liking to you. He hasn't got the time of day for most people so you are privileged.' Ma Fletcher smiled at the beautiful young girl. 'My, tha's a bonny lass, you take after your mother. Your mother and aunt will have to fight men away from your door before long.'

The young girl blushed, and removed her bonnet that was covered with delicate fabric violets the same colour as her long sweeping skirts. She sat down next to Ma Fletcher and put her bonnet

187

on her knee.

'I'll take that.' Mary-Anne took Victoria's hat and gave a warning glance at Ma Fletcher and the cat upon her knee that Victoria was about to pick up. 'Just be careful with that fleabag of a cat, he can be vicious.'

'He's not a fleabag mother, he's beautiful.' Victoria stroked the scraggy tabby cat and laughed as the cat purred and made bread with its paws on her skirts.

'He'll pull the threads in your skirts,' Mary-Anne said sharply as she poured the tea and sliced the cake.

'Leave her be, lass.' Ma Fletcher looked fondly at the girl and the kindness that she was showing her cat. She was clearly the opposite of her father, which was a blessing.

'You have a beautiful home,' Victoria said, balancing both cat and a slice of cake on her knee.

'You wouldn't have said that a few weeks ago before your mother came and saved me. She's worked hard, she always did, even when she was your age. I remember your Aunt Eliza and her coming to my stall when they were only little things, not much older than you. Even then they wanted better for themselves and now just look at your aunt. And your mother, with a bit of help from me, will soon be bettering herself.' Ma Fletcher glanced up at Mary-Anne, hoping that she hadn't said anything that she shouldn't.

Mary-Anne gave a warning glance to Ma Fletcher. 'I'm sure Victoria does not want to hear about when Eliza and I were young, they were hard times.'

'Oh, but I do. I remember how Aunt Eliza used to work every hour of every day and I can just about remember going to the old shed along Aberford Road when we lived in Pit Lane when I was really young. So I know that things got better when Miss Ellershaw bought the shop on Boar Lane, and that we have to be thankful for how she helped us both.' Victoria sipped her tea and ate her cake daintily.

'That Grace Ellershaw will have made your aunt work hard if she's anything like her father,' Ma Fletcher spat.

Mary-Anne scowled at Ma Fletcher. 'Ma, she's done well for Victoria and our Eliza. I owe her a lot. So don't you belittle Grace.' She smiled at her daughter. 'She's not like the rest, Victoria. Take no notice of Ma, she doesn't even know her.'

'All I can say is that she is always kind to me and my aunt. And the rest of them aren't so bad either – George can be so thoughtful.' Even though she had gone off George since she had spoken to John Vasey that day, she felt an urge to defend him. Victoria could tell that Ma Fletcher had a problem when it came to the Ellershaws.

'I hope you are not sweet on him, are you? At your age? That would never do!' Ma Fletcher looked hard at Victoria.

'Ma!' Mary-Anne placed her cup and saucer down hard onto the table.

'He thinks too much of himself. But he's a good man, and yes, I suppose I do like him...' Victoria blushed and stroked the cat that was still on her knee. There was something about him that meant she couldn't help but smile when she thought of him

'But you can't let it ever go any further than that, lass. It would be so wrong!' Ma Fletcher took Victoria's hand.

'I don't understand, what are you saying?' Victoria said, a quizzical look on her face.

'Victoria, take no notice of Ma Fletcher, she sometimes gets confused.' Mary-Anne glared at Ma Fletcher.

'Nay lass, I don't. It's time the cards were laid upon the table and the truth was told before there's any more harm done to you and yours. Don't you see, he's your half-brother, you can't have them sorts of feelings for your brother. It isn't right in the eyes of our Lord.' Ma Fletcher whispered to Victoria and then looked up at Mary-Anne. 'She needs to know else her heart would be broken due to yet another Ellershaw.' Ma Fletcher sat back and looked at the anger on Mary-Anne's face and the hurt and confusion on Victoria's. 'It's best she knows before she gets any deeper into that George Ellershaw's grip.'

'It wasn't your place to tell her, shut up,' Mary-Anne snapped at Ma Fletcher. 'Victoria, forget what you've just heard, Ma sometimes doesn't realise what she is saying.'

'I don't understand. George is my brother? How can he be? That would mean his father is my father. So then, Edmund Ellershaw is my father?' Victoria turned to look at her mother, tears in her eyes as she took in what she had just been told.

'Oh, Victoria, I didn't want you to find out this way. Ma Fletcher should never have said anything. I was going to tell you when you were old enough to understand and I had secured a better life for us both.' Mary-Anne bent down, wrapping her arms around the trembling Victoria.

'Grace and George Ellershaw's father is my father? Is that why they show so much interest in my aunt and me? Do they show us both charity because of their father's misdoings? If he's their father, how can he be mine? He's married and old and–'

Victoria was hurt, so hurt. She had wanted to hear the news of her parentage from her mother and lived in hope that her father had been distinguished and of good standing in the community. Whereas Edmund Ellershaw might have some wealth and be the owner of the Rose Pit, but everyone talked about him because of his dissolute lifestyle.

'Victoria, I love you. It doesn't matter who your father is. I'm afraid to say that Edmund Ellershaw is your father through my own stupid mistake, but out of that mistake came you, and I love you dearly. Ma Fletcher should not have told you, she had no right; she is bitter and angry after Ellershaw brought heartache to her family too. As for George, Grace and even William, they have no idea that you are their half-sister. Eliza has always kept your parentage a secret, unlike this one here.' Mary-Anne glared at now the regretful Ma Fletcher.

'So, I'm a heartache, am I? Is that why you left me with Aunt Eliza? At least I can trust her, not like you and this old crone.' Victoria reached for her bonnet and pushed past her mother, not even glancing at Ma Fletcher.

'Aye, lass, I should have kept my big mouth shut. But I told you for your own good, you couldn't ever give your heart to George Ellershaw.' Ma Fletcher pulled her handkerchief from up her sleeve and dabbed her eyes.

'I'd no intentions of losing my heart to George, we are just good friends. I'm far too young to even think of love yet and George would never be right for me anyway,' Victoria snarled.

'Victoria, let me explain. Stay and finish your tea and I'll tell you everything you need to know. Please let's not leave things when you are so upset,' Mary-Anne pleaded.

'Staying here would break my heart. I'm going back to the person who truly loves me. The one who has always been more of a mother to me than you will ever be. And you are right. I am better off not knowing my true father, no wonder you have never told me.' Victoria opened the door and ran out into the busy street.

Mary-Anne rushed out after her and pulled on her arm, urging her to return. 'Victoria, please don't think bad of me. I'd no choice. As you say, he was old and married and he took advantage of me. It was not my choice but then I found out that I was carrying you.'

'Why should I believe you? I think what happened was that you lowered yourself to be paid for his attention, and no sooner did you give birth to me than you decided to abandon me with your sister in order to go halfway around the world with your next fancy man. And that poor devil was broken and hurt because of you, so much so that he turned to drink and drowned himself. I'm ashamed that you are my mother, you deserve to live with that scheming old crone in your witches' coven because that is what you both are.'

Victoria pulled away from her mother's clutches, lifted her head up and walked down the street. An hour ago, she had walked up this street so glad to be visiting. Now she was walking down it with her heart broken and tears running down her face. She'd see what her aunt Eliza had to say about all she had learned. She knew Eliza would tell her the truth. She was the only one she could trust.

'Why couldn't you keep your mouth shut?' Mary-Anne slammed the door behind her and stood with her hands on her hips in front of Ma Fletcher.

'Aye lass, she had to know. What if George took advantage of her? Now, that would be a scandal, you'd be wishing that you'd have said something to her then.' Ma Fletcher put her head down. Despite her words, she did feel guilty at spewing forth Victoria's parentage without thinking about Mary-Anne's feelings. 'Get yourself down to Eliza's because that is where she will have gone. Go and sit down with her and tell her how it was, she'll understand once you both calm her down. Eliza will comfort her, after all, she has brought her up, and she'll know how to get her to see the truth.'

'I didn't want her to know just yet. And the way you told her? I could have bloody swung for you.' Mary-Anne reached for her shawl from behind the door. 'I'll go and find her, tell her everything

193

and tell her no matter what I love her more than life itself.' Mary-Anne held her shawl to her and nearly cried.

'Now then, lass, don't go soft on me. I'll give Victoria her due, she's got a temper and can stand her ground. Reminds me a lot of her mother, whether she knows it or not.' Ma Fletcher smiled at Mary-Anne and called for her cat, who had decided to hide out of the way until peace had returned to its home.

'No bloody wonder I have a temper. You deserve all the words that Satan himself could throw at you. You've broken my lass's heart. You and your big mouth.' Mary-Anne looked daggers at Ma Fletcher.

'You think you've got problems? Save your sympathies for Catherine Ellershaw. She's got a bastard for a husband, another bastard in her eldest son, a sour-faced old maid as a daughter and I don't like the sounds of that George either. Now that is a family you would not want to be related to.' Ma Fletcher stroked Mr Tibbs.

'You are beyond saving.' Mary-Anne shook her head and made for the door to go and mend her relationship with her daughter. 'Dinner may be late, so don't you bloody well complain because this is all your doing and don't you forget it.'

'Victoria, what on earth is wrong?' Eliza turned away from her latest fashion design and went across to her distraught niece who had entered the room like a hurricane, slamming the door after herself before sitting down and crying in the chair next to the window.

'Why didn't you tell me? Why did you let me make a fool of myself, going out to tea with George when all along you knew we were half-brother and sister?' Victoria looked up at Eliza, her eyes red and swollen with tears. 'Yes, I've found out that I am Edmund Ellershaw's bastard child, the old hag who my so-called mother lives with told me.' Victoria sobbed and flung her bonnet down onto the floor.

Eliza bent down and held Victoria's hands. 'She'd no right to tell you that, it was for your mother to do. Why do you think I've kept it a secret all these years? It was because your mother was waiting for the right time. I don't know what to say, my darling girl. I know that you will be upset by the news. Just what did Ma Fletcher tell you and where was your mother?'

'My mother was there with me, she couldn't stop her. It was as if Ma Fletcher was taking delight in being the one to tell me. Mother was angry with her but I could not stay another minute longer, I just wanted to flee. I will never be able to look at George and Grace in the same light again, and as for their father, I just don't know what to say.' Victoria trembled and sobbed.

'Oh, Victoria, I'm sorry, my darling. We have all tried to protect you for so long and for this to come out in this way... Ma Fletcher never was one for tact, but she'd have meant no harm. She's just thoughtless.' Eliza caressed her niece's arm and sighed.

'Thoughtless is putting it mildly,' Mary-Anne spoke softly as she opened the door and made her way into the fitting room. 'I'm sorry, my darling. Ma Fletcher never could hold her tongue. I didn't mean for you to find out that way. You are everything to me and I never wanted you to be hurt.' Mary-Anne looked with sorrow in her eyes at Eliza who stepped aside for her to be next to Victoria. She put her arm around Victoria and tried to kiss her.

Victoria put her head up and anger flashed in her eyes. 'Don't touch me! I don't want you anywhere near me. I can't bear to think about how I came into the world and was conceived. Did you make him pay for his pleasure? Were you like the common women down on the docks, who everyone despises?'

'No, Victoria, it was not like that. Believe me, it was not by choice that I let Edmund Ellershaw have his way with me. If I'd not done as he'd bade, Eliza and I would have been out on the streets, he owned everything we had. Our mother had just died, our stepfather had left us and neither of us had any money to feed ourselves or keep him from throwing us out of the rented cottage that he owned. I was so desperate I couldn't think of any other way than to do what he wanted. It was only the once. He was such a brute that I knew I'd rather see both Eliza and myself on the streets than suffer more humiliation in his hands. The one good thing that came out of that night was you, although I'll be honest – when I was carrying you, I didn't think so. But I am so proud of you, you are such a little lady, thanks to Eliza here, and Grace Ellershaw.' Mary-Anne smiled at her sister and watched as Victoria tried to control her sobbing. 'I'll give Grace her due, she is nothing like her father, so she must take after her mother. Which I hope that you do. You are loved by us all, Victoria, your father is not worth dwelling on, but I'm sorry that you were told in the way you were.' Mary-Anne felt her heart ache for Victoria.

'So he forced himself upon you? You did it to keep Aunt Eliza and you safe and together?' Victoria said.

'Yes, perhaps I shouldn't have done. But I could see no other way out of our predicament. And as you know, I left you after you were born with Eliza because John wanted us to get settled before you joined us in America. But that never happened and the years went by and Eliza and you had a good life here, and Grace Ellershaw was doing what her father should have done for you both. So I knew you were being looked after and that was all that mattered to me. Who your father was, you were better off not knowing.'

Eliza looked at her heartbroken niece. 'Victoria, I owe a lot to Mary-Anne. She was always there for me when I was growing up, and she put herself at the mercy of Edmund Ellershaw just so that I was protected. It is true you were not made out of love, but you brought love with your arrival into the world and your father is best forgotten. He is not worth the worry.' Eliza crouched down and kissed Victoria on her cheek. 'You are still young. When you're old enough I am sure a gentleman will swipe you off your feet,' Eliza smiled. 'Your mother and I love you and always will.'

Victoria wiped her eyes. 'I just don't know what to think. It came as such a shock. I've met Edmund Ellershaw when I've been out with George.

He's a rough, outspoken man, with little manners and I could tell he disliked me as he never looked at me or acknowledged me. Now I know why. He knows I'm his daughter.'

'Why do you think I never visit Grace at home? He hates the Wild family. We remind him of his transgressions and is frightened that his wife will find out just how wicked a man he is.'

Mary-Anne put her arm around her daughter. 'I'm sorry, my darling. You deserve better. I know I must be a disappointment to you, but one day that will change, I promise you.'

'At least I know now. I'm sorry I judged you. At least you knew who my father was. Half of the children of Leeds either don't know or their mother can't remember.' Victoria smiled wanly. 'You see, I'm not that precious.'

'That's my girl. You can live without Edmund Ellershaw in your life, believe me.' Mary-Anne kissed her on her brow and smiled. Victoria was tougher than she looked, and in that way at least, she took after her side of the family.

Chapter 20

'Don't you say another bloody word.' Mary-Anne put on her favourite green bonnet and looked at herself in the mirror to make sure she looked respectable and at her best before she set off on her way to meet William Ellershaw. She pulled on her lace gloves. 'You've done enough harm for this week without telling me how to dress.'

'Oh, stop moaning. I don't regret what I said,' Ma Fletcher tutted. 'Victoria needed to know who her father was. Besides, you said she was all right now, and it is all out in the open. You and Eliza need not skulk around the subject any more. Are you really going to meet William Ellershaw in that green bonnet? Isn't it a bit plain?' Ma Fletcher looked Mary-Anne up and down and decided not to say another word when she noticed the black look on her face as she picked up her posy bag.

'I'll be back for supper. All you need is on the table by your side. The coal bucket is full, so you don't have to move. Just bloody well behave yourself. In any case, I believe that time on your own will make you rue what you said to Victoria.'

Mary-Anne opened the door and left the old woman on her own, hearing her shout 'Bollocks!' as she closed the door behind her.

Could she stand living with Ma Fletcher much longer? That would depend if she could ever forgive her for telling Victoria the news that had been kept a secret from her so long. The atmosphere between her and Ma Fletcher had been frosty that morning, and on top of that, she had felt nauseous at the thought of her luncheon with William Ellershaw. It was what she had hoped for, but when it came to the meeting and sitting across from him in a well-to-do restaurant, she was suddenly nervous. Ma's comments about her attire hadn't helped and now she was doubting her choice of clothes as she walked down onto The Headrow and on to Briggate to make her way to Whitelocks, where the gentry ate and entertained.

Leeds was always busy but at lunchtime the streets were extra chaotic, with people in such a rush to get things done in the short time they were allowed away for their workplaces. Millworkers were doing errands before the mill's whistle warned them to be back at work; businessmen and bankers shoved their way into the many chop houses along the streets to share a grill with work colleagues.

Mary-Anne pushed her way through the crowds and stood next to the stalls on Briggate that were at the entrance to the alleyway leading to Whitelocks. One was a fish stall and the smell of dead fish churned her stomach, adding to the anxiety of meeting William Ellershaw in the next few seconds. She composed herself and prepared to put on airs and graces as she walked up to the elaborate façade of Whitelocks restaurant. Through the acid-etched windows of the lounge bar she watched the waiters, dressed in white shirts and black trousers with black aprons around their waists, serve the customers within. Whole fish were served on silver platters and bottles of wine were being poured and returned to ice-filled buckets. She had never before eaten in a place like this. Perhaps Ma Fletcher was right: she was a little underdressed for the occasion.

She was just doubting her courage to enter the premises and planning how to make good her escape when she saw William Ellershaw wave to her from a table in the corner of the main restaurant. It was too late to turn tail and run. She smiled and waved back before entering this elegant world of food and drink.

'Mary-Anne, you made it, how wonderful.' William rose from his seat. The waiter took Mary-Anne's mantle from her shoulders and pulled out a chair for her to sit upon before placing a napkin on her knee. 'I thought perhaps you might think twice about joining me, after all, I wouldn't blame you.'

Mary-Anne tried to relax and smiled at her companion. 'How could I resist? A handsome man, good food and distinguished company?'

'You are too kind, and I think a little teasing by the look in your eye. Besides, it is not that well-to-do. In fact, this place is a bolthole for those with secrets. Do you see the old man over there, sat with a very young, buxom girl?' William bent forward and whispered to Mary-Anne, glancing at what she thought to be perhaps an elderly grandfather and his granddaughter.

'Yes, I do,' Mary-Anne whispered back, forgetting her nerves.

'Well, that is Lord Westcliffe, magistrate to the West Riding, and that is his latest paramour.' William winked and picked up his cigar that had been smouldering in an ashtray. 'There's no fool like an old fool. Even though he's supposed to know every right and wrong in the land.' William laughed at the shock on Mary-Anne's face. 'Over there is Lady Ashmere. I bet her husband doesn't know that she's dining with his best friend, the Right Honourable Ronald Allen. I think he'd have a few words to say about the way he's looking down her cleavage.' William watched Mary-Anne follow his gaze around the room. 'Don't worry, there are some decent folk eating here as well, after all, there is you and me, and I want you to be assured that I'm just extending a hand of friendship, so you can stop thinking that I mean you any wrong. Although I am flattered that you called me handsome, I promise it will not go to my head. However, I beg to differ. Those days when I was once handsome have well and truly gone. Hard work and an empty-headed wife have seen to that. Surely you noticed my greying hair and tired looks? But, as for you, I think you are in your prime and outshine any of the women of note in this room.'

Mary-Anne sighed. 'Please, I don't need to be flattered. I'm here because I think both you and I have a lot in common. We both desire things and will do anything to possess them. Is that not why you married Priscilla? I'll be honest: I want more in my life, and now that I'm a widow I can start over and make a name for my daughter and myself. I'm no longer the innocent Mary-Anne that you once thought you could take advantage of, so please don't waste words of nonsense on me.' Mary-Anne still found William attractive but she could not weaken and fall for his charms if her plan was to work.

'You've still got spirit, Mary-Anne. You are not acting so much like a grieving widow. Perhaps you married the wrong person as well and the grass was not as green in America as you made it out to be? Now, let us both forget the unfortunate start to our friendship and start afresh. You never know, we may even develop a liking of one another. I sincerely hope so. Two lost souls in a sea of despair; plenty of money, perhaps, but not loved in a way that we would wish.' William summoned the waiter. 'Claret? It helps lift the spirits.'

Mary-Anne noticed the laughter lines around his mouth as he raised his glass for her to join him in a drink. She nodded to the waiter as he filled her glass and then she lifted it to join William's in a toast.

'To two lonely, misunderstood people with dreams that are still unfulfilled.' William clinked his glass to hers and then took a long sip of the dark-red claret, watching Mary-Anne as she politely took a small sip. 'I'm sorry, I acted like a bastard before you left for America. I was desperate, you were sending me mad and then I had to marry Priscilla to appease my grandfather. I apologise for my actions. I hope that we can become good friends, if not more.'

'But you are married!' Mary-Anne exclaimed, knowing it was expected of her.

'Look around you, so are half the people in here, but they are not here with their spouses. Life is too short to be miserable and Prissy is so fixated on her potions that keep real life at bay, she's rarely in my company.' William took another sip of wine.

'Perhaps she has to find comfort in her own world if you are as big a cad as I hear you are. Which leads me to wonder why I should look twice at you?'

William had a wicked twinkle in his eye and she remembered how smitten she had been when she had first met him.

'I'll admit I'm no saint. I like the comfort I find in my mistress's bosom. I've no other option. Priscilla does not show me any affection and nobody else will have me. Money, believe it or not, does not buy you everything. It can't buy you love and respect.' William went silent as he swirled the last of his wine around in the bottom of the glass.

'Now, don't you go maudlin on me, it doesn't suit you. Neither did the angry, demanding bastard that you once were. But yes, let us begin a friendship together, it will benefit us both and I will enjoy your company.'

Mary-Anne smiled, William Ellershaw was hers to play with as she liked and play with him she would. She had the upper hand this time, and had to ensure that he never found out that she was not all she seemed to be.

'To our friendship and wherever it leads us.' William nodded to the waiter to refill his glass.

'To friendship.' Mary-Anne raised her glass.

William urged the waiter to bring a plate full of oysters to the table

'I hope you don't mind. I took the liberty of ordering these as soon as I entered the room, to make sure we got the best to share. They are supposed to be a stimulant, but perhaps neither of us need such.' William took one of the pearly shells from off the plate and loosened the jellied mass of the oyster from its shell, before putting his head back and swallowing the delicacy. 'They truly are delicious. Do try one.' William pushed the plate towards Mary-Anne. 'A squirt of lemon perhaps?' William smiled noticing the look on

Mary-Anne's face.

She had never eaten oysters before and even though it seemed that William had enjoyed the revolting-looking treat, she didn't think she would. She wasn't sure she dared to try eating them without making a fool of herself.

'Just the one. I'm not that keen on them.' Mary-Anne picked up the smallest oyster and copied what William had done. She tried not to retch as the slimy oyster slipped into her mouth and she swallowed hard to get rid of the foul-tasting morsel. The liquid that had surrounded the oyster ran down her chin as she tried not to show her hatred of the seafood and she quickly raised her napkin to wipe it away.

'Not the easiest things to eat, are they?' William grinned as he helped himself to another. 'Would you like me to order you some soup? I recommend the blade of beef, it is always so tender.'

'No, please. I'm fine. You enjoy your oysters, the beef will be sufficient for me.' Mary-Anne sat back as William cleared the plate of oysters and drank his claret.

'Priscilla does not like oysters either, but then again, there is not a lot she does like. I made a terrible mistake marrying her. If it hadn't been for her wealth and contacts, I wouldn't have looked twice at her.' William went quiet as the waiter cleared the empty tray of oysters and brushed the table down ready for the next course.

'We all make mistakes. I should never have left and married John Vasey. I may have seen a part of the world that others would have loved to have seen but I have missed my daughter growing up and she struggles to find any feelings for me.' Mary-Anne sighed and tidied her napkin.

'Were you happy with your husband? He had obviously done well for himself by the looks of your clothes and the house that you are living in. Was he the father of your daughter?'

'John was a good man. He was an idealist and perhaps he should not have chosen me to spend his short life with. But, no, he's not the father of my child. I was taken advantage of by a letch. However, I do love my daughter, she cannot help her arrival on this earth.' Mary-Anne tried to avoid William's gaze and hoped that he would not pry any further into Victoria's parentage.

'I'm sorry, I'll not ask any further questions. Now, when are we to meet again?' William smiled at Mary-Anne as she looked at the plate of dinner put in front of them both.

'This is enough food to feed me for a week!' Mary-Anne gasped. 'Meet again? That would be wonderful. I'd like to get to know you better.' Mary-Anne picked up her knife and fork and started to tuck into her meal.

'Yes, Mary-Anne, I'm enjoying myself greatly, it is not every day I get to sit across from a beautiful woman. At least one I've not paid for!' William winked wickedly at Mary-Anne.

'Ah! But I am paid for. After all, I presume you are paying for my lunch? I hope you are not expecting payment in kind? As I say, let us keep it to friends for now, but who is to say that our friendship will not develop into something more?' Mary-Anne looked across at William and knew exactly what he was thinking. But the trouble was that she was thinking the same thing.

'Do you like going to the theatre? Perhaps you would like to join me next Friday evening at the music hall adjacent to the White Swan? I have my own private box and would enjoy your company.'

'I think I'd enjoy that. But I can't help but feel guilty about your wife.' Mary-Anne wasn't one bit concerned about Priscilla but she had to seem reluctant and let William court her.

'Forget her. She will be glad to see the back of me for an evening. Don't let her spoil our friendship, she means little to me and is not your concern.' William picked his knife and fork up and started to eat his dinner.

'Then yes, I'd be happy to be your guest at the music hall. What time are we to meet?'

'Eight, at the White Swan? We can pretend to meet in there by accident and then no one is any wiser.' William grinned.

'That's a good idea. I'll look forward to it.' Mary-Anne concentrated on finishing her lunch. Her plan was working; William thought he was hunting her when in truth he was the prey and he didn't even realise it.

'Well, madam, how did you get on with your web of deceit?' Ma Fletcher noted Mary-Anne's flushed face as she entered her home.

'I've had an excellent lunch and a glass or two of claret and to be quite honest I even enjoyed William Ellershaw's company.' Mary-Anne grinned as she pulled out her hat pin from the green hat that Ma Fletcher had disliked so much and hung it up on the coat rack in the hall.

207

'Don't you forget what he's really like and whose son he is. That look on your face is not what I wanted to see,' Ma Fletcher growled. 'Don't you go and fall for his charms, else you will forget what you are really after.'

'Now, don't go spoiling it. My belly's full, I feel content and I'm to meet him again next Friday.' Mary-Anne lifted the coal bucket up from out of the hearth and heaped a few more lumps onto the fire before slumping in the chair across from Ma Fletcher. She yawned and pushed her shoes off. 'I'm knackered, I could do with a nap.'

'This is only your first meeting with him, lass, what are you going to do a few months in? Where are you meeting him next Friday? Because don't have so much to drink next time. By the looks of those flushed cheeks, he's plied you with enough wine to get exactly what he wants already.' Ma Fletcher pulled her shawl around herself and pulled a face at Mary-Anne as she closed her eyes.

'Hold your tongue. He got up to nothing, but I was sorely tempted. He's quite handsome is our William.' Mary-Anne closed her eyes and smiled, thinking of the good-looking man whose company she had greatly enjoyed.

Ma Fletcher wagged her finger at Mary-Anne. 'Now, don't you be forgetting that he's almost as much of a bastard as his father.'

Mary-Anne just kept her eyes closed and nodded her head. He might be a bastard and a rogue but she was going to enjoy herself with him.

Chapter 21

A crowd was gathered at the bottom of Hyde Park Lane. Ordinary working-class men and women were listening to those with something to say about the state of the nation and local affairs. Mary-Anne stood at the garden gate and listened as the crowd yelled their agreement with the speaker or booed when they did not agree with what was being said. She pulled her shawl around her shoulders and set off down the street in the hope of talking to Tom Thackeray. She'd left Ma Fletcher asleep in front of the fire and a stew was simmering nicely on the fireside, ready for dinner on her return. She followed the cobbled street. As Tom stepped up onto an upturned wooden crate to give his talk about pit safety, the onlookers clapped. She pushed her way to the front of the crowd and looked at the man her sister should have married. Although years older, Tom had not changed a great deal. He cleared his throat and started to speak.

'Thank you, thank you, good people.' Tom looked at the crowd. The woman who'd made her way to the front of the looked vaguely familiar, and then he realised who it was. Mary-Anne Wild, back from America. How long had she been back in the country and why was she there listening to him?

Tom concentrated on the matter at hand. 'This

morning, people, I was going to talk about the safety of our mines and the lack of care given to us mine workers by pit owners. However, firstly I need to tell you of the latest grave news.' Tom heard a mumbling in the crowd. Those who already knew what had happened in the Black Mine in Lancashire were telling others the news. 'Fifty-four men and boys have perished in the Astley Deep Pit over these last few days. This, my friends, is due to the mine owner's love of money over human lives.' Tom saw the anguish on the crowd's faces. 'A roof collapsed seventy feet below ground and released a large amount of firedamp. Because the owners would not invest in Davy safety lamps, a lot of the miners down at the face were wearing open lanterns with candles lit for light.' Tom looked down at his feet for a few moments before looking back up at his audience. 'I don't have to say much more, you can guess the rest. That the natural gas in the firedamp exploded when it reached the lit candles. The explosion and fire raged through the pit, making further shafts collapse and taking the fifty-four poor souls to their death. The fire is still raging and many more men have been injured. You can understand the hurt and pain that is going through the community of Astley, but the trouble is any pit could have a disaster like this. The pit owners must be made responsible for their miners' safety and stop thinking solely of their own pockets! Much like local pit owner Edmund Ellershaw at the Rose. I lost my position there because he wouldn't listen to my concerns about his penny-pinching. Then, when an accident happened because of inadequate spending on pit props, he told me it was all my fault. He had not one care for his workers, he just wanted to save his own skin from any retribution there might have been from an inquiry, so I got the blame. We can't let this continue. It is your husbands, sons – aye, and in some cases your daughters – who are dying for the lack of basic safety.'

The crowd were all nodding their heads in agreement and clapped him loudly as he continued his litany of crimes of the local mine owners, especially those of Edmund Ellershaw, finally finishing with a minute's silence for the lost souls of the Astley Pit before he stood down off his crate.

Tom shook the hands of those who had agreed with him and gave comfort to those who were moved by the deaths. Mary-Anne made her way towards him.

'Hello, Tom Thackeray, it's been a long time. You spoke well, the people listened to you, and know what you say is right.' Mary-Anne smiled as he shook her hand.

'Thank you. It's been years, Mary-Anne. Now, what brings you back to Leeds? I thought America was your home now.' Tom remembered the hours spent in the parlour of Pit Lane when he had lost his heart to her sister.

'My daughter, Victoria, among other things. Eliza, bless her, has been like a mother to her, but now it is time to rectify things.' Mary-Anne looked at the surprise and hurt on Tom's face.

'She is yours, then. I didn't believe her when she begged me to believe that she hadn't been un-

211

faithful. I didn't even believe old Bill Parker when he told me the baby wasn't hers, thinking she was lying to them as well. When I told my mother that Eliza had lifted her skirts to someone else, she was delighted, and she took the opportunity to pour more of her poison in my ear.' Tom bowed his head, thinking of all the years that he had loved Eliza. He'd never been able to love anybody else. The hurt he had felt had been unbearable.

'Yes, Victoria is mine, born in disgrace. She, until recently, was ignorant of who her father was. Now, I've returned to secure her something of what should rightly be hers.'

Tom looked puzzled. 'I knew she wasn't John Vasey's, else you wouldn't have left her behind. Go on, tell me what I think I've known for a few years now. I've had my suspicions as to what was happening at the Rose.' Tom took Mary-Anne by the arm, guiding her away from the crowd to a quiet place along Hyde Lane.

'Yes, we have a lot in common, Tom. Edmund Ellershaw ruined your prospects just as he ruined mine. He took advantage of me when we could not pay the rent. I'm ashamed to admit that I lowered myself to let him bed me so that we could keep a roof over our heads. He's a bastard. He would bleed his own mother dry.' Mary-Anne held back the tears as she confessed her past to him.

'Mary-Anne, I should have realised sooner … there were rumours that he had that arrangement with quite a few of his worker's wives. I used to wonder why the women of the family were com-ing to pay the rent. I was innocent back then, not realising what sort of man I worked for. You must have gone through hell.' Tom put a comforting arm around Mary-Anne. 'Now, where is John? Are you living back here? I'd like to catch up with you both.'

'Oh, Tom, I left him back in New York, only for him to follow me here. I couldn't live with him any longer but, unfortunately, he couldn't live without me. After I refused to return to America with him he was found drowned in the cut. I have caused so much hurt to so many people, including yourself. If it hadn't been for me you would be happily married to Eliza, in a house of your own and with your own children.'

'Nay, it wasn't just you. My mother would never have agreed to our marriage and I was stupid enough to listen to her poison more than my heart. I'm sorry to hear about John, he was a good man.' Tom sighed. 'Is Eliza all right? I see she's doing well for herself.'

'She is. She always did have the better business head on her. She misses you though, I know she does. Even after all these years. You know she's never married? She often told me in her letters how much she loved you and missed you and I believe she still does.' Mary-Anne noticed a spark light up in Tom's eyes.

'She does? I thought I'd be long forgotten. Especially now when she's doing so well for herself.'

'Get yourself along to see her, she'd be so happy to see you. I will give you her new address. I still think she loves you deeply, it would be a shame for you to miss out again.' Mary-Anne linked her arm in Tom's as she started walking

213

towards her home. 'I'm living with Ma Fletcher, just here. We are plotting Edmund Ellershaw's downfall between us. She hates him just as much as we do.'

'Ma Fletcher lives here in this grand house? Bloody hell, she must be worth a bob or two!' Tom whistled as he looked at the double-fronted house.

Mary-Anne grinned. 'She is, but she's not well and she's a nightmare to live with.'

'I can imagine. She always was an awkward old bag when she stood in the market. Do you really think Eliza would accept a visit from me?'

Tom let go of Mary-Anne's arm as she opened the garden gate to go back into Ma Fletcher.

'I sure she will, Tom Thackeray. It is time two broken hearts were mended.' She kissed the man that she had wronged on the cheek. 'It would make me very happy.'

'Then I will pluck up courage and visit her and beg forgiveness.'

'Good, make sure you do.' After giving Tom Eliza's address, Mary-Anne left him standing at the gate. She hoped that Eliza was going to get her true love back into her life.

'Victoria, have you seen the other of these invitations for the Guild Ball? I seem to have mislaid one.' Eliza picked up the solitary invitation and hunted through the pile of correspondence that was on her desk.

'No, I'm sure I put both back together after I had shown my mother them. But I can't say for certain as I thought nothing about it when I

214

replaced them back in the desk after leaving them on the fireplace.' Victoria looked worried. 'Have we lost one, does that mean I won't be able to go?'

'No, I'm sure I will be able to secure a replacement, but I just find it strange that I have one but not the other. Did you leave your mother alone with them?'

'Only to get her a drink of water. She had a cough.' Victoria raised her head from her book and looked across at her aunt hunting through her desk.

Eliza knew exactly where the invitation had gone to but didn't want to admit it to Victoria. The discovery of who her father was – and how she had been told – had hurt her enough.

'Blind me! Look here it is, it was hiding under this pile of correspondence. Thank heavens for that.' Eliza quickly put the desk lid down. 'Shall we go and visit your mother? It's a lovely spring day and I've not been to see where she lives yet.'

'But it's Sunday, mother, and I am reading my book. George recommended *The Tenant of Wildfell Hall* to me. I can't believe that he has read it. The content is so romantic.' Victoria didn't really want to visit her mother. She felt vulnerable and hurt after the admission of who her father was. She had found it particularly hard when George had asked her to join him for tea at Highfield House and she had made an excuse, frightened that she might give herself away.

'You can read that anytime. Come, we will get a Hackney cab from Aire Street. A good horse will have us there by two and we will return for supper.' Eliza took the book out of Victoria's hands. 'Stir your stumps. It will do you good to get out of the house, you can't hide away in here for the rest of your life. No one knows who your father is, and even if they did they wouldn't give a damn.' Eliza's patience with her niece was running thin. Victoria's long face and the surly mood were beginning to test her.

'I don't want to go and see her. I hate her! She is no better than a common whore!' Victoria shouted. 'How could she let Edmund Ellershaw do that to her and why didn't she think about his family and wife? All she thinks about is herself.' Victoria threw her book down into the chair across from her and crossed her arms like a petulant child.

'Victoria, don't you ever say that. She did what she thought was right, keeping both her and me out of the gutter. You seemed to accept that when we explained that to you the other day. What's changed? Nothing. She loves you and has come back to be the mother that she has always wanted to be, given the chance. Now, put that petted lip away and get your shawl. The more that you see of your mother, the more you will get to know her.'

'If I must go, I will. But I can't guarantee that I will be civil. She doesn't deserve it.' Victoria stood up and made her way to the hallway.

Eliza picked up the discarded book and placed it on the small table. Ma Fletcher and her big mouth. Why couldn't she have kept the secret to herself for just a little longer? She heard Victoria open the door and slam it behind her. Eliza sighed as she picked up her gloves and bonnet. How she wished that her parentage had remained a secret at least until her mother had won her love and respect. Now all her niece was feeling was resentment and shame and she was on the receiving end of Victoria's frustration.

'Who's this knocking on our door now? I was just going to have a nap after my dinner.' Ma Fletcher moaned as Mary-Anne pulled the net curtains back from the window to see who their visitors were.

'It's Eliza and Victoria, what a lovely surprise.' Mary-Anne checked around the kitchen to make sure all was tidy and then went to the door with a wide smile on her face.

'It's lovely to see you both. Especially you, Victoria.' Mary-Anne reached to kiss her daughter on the cheek but was ignored, as Victoria pushed past her.

Eliza shook her head as she kissed her sister on the cheek and removed her hat, passing it to Mary-Anne to hang up on the stand next to the door. 'We thought as it is such a lovely day we would pay you a visit, didn't we, Victoria?'

Victoria said nothing as she stood with her coat still on. She didn't want to be there, with an old woman who had ruined her life and a mother that she had no respect for.

'I tell you what, Victoria, while you have still got your coat on, would you like to go to the house we just passed at the corner of the street? The woman had her front door open and was selling baking of some kind. See if she has any of her bannocks for sale. I think I noticed some when we drove past in the cab. They will be a real treat for us with a drink of tea.' Eliza felt in her bag for a few pence, placing them in Victoria's hand, who said nothing as she made her way out of the kitchen, glad to get away from her mother and aunt and especially the old bag that had broken her heart.

'Well, she's not got much to say for herself!' Ma Fletcher said.

'What do you expect, when you opened your mouth and told her things we had protected her from for years?' Eliza said curtly before sitting down across from the old woman who she hadn't seen in years. 'Now, while she's not here. Did you pinch an invitation to the Guild Ball, our Mary-Anne? We seem to have it missing and I know it is a trick that you'd do, even if it would break your daughter's heart again if she found out.' Eliza looked blackly at her sister.

'I don't know what you are talking about. It's nothing to do with me!' Mary-Anne tried to show no sign of guilt.

'Nay, lass, come on, be right with your own. Aye, she's got your invitation, she's going to use it to seduce William Ellershaw, but if you ask me she'll not be needing it. He's already smitten. He'll invite her himself!' Ma Fletcher grinned.

'Ma, do you never know when to shut up!' Mary-Anne growled.

'You don't lie nor pinch from your own. Now give it back to Eliza before you lose your sister's respect and all.' Ma Fletcher knew that the two sisters were strongest when they stood together united. 'You've caught him already, you don't need a fancy frock and the trappings to catch him, and he's ruled by his dick, just like his father.

218

That's the Ellershaw family's downfall, their love of women.'

'What am I to do with you? I can't tell you anything!' Mary-Anne marched off to retrieve the ticket and hand it back to Eliza before Victoria returned.

'Well, at least you are straight, even though you don't realise the harm you've done to my family.' Eliza stared at the old woman. They waited in silence until Mary-Anne returned.

'Thank you,' Eliza said when Mary-Anne handed the invitation to her. 'If you'd have asked, I'd have given you it, but as it is now, I'll be able to take Victoria with me. Don't even think of stealing from me and mine again, just ask if you need anything. Now, what's this about you trapping William Ellershaw? Will it reflect badly on Victoria? Because I don't know how much more of her sulking I can put up with. You've seen the state she's in.'

'We are to go to the theatre together this Friday, he's playing right into my hands, Eliza. Don't worry about Victoria, she will come round, I'll make a fuss of her once she comes back in. William is nothing to do with her anyway.' Mary-Anne reached for some cups and saucers and set them out on the kitchen table.

Ma Fletcher glanced across at Eliza. 'She's a lot harder than she used to be your sister, and she's got her head set on what she wants, nowt's going to stop her.'

'I've gathered that.' Eliza sighed and looked down at her gloves that she was still holding in her hands. 'I sometimes wish she hadn't turned

219

up on my doorstep and that Victoria was still living in ignorant bliss.'

Mary-Anne stopped in her tracks. 'Eliza, I love you and Victoria. What I'm doing is for us all. Don't worry about Victoria. It's been a shock to her but she had to know sometime.' Mary-Anne finished laying the tea table and caught a glimpse of Victoria coming through the garden gate. 'Shush now, she's back.'

'You can stop talking about me now.' Victoria closed the door behind her and took off her bonnet, placing four small currant bannocks wrapped up in brown paper on the table before she sat down across from her aunt.

'Nay, we might have been talking about you but only because your aunt was saying that you will both be attending the Guild Ball. That's quite a party you'll be going to – and at your age as well. Can you dance, lass?' Ma Fletcher enquired as Mary-Anne placed four gilt-edged tea plates on the table and buttered the bannocks before passing them to her guests.

'I like to waltz. Aunt Eliza has taught me most of the steps.' Victoria mumbled.

'If you wish, after we have had our tea I'll teach you the two-step. It is a dance they all love in America and I believe it is just as popular here. Although I've got two left feet most of the time.' Mary-Anne smiled at her daughter.

'You haven't, our Mary-Anne, you always danced beautifully. Let her show you, Victoria; I don't know the steps. That and the polka are all the rage, from what Grace tells me.'

'I don't know.' Victoria hung her head. She'd

like to have learned the dance but not with her mother.

'Well, let's have tea and then you can decide.' Mary-Anne poured the tea and offered everyone a plate.

'Come on, then, I'll show you the steps and I'll also hum the tune so that we don't look like complete Charlies.' They had finished the tea and bannock buns, and Mary-Anne urged Victoria to follow her into the front room parlour. She smiled at her daughter, noting how uncomfortable she looked as she grasped her mother's hand. 'I promise I won't bite and I don't need your hand.'

Victoria dared not look at her mother in the eye.

'Now, you just follow me and watch my feet, you'll soon get the hang of it.' Mary-Anne hummed a tune that she remembered from her time back in America and grinned as Victoria watched her every move. She held her tightly and thought how much she loved her precious daughter as she slowly taught her the steps. Their skirts swirled around them and before long, both mother and daughter were dancing and laughing together as they paraded around the parlour.

'Sounds like those two are having fun and have made their peace.' Ma Fletcher leaned forward in her chair and watched as Eliza cleared the table.

'For the moment. Let's see if it continues. And if our Mary-Anne can behave herself.' Eliza stood back against the sink and dried her hands on the tea towel, wistfully wishing that the frolicking would build bridges between mother and daughter.

221

Chapter 22

'Well, how do I look?' Mary-Anne stood in front of Ma Fletcher and fidgeted. She felt like a young girl again as she thought of the reaction on William Ellershaw's face.

'You look like a trollop! A well-to-do trollop, but a trollop nonetheless! Those dumplings of yours are nearly falling out of your bodice. You'll blind him if you are not careful.'

'That's what I aim to do. Blind him with lust and passion but keep him at arm's length, just to make him really want me and only me.' Mary-Anne squeezed her breasts together and pulled her bodice up.

'He'll be trading you in at a brothel if you aren't careful. You need to be a little more modest, else he'll only do what his father did before him.' Ma Fletcher couldn't believe just how forward she was going to be with William.

'No, he'll not. He thinks I'm wealthy, so he will have to show more respect. Besides, we will be in company tonight at the music hall. I'm sure there will be people he knows there, I only hope his wife does not find out about our evening together. The poor cow.' Mary-Anne picked up her black and green lace fan and put her small posy bag on her arm and looked down at her silk skirts and tight, nipped-in bodice. 'Do you think this peacock-feathered brooch looks right in my hair?' She put her hand up to her head and felt the hair adornment.

'Aye, but it'll not be in for that long, he'll pull it out when his hands are all over you in the carriage. You hadn't thought about that, had you?' Ma Fletcher was worried, Mary-Anne was playing with fire. 'Alone in his carriage, no wonder he said he would send one to you. Just mind what you are doing.'

'It's here, listen, I can hear the horses! Oh, Lord, you've got me worried now.'

There was a loud knock on the door.

'Well, open it then lass, he's waiting!'

Mary-Anne remembered the last time she climbed into a carriage with a member of the Ellershaw family. Edmund Ellershaw's hands had been all over her as soon as the carriage door had closed and she had wished herself dead by the time they had reached his gentleman's club. She breathed in deeply and opened the door to her visitor.

'Mrs Vasey? Mr Ellershaw has sent me to escort you to the music hall. He sends his apologies for not being here in person.' The groom was short with a round face and red cheeks. He coughed slightly as if embarrassed by his master's message.

'Yes, I'm Mrs Vasey. I quite understand.' Mary-Anne picked up her skirts and looked quickly behind her at Ma Fletcher. She closed the door and made her way to the steps of the carriage. She could breathe easier now. There would be no fondling or groping on this journey at least.

She sat back in the darkness of the carriage and the team of horses took her into the bustling city of Leeds. The hostelries and gin parlours were alive with roars of laughter and singing, while women were selling flowers and matches on busy street corners in order to keep their families fed. Some were touting for other trade and were not ashamed of letting people know what they were about with jeers to drunken men and a quick flash of flesh to show them their wares. Mary-Anne decided to wrap her lace shawl more securely around her shoulders. Perhaps Ma Fletcher had been right and the dress was a little too revealing. The carriage pulled up into Swan Street and the carriage driver was dodging people of all classes to open the carriage door for her to alight.

'Thank you.' Mary-Anne took the hand of the coachman and stepped out onto the busy street. She looked down the narrow cobbled yard that lead to the White Swan and the building that was now known as Thornton's New Music Hall. Most of the ladies were dressed in their finest, with wide-brimmed hats adorned with flowers, feathers and even stuffed birds, and their sweeping skirts rustled as they hurriedly walked to get to the best seats, arm and arm with their partners dressed in full evening dress or their Sunday best.

'Mr Ellershaw told me to say he's already in his own box. All the stewards know where he is, you have just to tell one of them whose guest you are.' The carriage driver tipped his hat and left her to make her own way down the cobbles of Swan Yard and into the wide arched doorway of the music hall along with the other excited theatre-goers.

Mary-Anne stood looking around her. She'd

never been in a place like it before. She may have made costumes for performers in New York, but she and John never any money to take in a show. The music hall was decorated in bright colours with posters on the walls and an orchestra was tuning up somewhere within the walls. The gold painted ceiling was hung with gas lights that flickered with the draught created by the crowds of people coming in to the theatre. People were queuing up excitedly at the ticket box offices and couples were smiling and giggling as they made their way through to the main auditorium.

'May I help you?' A young steward dressed in a navy coloured uniform with brass buttons in two rows on the front of his jacket made himself known to Mary-Anne as she stood in awe of the magnificent building.

'Thank you. I'm Mr William Ellershaw's guest. I believe he has his own box?' Mary-Anne didn't quite know what she was asking for. What was a box? she thought to herself as the young steward smiled and asked her to follow him up winding stairs to somewhere above the main stage.

The steward pulled the heavy red velvet curtain to one side, revealing a small private seating area. William was sitting in one of the four chairs, leaning over the ornate gilt edge of the box, look-ing down upon the gathering crowds and stage. He turned round.

'Mary-Anne, you made it! I'm so glad. I hope you will forgive me for sending my carriage to pick you up. I thought it was perhaps best. People talk and I knew once you were here, we could be reasonably private.' William rose from his seat,

225

took Mary-Anne's hand and kissed it gently.

'I hope you are not insinuating that we are doing anything wrong? After all, are we not just good friends?' In the surroundings of the theatre, William looked even more handsome – the picture of the perfect Victorian gent, one that any self-respecting woman would be proud to sit next to. A ruby stud glistened in his collar and an expensive-looking gold pocket watch hung from his waistcoat pocket. She sat down in one of the red velvet and gilt chairs that he offered to her and smiled at him as she noticed his eyes take in her low-cut bodice under her shawl.

'Of course, if that is what you wish. However, I will have to try and control myself, you look so wonderfully seductive.' William let his hand linger on her shoulders as he sat down next to her.

'And you look devilishly handsome, Mr Ellershaw. I don't think I'm worthy of sitting next to you, and people will be talking. Perhaps we should keep our distance while we are sat up here.' Mary-Anne pretended to be bashful, but at the same time, she was thinking of her next move once outside of the music hall. 'Besides, you must consider that you are a married man and that your wife will be waiting for you to return to her arms.'

William's face darkened. 'That she will not! Gone are those days and they were only a fleeting moment when she did make me welcome.'

'I didn't mean to cast a shadow over our evening.' Mary-Anne reached out her hand to William and squeezed it. She looked around her. 'I've never been in a music hall before, it is truly fascinating.' She looked down at all the people waiting for the first act to appear on the grand stage. Palm plants in jardinières stood at either side of the stage and the rich golds of the decorated ceiling and balconies shone in the gaslight. The crowds erupted with clapping and shouting as the host of the evening climbed the small wooden stairs from the music pit where the orchestra was playing a favourite tune of the day. He struggled to make himself heard above the excited spectators as he stepped to the centre of the stage. He was dressed in an evening suit, his dark hair in a perfect centre parting. He had mutton chop sideboards and a sporty little black moustache and he glanced around him before putting his hands up into the air to quieten the crowd.

'My lords, ladies, gentleman and most beautiful women of Leeds. It is my pleasure to welcome you to Thornton's Music hall, where tonight we have a wonderful selection of artists to titillate and amuse.' He stopped for a second as the crowd whooped in anticipation.

'Without further ado, please put your hands together for the sorrowful, heartbroken Mr Henry Clifton.'

The host bowed as the curtains were pulled back to reveal a beautiful gentleman dressed as a milkman. He came to the front of the stage and started singing:

I am a broken-hearted milkman, in grief
* I'm arrayed*
Through keeping of the company of
* a young servant maid*
Who lived on board and wages, the hose

227

to keep clean
In a gentleman's family near Paddington Green

She was as beautiful as a butterfly and
proud as a Queen
Was pretty little Polly Perkins of Paddington Green

He smiled around at the audience holding his arms out and urging them to join in with him on the next chorus as he continued in the popular song about his unrequited love for Polly Perkins.

She'd an ankle like an antelope and a step
like a deer
A voice like a blackbird, so mellow and clear
Her hair hung in ringlets so beautiful and long
I thought that she loved me but I found I was wrong

'Altogether now, everybody sing:

She was as beautiful as a butterfly and
proud as a Queen
Was pretty Polly Perkins of Paddington Green

Mary-Anne looked across at William and saw him laughing as the singer carried on with the next verse and watched as he sang along with the chorus. She could get used to having him by her side and enjoying evenings like this one. She listened to the next verse and then grinned as she joined William in the last chorus, both of them laughing and cheering as the singer finished his performance. All thoughts of revenge were forgotten as she enjoyed act after act.

The last act to be announced was the most popular, and clearly beloved by the audience. Mary-Anne sang happily along with William. His name was George Leybourne and he swayed about the stage – always in danger of toppling over, pretending he was drunk – amusing the crowd as he pretended to swig from an empty champagne bottle in his ragged evening dress, singing a song even Mary-Anne had heard of, 'Champagne Charlie'. The crowd bayed for more as his performance came to an end and the host of the show called for everyone to make their way out of the theatre.

William couldn't help but notice how enthralled Mary-Anne had been with the evening. 'I come here at least once a month, it would be my pleasure for you to accompany me on my visits.'

Mary-Anne pulled her shawl around her. 'I'd very much enjoy that. I have had a most enjoyable evening.' She took William's hand as they made their way out of the box and down the stairs to the busy crowds and the fresh air of the dark night.

'May I be like Burlington Bertie, and offer you a glass of champagne before we both retire? After all, to quote the song, "By Pop! Pop! I rose to fame, I'm the idol of barmaids and Champagne Charlie is my name."' William sang as he took Mary-Anne's arm and escorted her along Swan Lane.

'I thought we were not to be seen with one another?' Mary-Anne glanced up at him as he walked up the cobbles with her on his arm, in full view of the busy crowd.

'What does it matter? I have a feeling that we will be seeing a lot of one another over the coming months. This time I aim to court you correctly. I don't see you arguing about me taking your arm.'

'But your wife, William! You are married.' Mary-Anne stopped in her tracks and acted surprised at his admission of wanting to court her.

'She means nothing to me, we are only married in name. We never loved one another – or at least I never did. We were both just eager to prove our worth to our parents.' William stood face to face with Mary-Anne and held her arms tight. 'Now, why don't we stop fooling one another and be truthful: we both desire one another. The chance of us both remaining just friends is very slim.'

Mary-Anne looked into William's eyes, remembering how she'd looked into them once before and had fallen for the warmth she had seen in them. But she remembered too that she'd also seen a wicked man who had to have his way. However, this time it was what she wanted, this is what she had planned, and he was hers to take. She should kiss him now, but everyone would see.

'It's true I do find you handsome and if you are willing to accept the gossip and slander that we will endure if we do become more than friends than I am willing to also.' Mary-Anne put her arm back into his and walked by his side. The smell of his Bay Rum cologne filled her nose as she placed her head on his shoulder for a brief second. She knew the herby cologne was expensive and only the very rich wore it.

'We were made for one another and I have

always regretted my hasty actions towards you. Now let us have a glass of champagne to celebrate us becoming more than friends and put the past behind us.' William stopped outside The Grand hotel and bar.

'Never mind the champagne, follow me.' Mary-Anne led him up the darkened alley between buildings. 'Now, don't you get too carried away but let us seal this night with a kiss away from prying eyes. I've no need of champagne. My head is dizzy with the excitement of the night already.'

William pushed Mary-Anne against the wall and held her tight, kissing her passionately before untying her shawl and caressing her breasts.

'Now, just a kiss, that's all for now. I'm not one of those whores on a street corner and don't you forget it.' Mary-Anne pushed him back and pulled her shawl around her shoulders.

'You are teasing me. Don't tease me too much, Mary-Anne. I won't be able to help myself.' William kissed her neck and smelt her perfumed hair.

'Enough, William. If we are to see one another again, that is enough for tonight.' Mary-Anne pushed her way past him back into the gas-lighted street and hailed a horse and cab that was standing just outside The Grand, waiting to take worse-for-wear revellers home. It was time to leave her conquest and to keep him wanting more.

'Have lunch with me next Monday, at Whitelocks?' William asked as he gave her his hand to steady her climb into the carriage. 'One o'clock, I'll wait for you.'

'If I can make it I'll be there, William. Thank you for a lovely evening and goodnight.' Mary-

Anne blew him a kiss before sitting back in the cab and smiling to herself. Her first flirtation with William had shown her just how much he wanted her, but it had also brought old longings back to her. Perhaps she was playing with fire. No doubt time would tell.

'Well, at least you've returned in one piece and you look as if you've had a good night.' Ma Fletcher leaned on one elbow in her bed and watched as Mary-Anne threw down her shawl and hummed to herself as she placed the copper kettle on the dying embers of the kitchen fire. 'Did he try anything on with you? I hope you told him where to go, if he did.'

'I've had a wonderful night, Ma. William Ellershaw can be quite a gentleman when he wants to be. It was me who had to do all the tempting.' Mary-Anne sat down in her chair and reached for the button hook to undo the buttons on her boots while she waited for the kettle to boil.

'Now, don't you be forgetting who he is and lose sight of why you are doing this. He's still a bastard and don't you forget it.' Ma Fletcher laid back in bed and pulled her covers over herself, sighing at the excitement she could see in Mary-Anne's eyes.

'Don't worry, I won't forget. But I'm going to enjoy myself while getting even, of that you can be sure.'

Chapter 23

'Why are you still awake?'

William walked into the drawing room of Levensthorpe Hall to find Priscilla sitting in her chair next to the fireplace. He walked over to the sideboard and took the key that unlocked the Tantalus from his waistcoat pocket before pouring himself a large whisky and swigging it back in one, then pouring himself another and sitting across from his wife.

'Your father called, he wanted to see you. I told him you were still at the mill, but I can smell the whore you've been with on you. The smell of her cheap perfume is filling the room. Heaven only knows why I lie so much for you.' Priscilla sobbed as she looked across at her husband who gazed unfeelingly into the fire.

'Because you've no option if you want to stay a member of society. Just look at you. Why I return home at all is unbelievable. There's no love to be found in your arms, no wonder I look for it elsewhere.' William scowled. 'What did the old bastard want anyway? He's not in the habit of visiting his loving son, something must be afoot.'

'He wouldn't tell me, but he asked that you pay a visit to him at the pit. He emphasised not to visit at home. He seemed very on edge.'

William shook his head. 'He'll be bloody lucky – if I can't visit him at home, then why should I visit him at the pit?'

Priscilla stood up and wiped her eyes. As convention dictated, she stopped down to kiss her husband goodnight.

'That's as good as it gets between us two, isn't it? You'd be better off without me, Priscilla, and I definitely would be better for not having you sobbing and hanging around my neck.' He sneered at the unkempt and miserable creature he had married. It was hard to believe that she had once been beautiful.

'But I love you, William,' Priscilla whispered back quietly.

'Then you are a fool,' William said.

Prissy sobbed and fled the drawing room, running up to her bedroom, heartbroken yet again.

William sat forward in his chair and stirred the dying embers of the fire with a poker, wondering what had brought his father to his door and what business he was wanting to discuss. Why did he want to meet him at the Rose Pit? His father's request was soon put to the back of his thoughts though as he recollected his night with Mary-Anne Vasey. Now that was a woman who turned men's heads. He hadn't been able to take his eyes off her all night. She knew what a man wanted. His blood had raced through his veins when she had kissed him and tempted him with her ample cleavage. He would bed her, but perhaps this time he would do it correctly, take her as a mistress and get rid of Ruby Bell, who no longer kept him satisfied anyway. But tomorrow, if he had the time, he would see why his father needed to speak to him. It wouldn't be because he was concerned about him, his son, that was for sure.

William walked through the gates of Rose Pit to find a scene of complete disorganisation. Coal was stacked in every corner of the yard, un-bagged and un-delivered to customers who must have been in need of it. The ponies that helped deliver it looked half-starved and miserable, hanging their heads in despair, and the miners scowled at him as he entered his father's office.

'So, will wonders never cease? You came and visited me when I asked you to.' Edmund lifted up his head from the books that he was trying to make sense of and glared at his son.

'What's going on, Father? What have you done for the yard to look like it does? Is it because of the accident I heard you had a few weeks back? Why isn't Tom Thackeray sorting things for you?' William sat down across from his father. The older man opened his desk drawer, took out a hip flask and swigged its contents.

'I sacked the bastard. He gave me too much lip, said the accident was all my fault, that I'd used substandard pit props – said it in front of the men too.' Edmund waved his hand dismissively at the yard and the miners who had lost all respect for him.

'And had you? If so, he was right to say what he did.' William took the flask out of his father's hand, replaced the stopper and put it in front of him. 'That stuff's not the answer to your prob-lems. Even I know when I need to focus on work.'

'You bastard, give it back.' Edmund leaned for-

235

ward for his flask, as William snatched it and put it in his pocket.

'Did you put your workforce in danger with your penny-pinching? It sounds like a thing you'd do. I don't know why. You've never been short of brass, even though you always say you are.'

'Know your place, William, I'm your father. You can't talk to me like this.' Edmund slurred. 'You know nowt. I've lost it all, lad, your father's penniless. The banks are yelling at me, your mother thinks she can live like a lady, and your younger brother spends money like water. At home, there's only our Grace who's worth anything and I'm not asking her for any of her brass, you'll not get me begging around a woman's skirts.'

'So, that's why I'm summoned. You want some money!' William rose from his chair and leaned against the small filthy office window and looked out at the un-loved pit yard. 'How much do you want? Although I don't see why I should bail you out, you've never been there to help me, unlike grandfather, who did right by all of us. We've nowt to thank you for.'

'Now, lad, I sent you to college, I fed and clothed you. When times were better you wanted for nowt.' Edmund grunted and his face flushed with suppressed anger as he watched his arrogant son sit back down across from him.

'I'll give you some money, but on one condition. Take Thomas Thackeray back on as your manager. He'll keep you straight, the men respect him and he wouldn't have the piles of coal growing in every corner of the yard undelivered. How do you expect to make brass if you aren't selling owt?'

His father's face turned purple with anger at his son dictating terms of his loan. 'Tom bloody Thackeray. You'd think he was the only man on God's earth, that's all I hear them lot out there mutter under their breaths.' Edmund banged his fist down on the desk.

'How much do you want? And don't take me for a fool. I'll know if you don't take him back on and offer him a decent pay because it's obvious you can't manage without him.' William reached inside his jacket pocket and took out his chequebook.

'But what if I can't find him? He's no reason to stay now his mother's died. Just give me the money, William, have pity on your father.' Edmund pleaded.

'He's working for the Bentleys at Eshald Mansion. I'll offer him the position when I return back to Leeds. He'll no doubt bite my hand off as he loves mining, it is in his blood. Now, will two hundred set things straight?' William gave his father an icy stare as he lifted his hand to write the cheque.

'You've bloody got me over a barrel. I hate the bastard, but if that's what it takes to get me back right with the bank, I've no option. Make it two fifty lad, that'll give me time to get myself straight again and keep everyone off my back. I'll try and sell that useless pit at Wakefield, not that it's worth a lot.'

'Square yourself up father, for all our sakes,' William said as he signed the cheque and held it out to his father. 'You don't look well. Mother must be concerned for you.' Now that the pressing matter of the pit had been settled, William saw that his father was bloated, with a strange colour to his complexion and his lips looked almost blue.

'She isn't bothered about anybody but her fancy tea parties and her precious George. Grace keeps herself busy with that Wild woman and she isn't bothered about me. I thank you lad, for this, I should be able to manage now and if Tom Thackeray is part of the deal, then so be it. Perhaps he was worth his weight in coal at any rate.' Edmund smiled at his son, who he had always thought as spoilt, but he needed his help so badly at the moment.

'Take care, Father, watch the drink and other pastimes that I know you get up to. You are not getting any younger.' William put his top hat on his head.

'Aye, you take care and all, lad. Get rid of that mistress and take care of that wife of yours – your mother tells me she looks ill.'

Edmund held his lifeline of a cheque in his trembling hands and sighed. Thank God for that – he'd live to fight another day, even if Tom Thackeray was part of the deal, and even though it meant losing face to his arrogant bastard of a son.

Tom Thackeray took a deep breath and stepped back into the yard of Rose Pit. He closed his eyes for a moment to summon up courage before he made his peace with Edmund Ellershaw and to see what the bastard demanded of him. There was plenty to do. By the looks of it the place had gone to the dogs since he had left.

'You are back then. My lad's talked you into seeing sense.' Edmund Ellershaw bluffed his way with Tom as he stood in front of him, cap in hand.

'Your William said I was wanted back here and I was to be reinstated as the manager and paid ten shillings a week. Now, if I've got it wrong, I can turn around and go back to my gardening.' Tom wasn't going to stay and be made a fool of.

'Ten shillings, you say? You'd better be bloody worth it, I'll expect you working every waking hour for that pay. I didn't want you back but it seems my lad and them out there think I'm past running this bloody mine, so you'd better get your arse out there and show me that you are worth this money my lad's promised.' Edmund glared at Tom Thackeray. He was everything he hated: clean cut, clean living and one to stand up for his rights and that of his fellow man. He was a sop and a troublemaker, and definitely not worth ten bob a week. What had his lad been thinking about when he'd offered him that?

'Right, Mr Ellershaw, as long as we know where we stand. I'll do my job and get this place back in action and you leave me alone to do it. You'll not regret sending your son to me, that I can assure you.' Tom put his cap back on his head and went to the door.

'Don't you give me any bother, Thackeray, else it'll be the worse for you,' Edmund Ellershaw shouted after him.

Tom stood on the steps of the office and looked across at the hungry pit ponies and decided that was his first job. He shouted at one of the yard hands to go buy some hay and get them fed before they dropped. He was officially the manager now. One day, if he was careful, he hoped to own the Rose Pit, and there was money to be made there if it was run properly and Edmund Ellershaw gone.

Chapter 24

'Was that the post-boy I heard at the door, Victoria?' Eliza looked up from her tea as her niece entered the parlour, reading a newly delivered letter and looking flushed.

'Yes, Aunt Eliza, it was for me. It's from George. He's asking me to tea on Friday.'

'Oh, and how do you feel about that? Will you be attending? I'm sure your feelings regarding George have changed now that you know he is your half-brother. However, I realise that you are good friends and a friendship should never be thwarted.' Eliza smiled as her niece sat opposite her looking perplexed.

'I don't think he's ever been that sweet on me in that way, Aunt, he thinks I'm a child still ... which I know I am. It's more of a friendship that we have, but to have tea at his home will certainly be strange, especially if his father is there, or should I say our father? I don't know what I'd quite do with myself.' Victoria sighed and bowed her head.

'Then you have not got a problem. You've seen

his father before, just treat him like you did previously. Anyway, George will keep out of his way, if what Grace tells me is true. I believe his father and he spend as little time as possible in one another's presence. I fear your father is not a well-liked man, Victoria, not even by his legitimate family. They have no time for him and he has no time for them, so he won't give you a second glance.' Eliza patted Victoria's hand. 'Go. Don't forsake George for the sake of his father's mistake, you enjoy one another's company too much.'

'I might, out of curiosity. I'd like to see his home, now I know what I do. But, I must confess, I don't wish to see anyone else but George, in fear that they may recognise any family traits, now I know my parentage.' Victoria swallowed hard.

Eliza smiled at her niece. 'No one would ever guess, Victoria. You take after your mother and me. Go and enjoy yourself.'

'Aunt Eliza, can I ask you something? When I last saw George, I heard some ladies gossiping about him and I didn't understand what they were saying. They said that he prefers mollies to ladies... Is it because he dresses like a dandy? Is that what a Molly is?'

Eliza looked at her young niece wondering how to best explain what she had overheard. 'I... Well, I think they're suggesting that George prefers the company of men to ladies, Victoria. Which is quite a turn up for the books and I'm not sure what his father would think, if he knew.'

Eliza couldn't help but laugh, though her expression softened as she glanced at her baffled niece.

'He won't ever fall in love with a lady, Victoria.

They don't … stir his blood in the way that his male friends might.' Eliza realised her niece had started to understand. 'I guess we might have realised. As you say, he does like his fine clothes and he's always worried about his looks. And there was your mother, worried that he had designs on you. Well, what comes around goes around: Edmund Ellershaw has a bastard for one son and a Molly for another. It's his good fortune that he has two fine daughters in you and Grace, both of whom he won't give the time of day to. I'm afraid your father is a fool and you are better off without him my dear.' Eliza sat back still laughing at the thought of George being homosexual.

'You'll not say anything, Aunt Eliza, will you? He's still George and he's my friend. I don't mind if he likes boys, but from what you say, it's something his family would be ashamed of if they knew the truth.' Victoria looked alarmed.

'I think he would be shunned by everyone if it was common knowledge,' Eliza said gently. 'But I'll not say anything. Now, you go and have tea with him, hold your head up high and enjoy every penny that he spends on you. By rights, it's partly your money that he wastes on his male friends and clothes.' Eliza shook her head thinking about George. Mary-Anne would find it so amusing when she told her.

'I really am so pleased that you have joined me here today, Victoria. I do relish our friendship.' George looked at himself in the long gilt mirror that hung in the drawing room of Highfield House, preening himself before turning and smiled at his young guest as she gazed around her. 'Mama is pleased that I have you as a friend too. She wished to meet you, but alas, she has had to go and see my sister-in-law, Priscilla. She is of a very nervous disposition, and her note this morning begged Mama to visit.'

'I'm sorry to hear that, George, I do hope that she all right. She and your brother live in Levensthorpe Hall, don't they? I've seen your brother on the odd occasion but never your sister-in-law. Is she always nervous?' Victoria wanted to know more about the family that she now knew she was part of but didn't want to seem as if she was prying.

'She's always having a fit of the vapours. But then again, my brother is such a selfish man and only thinks of himself. No wonder she's nervous. Anyone would be who was married to that boor.' George sat down across from Victoria. She was a pretty thing and her aunt always made sure she was well dressed. He could see she would be a beauty when she was older and he liked the fact that she clearly doted on him.

'Your sister Grace is lovely, she is just the opposite. Aunt Eliza says we owe her everything. She treats her just like a sister, they get on so well.' Victoria blushed, realising what she had just said connected the two women together.

'They are close because they need one another in business. Of course, your aunt only works for my sister. We should never forget that. However, I'm sure they have a strong friendship as well. Just like we have. I really do enjoy your forthright views and fashion sense that you have obviously

243

inherited from your aunt.' George pulled his highly embroidered waistcoat into place over his rotund stomach. 'What do you think of my tailor's latest creation? It is of the best Parisian silk, the embroidery is exquisite, don't you think? I haven't dared wear it in front of my father or tell him the expense of it. I'll suffer his wrath when the tailor sends his bill.' George sat back in his chair and looked smug at the thought of getting away with his costly buy until the bill was delivered.

'It's truly spectacular, George. Just like your home. I don't think I've ever been in such grand premises.' Victoria looked around at the expensively decorated walls and the fine furnishings of Highfield House.

'This is nothing compared to my brother's home. He has ten bedrooms and fifty acres of grounds. Mama is always complaining to father saying that we have nothing compared to some families in the district. She is never satisfied.' George sipped his tea.

'When we lived in Pit Lane, we had nothing. Poor Aunt Eliza struggled to feed us both until your sister came along and saved us. When we moved into Aireville Mansions we both thought we had died and gone to heaven, but it is nothing like here. My mother, when she first came to find us both after returning from America, couldn't believe that we had such a big house. You should have seen the look on her face when she was shown around it.'

'Your mother's here and no longer in America? You never told me.' George gasped.

'I'm sorry, did I not? She returned about two

months ago and I've just been getting used to having her here and getting to know her. She is not quite what I expected my mother to be, but I suppose I will grow to like and love her. After all, she is blood.' Victoria gazed at her half-brother over the top of her tea-cup.

'I wouldn't count on that for anything. I hate my father, he's a bastard and he just doesn't understand me.' George sighed. 'I must meet your mother and then I'll tell you what I think of her. She can't be worse than my father.'

'I don't know, I've never spoken to your father either. However, it seems we have a lot in common, George, probably more than you realise.' Victoria placed her tea cup down wanting to tell George everything about his father and her mother but refrained, she was only just getting used to the news so why ruin George's world? It would wait until their friendship developed, a strange friendship between two unloved children of Edmund Ellershaw.

Catherine Ellershaw sat across from her daughter-in-law and tried to seem sympathetic to her gripes and moans as she belittled her marriage to her son. 'Really, Priscilla, you are going to start to appreciate just what you have got in your life and realise how lucky you are. William works hard to keep you in a decent lifestyle, surely you can forgive him for a few misdemeanors.'

'But he doesn't love me, Mama, he treats me so badly. I know he has another woman that he goes to at least two nights a week and he expects me just to turn a blind eye to all his assignations. He never ever looks at me with any love, or indeed touches me.' Priscilla had contacted her mother-in-law in desperation, as there was no one else to turn to with her problems.

'I'm afraid, my dear, William takes after his father in some respects. They both have manly needs that a normal marriage cannot fulfill. You will just have to ignore his lustful ways and be thankful that he isn't demanding your attention every night. I have done just that for years, and to be quite frank my dear, I'm grateful for the nights Mr Ellershaw and I sleep apart. Otherwise, I'd have to lie back and think of England and put up with his heaving which I find quite repulsive these days. I still love my husband, just like you, so I do have some sympathies. Just be grateful that you have still got a roof over your head and are kept in a very good fashion. A fashion that you would not have had if my son and my father had not saved your family from financial ruin.' Catherine Eller-shaw hadn't time for her scatty daughter-in-law's complaining. Priscilla's appearance had got worse of late and she was more hysterical than usual, but she would just have to buck up and live with her circumstances.

'I love him so much, but he treats me so badly. Some mornings I wake and don't want the day to happen. I have nothing and no one to live for,' Priscilla sobbed.

'Don't be so dramatic, Priscilla, there are hundreds of wives in exactly the same position as you. Men will do what men will do and we have to grin and bear it. Now get on with your life, find a new hobby, get out more and stop moping.

246

My William was a good catch and I'll not hear another bad word about him or your marriage. You have got to smarten yourself up and give him something to come home to. Looking at you now, I can fully understand him taking a whore, even they look more presentable than you. Your husband has a position of power. Make him proud to have you on his arm, instead of this unstable wretch that is standing in front of me at this minute. Are you going to the Guild Ball at the end of this month? That will give you an opportunity to shine. Treat yourself to a new dress. Grace and her partner Miss Wild will dress you in something spectacular of that I'm sure.'

'Oh no, William won't want to take me there, I'll only show him up. He usually goes on his own. At least that is what he tells me.' Priscilla looked fearful at the proposition of attending such a prestigious event.

'Well, this time go with him and prove that he should still be proud of having you, and charm everyone. Act like the lady that you are, Priscilla.' Catherine rose from her chair. 'You know, I would relish this house. You have everything I ever wanted. Now look after your husband and make your life complete. You don't realise how lucky you are, that's your problem, Priscilla. Try and keep your spirits lifted. No man wants a woman who is constantly moaning. William will always have his needs and you must learn to live with them. Now, I must be away, I promised to call in at Mrs Hutchinson's. She has just lost her husband, died after a bout of pneumonia, poor soul, and him only forty-two. She's going to be lonely without him, so count your blessings, madam. Things could be worse.'

Priscilla sat in her chair sobbing. She should have known her mother-in-law would have no sympathy for her because, after all, she was in the same situation. Everyone knew that Edmund Ellershaw was a bastard when it came to using women and that his wife had married badly and below her standing, causing her father to bequeath his estates to his grandchildren upon his death. Catherine, however, could live without her husband's love and attention, unlike her. Her heart was broken and so was her self-esteem and her love for life. Life itself meant nothing to her and she no longer wanted to face the world.

Chapter 25

Tom Thackeray whistled as he walked along the cobbled street down into Woodlesford. He'd gone to chapel as always on a Sunday and now he was going to do something that had been playing on his mind ever since he had seen Mary-Anne Wild. He was about to put right a wrong of the past twelve years and hopefully make both his and Eliza Wild's lives more fulfilled. This time there was no interfering mother and no phantom lovers and both of them were in positions of responsibility and respect.

His heart had been broken at the thought of Eliza being untrue to him all those years ago, while his mother had selfishly kept him for herself, making sure that any woman that came courting soon realised that Tom was his mother's and she was not willing to share him. Now, a year on from her death, he was free to court whom he wished, and the words that Mary-Anne had said to him had made him determined to right a wrong and try to rekindle the love that Eliza and he had felt for one another.

He breathed in the warm spring air and strode to the area of Woodlesford where the business folk lived in their smart bay-fronted terraced houses with tended gardens surrounded by iron railings, a million miles from the small pit cottage that the Wilds used to live in. He opened the garden gate and stood for a second on the pristine doorstep before he tugged on the bell pull, nerves flitting about like a frantic butterfly in his stomach as he doubted his actions. He heard someone come to answer the door.

'Can I help, sir?' The maid employed by Eliza looked at the man she did not recognise and noticed a flush on his cheeks.

'Could you tell Miss Wild that Tom Thackeray would like to pay his respects?' Tom took his cap off and screwed it up in his hands, worrying if he had made a mistake.

'Would that be my mistress Miss Eliza?' The maid enquired.

'Miss Eliza,' Tom answered, as a voice was heard asking who was at the door.

'It's a Mr Tom Thackeray, ma'am.' The maid turned and informed Eliza as she came to the door.

'Tom, now this is a surprise! How long is it since I've seen you?' Eliza pushed past the maid and looked at the man she once loved standing on the doorstep. 'You can go now, thank you, Lucy.' As she looked at Tom, her heart missed, a beat as all the memories of the love they once shared came flooding back.

'I hope you don't mind me calling, but I bumped into your Mary-Anne and she said that she thought that you would be pleased for me to call on you, even after all these years … and perhaps renew our friendship, if that is possible.' Tom stood on the doorstep looking at the beautiful, well-dressed woman and remembering her wicked amusing laughter and cheeky innocence of youth.

'Did she now? Well, she was right, nothing would delight me more, please come into our home and let us catch up with one another.' Eliza held the door open and let Tom brush past her. He had hardly changed from the lad that she had strolled out with down Pit Lane. He still smelt the same and still had a liking for checked jackets and breeches she noticed as she showed him into the parlour.

'Victoria, may I introduce you to Mr Tom Thackeray? Tom and I used to be friends long before you were born. Tom, this is my niece, Victoria. I'm sure Mary-Anne will have told you all about her if you've already spoken to her.' Eliza smiled quickly at Tom. She was aware of a sudden warmth in her cheeks.

'Aye, she did that, told me all about you and how she was proud of both you and your aunt.

250

She sounded as if she had regretted every moment away from you both, even though she's seen things that we can only dream of.' So it was this young woman whose parentage had caused such confusion and consternation all those years ago? She was the spitting image of Mary-Anne – it was clear whose daughter she was.

'It's nice to meet you, Mr Thackeray. My aunt has mentioned you in the past and she is always complimentary when she speaks of you. Now, if you'll excuse me, I'll go to the study and write one or two letters. I'm sure you have a lot to catch up upon.' Victoria glanced at her aunt's flushed cheeks and guessed that there had been more than a friendship between them in the past. She was not about to come between a re-kindling of such a flame.

'Please do not go on my account, it is only a short visit, just a few minutes to pass a long Sunday afternoon.'

'Nonsense, you must sit down and join me for tea. Victoria, when you go up to write your letters, tell Lizzie we would like tea and biscuits and then we are not to be disturbed.'

Tom spluttered and then came out with the words that he had rehearsed so many times already in his head. 'Eliza, I'm sorry. Mary-Anne told me everything. I was young and I was foolish. I was also madly jealous and my mother thought nobody to be good enough for me and she didn't want to share me. There's not a day goes by that I don't think of you. I've regretted thinking so low of you, back then. I don't suppose you have it in your heart to forgive me?' Tom stood up and went

251

to the window not daring to even look at Eliza.

Eliza hung her head and recalled the hurt that she had felt when rejected by her one true love. 'You broke my heart. You wouldn't listen that I loved you and you alone. When Victoria arrived and after Mary-Anne had left us both, for nearly three years I struggled to keep my head held high and wait for Mary-Anne to re-claim her child so that I could resume my life again. But that never happened. Instead I brought Victoria up to what you saw before you today. Without the generosity of Grace Ellershaw and my hard work, we would not have survived. The times that I could have done with your shoulder to cry on and for you just to say how much you loved me, I've lost track of. There's only ever been one man in my life and that has always been you. So, Tom don't play with my heart again. If you are truly here through love and friendship, do stay, but I couldn't bear to be hurt again.' Eliza was near tears. She still felt for Tom deeply. There had been nobody else since the day he had walked away from her.

Tom turned and looked at Eliza. 'It seems we have both been fools, but I have been the biggest one. We have wasted the best years of our lives doing others' bidding when we could have lived out happy lives together. Eliza, let's put the past behind us and from this day go forward with our friendship, it's not too late for us to find happiness. My mother died last year and she left me the cottage on Wood Lane and Edmund Ellershaw has just made me his manager again at the Rose. He still treats me like he always does but at least he is paying me slightly more pay after realising he can't run the pit without me.' Tom sat in the chair next to Eliza and was about to take her hand, but was interrupted when the maid knocked on the door and entered to put the tea tray in front of them.

'Thank you, Lizzie.' Eliza smiled at her maid as she curtsied and left them together again. 'Edmund Ellershaw, how that man is hated in this house. Did Mary-Anne tell you that he is Victoria's father but has never admitted to her existence, let alone given her any support? The poor girl got told of her parentage just lately and is still finding it hard to comprehend, especially with me being both friends and in partnership with Grace. Victoria too is friends with George, his youngest son; indeed I worried at one time that their friendship was perhaps not healthy, but Victoria tells me that would never be the case for many reasons.'

'Aye, I don't think that you've any problem there. From what I've seen and heard about him, he's not a ladies' man, unlike his father.' Tom grinned at Eliza as he took his cup and saucer from her.

Eliza sat back and looked across at Tom and then laughed. 'What goes around comes around. It serves the bastard right.' She giggled like a schoolgirl.

'Aye, and he doesn't hide it that much, but I don't think his father's cottoned on to the fact that his youngest prefers men to women. You should hear the lads at the pit, they don't half have some laughs about him behind old Ellershaw's back.' Tom laughed and looked across at the woman he had always loved. Now, after nearly twelve years, they were talking to each other as if he'd never been away.

Eliza smiled and sipped her tea. It was good to have Tom back in her life. Somebody who knew her from the old days, who knew everything about her and with whom there was no need to put on airs and graces to entertain and keep them amused. She might now have plenty of friends in high places, people who respected her for her business skills, but Tom knew who she really was and had re-entered her life like a breath of fresh air. How she had missed him. And now he was back, and she was not about to let him disappear again.

Chapter 26

Mary-Anne hummed contently to herself as she reached to open the garden gate on her return home from lunch with William. Earlier, she had visited Eliza at the shop, with the added bonus of seeing Victoria. Life was good: Victoria was beginning to accept her and trust her, and Eliza was full of the news of Tom's visit. Her face had shone with the love that her old flame had re-kindled, and Mary-Anne was pleased that her words had not fallen on stony ground when it had come to her matchmaking. As for William, well, she had him just where she wanted him. He was smitten and she was finding it amusing just how far she could tease and keep him on edge for her company and favours.

Mary-Anne suddenly stopped in her tracks. She was about to unlock the door into her home with Ma Fletcher, only for it to open, and a tall sombre-looking man made his way out.

'Good afternoon,' the man with papers under his arm said to her before walking away.

'Who was that then? I didn't know you were having visitors.' Mary-Anne hung her bonnet up.

'He's from Capstick and Sons, on The Headrow. He's my solicitor. I sent for him the other day. I didn't say anything to you because I wanted to talk to him on my own about my will. So I sent that gormless lad that always stands on the corner with a message for him to call today while you were out.' Ma Fletcher sat back in her chair and sighed. 'Aye, you needn't look so worried, I've not done owt daft. I've just made sure my wishes will be carried out after my death. I thought I'd better have it in writing, then there's no misunderstanding.

'But you are feeling all right? Are you ill?' She might be an old cantankerous woman, but Mary-Anne was fond of the old so-and-so all the same.

'Aye, apart from my pins are bad and sometimes I get this pain in my chest. But I'm tired of life, lass, this old body has seen enough. I watch you and think, I wish I was that young again, I'd have lived my life so differently. Now, lass, let me tell you what I've done. I've made the whole lot yours after my death; there's nobody else I could think I would want to leave anything to. But you can guarantee some grovelling worm will appear

255

out of the woodwork after my death. So I'm straight with myself and you now.' Ma Fletcher closed her eyes and swallowed. 'If nowt comes of your carrying on with William Ellershaw, at least I know you'll not want for owt and your Victoria could come and live with you here, now we are all tarted up.'

'But we aren't related, and you owe me nothing. I've only been here a short time. It's not that I'm not grateful, because believe me, I am. I could never have afforded a house like this, nor its contents.' Mary-Anne sat down next to the old woman. 'I know our original pact was to get even with Edmund Ellershaw and to give him something to worry about while I flirt with his son, but I've only just started leading him on.'

'Lass, I've been looked after the best I've ever been looked after all my life these last few weeks. You deserve it all, now leave me be, so that I can have forty winks. Besides, you look as happy as the cat that got the cream. I think you are enjoying your time with William Ellershaw a little too much. You do what's right by your own heart and forget about this stupid old woman's schemes, nowt matters when you are six foot below in a box.' Ma Fletcher pulled her shawl around her, keeping her eyes closed. She was tired and she had not told Mary-Anne the whole truth. She knew that her health was failing, she could feel it in her bones, and there was little time left to seek revenge upon Edmund and William Ellershaw. Better she go to her maker with purer thoughts in her heart.

Mary-Anne sat at the kitchen table, shaking her

head. Was she really the heir to Ma Fletcher's small fortune? All for the sake of a few weeks' care and the same loathing of the Ellershaws. Mary-Anne stopped herself from being excited about the prospect of inheriting it all. After all, it wasn't to be celebrated as it would mean the death of the kind old woman. She also mulled over the words that she had said regarding William Ellershaw. She didn't miss much, despite her years. She'd been sharp enough to recognise that yes, Mary-Anne was beginning to enjoy William's company a little too much and, if she were to be honest, sometimes she forgot the original plan of getting even with the Ellershaws. Now, no matter what happened, Mary-Anne would have security, thanks once again to Ma Fletcher. She would never be able to thank her enough.

Edmund Ellershaw sat awaiting his son's appearance at his office at Highwater Mill. He tapped his stick and continually looked at his pocket watch as William's clerk kept apologising for the absence of his boss. Edmund grew more and more frustrated with his son. Work was obviously more important than the fact that his father was here to visit him, a visit it was unusual for his father to make.

'Are you sure that bit of a lad has gone to find him? He's taking a hell of a time to get his arse back here.' Edmund stood up and hovered over the clerk before looking out of the glass-windowed office down onto the spinning looms and the operators that had no time for anything but concentrating on their jobs, or risk losing a limb or fingers to the unguarded machinery.

'I assure you, sir, he'll be on his way. He's just seeing to the new delivery.' The clerk put his head down and concentrated on his books as Edmund swore under his breath and went back to his seat in front of the green leather-topped desk that was littered with correspondence and wool samples.

'Father, what gives me this pleasure? Or, by the looks of your face, is it not going to be a pleasure.' William closed the door behind him as he sat across the desk from his father.

'Time's bloody money lad and what I've got say will not wait a minute longer.' Edmund leaned back in his chair and hinted for William to find his clerk a job outside the office walls.

'Turner, just go and see if I've left the correspondence for the latest delivery of bales down in the warehouse. I don't seem to have it on me.' William felt his pockets, knowing full well it was within his inside pocket.

'Yes, sir.' The clerk left his desk, looking relieved that he was not going to have to sit and endure a family dispute.

'Now, what is it? You look as if you have a mouthful of wasps. Is it money? Surely you've not spent what I lent you already?' William sat back in his chair and looked at his father's red- and purple-coloured cheeks and noticed him pull the face he had seen many a time when he was going to raise his temper.

'It's nowt to do with brass. I've heard that you are the talk of Leeds, been seen a time or two with one of those bloody Wild hussies,' Edmund spluttered. 'It's not enough that our Grace hasn't the sense she was born with, but I didn't expect anything else seeing she's a lass. But you, cavorting about with a woman who is no better than a whore, while your wife's at home and you supposed to be the pillar of respectability.'

'So what if I have been seen out and about with Mary-Anne? It's nobody's business but mine, and you're definitely in no position to comment.'

'Don't you lecture me, lad. When it comes to having a little pleasure, at least I'm discreet. I don't flaunt them at the music hall or in broad daylight and let everyone know what I'm about. A man has to have a distraction, but discreetly and preferably not with a penniless tart.' Edmund puffed and caught his breath.

'She's not penniless, nor a tart. She's recently widowed and lives up near Speakers' Corner. She's rich, Father, and beautiful, and provides me with a distraction from the poor wizened thing that waits for me at home. God knows I was lost until I met her again, I always did think she was the one for me.' William paced back and forward in his office, wondering just why his father was complaining this time – after all, he'd never said anything about his other transgressions, of which he was sure he had known about.

'You don't go near her, do you hear! She's rotten to the core, just like her mother,' Edmund blurted.

'Her mother? How do you know about her mother? Was she one of your fancies, or worse than that?' William turned and glared at his father. 'If my mother knew half of what I hear and know about you, she would leave you and be better off for doing so. You are a dirty manipulative man, who has used women all your life.' William stood in front of his father and watched the rage in his eyes. 'Who are you to lecture me?'

'You leave your mother out of this. And, aye, I poked Sarah Parker, just like I did her daughter, the one that you are so keen on showing off around Leeds. Why don't you ask her how you compare to your father? I'm sure she will remember the night I took her, more ways than one, at my club. She was such an innocent young thing then, and a virgin. Stop calling the kettle black, William, and look at yourself. There's nowhere you've been that I haven't been there before you, including Mary-Anne Wild. I'm trying to protect you from such a reckless life, it does nowt for you in the long run. Keep your dick and your nose clean, especially when it comes to that tart.'

'Get out, get out of my office. I never want to see your face again. How could you take pleasure in ruining my life and gloating over a past conquest? I'm your son, or do you want to forget that as I do at this moment?' William glared at his father.

Edmund pushed his chair back. 'You always were bloody stupid,' he shouted. 'That can be easily arranged. Don't expect me to leave you a penny of inheritance, I will leave it to George. He is twice the man you are.' He went to the office door and held his hand over the handle.

'Don't make me laugh, Father. What money will you have left in any case? And your precious George prefers the Molly house to the pit. He's more precious than any woman.' William leaned back and watched as his father slammed the glass-panelled door behind him, nearly shattering the glass with the slam that put an end to the relationship between father and son.

William sat back in his chair and fumed at his father's admissions. So, that was why his father hated the Wild family, they knew his dirty secrets. How many times had he taken Mary-Anne's mother, and had Mary-Anne gone with him more than once, and was it of her own free will? He would find out, but for all his father's warnings, it would not dissuade him from pursuing Mary-Anne Vasey. He would speak to her and find out if it was the truth he was ranting. He regretted the things that he had said about his younger brother. George was George, and he should not have told his secret to his father. George had never done anything against him and now he was sorry for his words said in haste, which would have huge consequences on how his father treated his youngest son.

Chapter 27

'It's all your bloody fault. Whenever I was laying the law down to our bloody family, you were undermining me. Pampering them and seeing to their every need. No wonder our George is the way he is, he's always hiding behind your skirts.' Edmund Ellershaw paced the floor in the study at Highfield House. He'd returned home from his meeting with William in a foul mood and was looking for someone to blame for his ruined family.

'And, I suppose, none of this is your fault,' Catherine Ellershaw spat back. 'You, you'd like me to believe, are entirely blameless. After all, you are the pillar of society, with your charitable ways and treatment of your staff, and don't get me started on your understanding of the women of the world. You have few or no morals, Edmund Ellershaw, so don't you preach to me about our children. It is my love and hard work with them that make them as fit for genteel society as they are.' She would not be blamed for her husband's shortfalls.

'Bollocks! Fit for genteel society! Grace thinks herself as good as a man when it comes to her business. And she never even looks at a man. William, well, he's always been a bastard, and now I find out George is a faggot. I should have realised, I've been bloody blind.' Edmund sat down. He heart was beating fast and his head was pounding with rage and the upset of suddenly realising his world was falling apart.

'And who have you to blame for all this? Yourself, Edmund Ellershaw. Look to yourself. None of your children have any respect for you, all they see is a dirty old lecher who uses and abuses people for his own good. At least my children do have a caring side – especially Grace, you can't say you are not proud of her. She has made more of the money given to her by her grandfather than you ever would. George can't help being what he is, he's a sensitive soul. William is a thriving businessman, though unfortunately I know that he does share some of your traits. Perhaps that is why you dislike him so much. He's a threat to you, and he has money, unlike you.' Catherine flashed her eyes at him and stared at her husband while he caught his breath. 'Go and apologise to William, you need him, he's your son.'

'Never!' Edmund jumped to his feet. 'He can rot in hell.' Edmund clenched his fists and stared at his wife before stomping out of the study. 'I'll never speak to him again and he's not to be made welcome in this house. Understand?'

Catherine stood at the fireplace and sobbed. She used to love her husband, but that was when she was ignorant about his ways, but of late he had tested her to her limit and her love for him was nearly dead. The pity shown on her close friends' faces for her plight made her uneasy in her friendships with them; it was as if everyone knew of the things she had to endure. Her tears suddenly stopped as she heard a thump coming from the hallway and a groan of a body in pain.

'Edmund, Edmund are you all right?' Catherine rushed to the hallway to find her husband slumped on the tiled floor way, unable to talk and move. His body seemed paralysed, his face distorted, and there was panic in his eyes.

'Help!' she shouted. 'Someone help me! Edmund has collapsed.'

Dr Greaves stood over Edmund Ellershaw in his bed and looked at his distraught wife, while he checked his pulse one more time. 'I'm afraid he's suffered a stroke. I've warned him on numerous occasions that he was not doing his body any good with his drinking and excesses. I think he still thought himself a young man, but I'm afraid time catches up with us all.' The doctor placed Edmund's hand back under the bed covers and shook his head. 'The next twenty-four hours will let us know if he is to stay in the land of the living or depart this good earth.'

Catherine Ellershaw sobbed and sat down on the edge of the bed next to her slumbering husband. 'I'm sorry, Edmund, I'm sorry we argued over our children. Please don't leave me, we didn't mean the things we said to one another.' She looked up at the doctor for assurance but he could not give her any.

'It's out of my hands, I'm afraid. The good Lord will do what he wants; I can do no more for him.' The doctor closed his Gladstone bag and stopped at the doorway. 'If he worsens, send for me. I'll come straight away. But for now I'll leave him to sleep, rest is what he needs. That and to be kept away from alcohol. He's drunk far too much over the years. Good day, Mrs Ellershaw.'

Catherine might sometimes despair of her husband and his morals, but deep down she still cared for him. Besides, she needed him. She hadn't a clue on how to manage the pit and keep the house affairs, he had always done that.

The bedroom door opened quickly. 'Mother, Agnes just told me now, when she took my coat. I'd have come home earlier if I'd had realised that father was ill.' George rushed to his mother's side. 'How is he?'

'Not good. The doctor says the next twenty-four hours will see if we are to keep him with us.' Catherine paused, she had to ask George if what his father had been told was true. 'He had a row with William and got himself worked up over it. Is it true what William told him? That you are not drawn to the fairer sex, that you prefer men? I always thought that you were a sensitive child but I never thought that of you.'

'Is that what William told him? He had no right. I don't say anything about where he goes and what he does. The bastard. He hates everybody and loves to make bother for me.' George glanced quickly at his father as he let out a low groan. 'I don't judge anybody else, so why should anyone judge me?'

'George, it doesn't matter to me whom you prefer, but I'm afraid your father was more than disturbed. You know what he's like. You will always be my son, no matter what your preferences, but I'm afraid your father will never understand. That is, if we are lucky enough to keep him in this world. Now, can you tell one of the servants to inform Grace of her father's illness, and William too. Never mind that your father has made him unwelcome in our home after his row over you.'

Edmund grunted to show his annoyance at Catherine's request. Even though the doctor had given him laudanum he could still hear and show his anger at his wife's actions.

Catherine reconsidered. 'Perhaps not William, but definitely Grace. She's visiting Jessica Bentley at Eshald Mansion today, they will find her there. She had gone to discuss their dresses for the Guild Ball.' Catherine sighed and patted her husband's hand under the bedclothes. 'This year, I'm afraid, we will not be attending my dear. Perhaps next, if we are lucky.' She held back the tears and watched as George made for the door. 'Could you go to the Rose Pit and inform the manager there? I've heard your father mention a Tom Thackeray. I suppose they will have to know, I don't know the first thing about mining. How I wish you had shown more interest, George. The pit would not be a problem then. Anyway, we will take each problem as it presents itself. The main thing is to nurse your father back to health.'

She watched George close the door behind him. How she was going to manage everything she didn't know, and how she regretted her words said in anger, but it would seem that William was right by the shame that she had seen on George's face and his anger at his brother.

'You. Are you Tom Thackeray?' George walked into the yard of the Rose Pit and looked around him with disdain at the dirt and roughness of the pit. The man he was shouting at was telling some miners to move some coal buckets out of the way of the upcoming cage.

'Aye, that I am. What can I do for you? Aren't you Mr Ellershaw's son?'

'I am indeed. I need to speak to you with some urgency and in private.' George indicated his wish to speak in the wooden office out of the way out of prying ears and eyes.

'Tha looks worried. Is anything amiss, Master George? We've not seen your father today, which is unusual.' Tom walked across the yard with

George and opened the door into the office.

'You'll not be seeing him for some time. He was taken ill this morning. The doctor says he's had a stroke. My mother is with him at home, but he's in bed and can't speak.'

'That's a bugger, I'm sorry to hear that. You mother and your family must be worried sick. If there's anything I can do just say. What do you want to do with the Rose? You surely can't close her, we employ fifty local men, and they can't be without their wages.' Tom's first thought was what Edmund's health issues would have on the pit and he hoped that his family would think the same. As for Ellershaw himself, well, he'd seen his demise coming for some time. No man could live the kind of life he had and not suffer the consequences.

'What are their concerns to me? If I had my way, the whole lot would be up for sale and the men laid off. However, while my father is ill and until we know how bad he is, we should keep the mine open. Would you be in agreement to being placed in authority and ensure its running until a decision has been made about its future?' George sat back on the edge of the desk and looked at the man he'd heard his father complain a bucketful about. He'd also grudgingly admitted that he was a godsend when it came to handling the workers, though. 'I take it that you can keep good accounts? I'd want to see them each month.'

'You assume right. I have a good head for figures and I know how the pit works like the back of my hand.' Tom knew an opportunity when it came his way.

267

'Right, take charge. If you need to spend any money that you can't make through the pit, let me know. Otherwise, I will be in touch weekly. And keep your fingers out of the till, Thackeray, I will be watching you like a hawk.' George stood up, not even bothering to look at the account books or to request a tour around the pit. He wasn't bothered by the Rose and its workers, but he knew he had to do his duty while his father was ill or until it could be sold. In another few months, George would come into his grandfather's inheritance and then he had no worries. It would be best all round if the pit went up for sale. Which would be the first thing that he would do on his father's death.

'Yes, Master George ... sir, it would be an honour. I'll do my best.' Tom tugged on his cap and looked down at the wooden floorboards of the office.

'I know you will, Thackeray, else I'll have something to say about it.' George brushed his gloved hands that had a covering of coal dust on them from just leaning on the desk. 'This place is filthy. How anyone can enjoy running this place, I don't understand. We will come to an arrangement regarding a rise in pay when you have proved your worth.' He glared at Tom before leaving him standing shocked by how little care that George had shown for the pit and indeed his father.

Tom looked around the cluttered pit office and couldn't help but grin. He was in charge of the Rose, he was his own boss! He walked around to the back of the desk that Edmund Ellershaw always sat at and rubbed his hand over his seat.

Nobody had ever dared sit in the chair, it was old Ellershaw's and was almost like a holy shrine. He pulled the leather-backed chair out, sat down in it quickly, looked around his domain and laughed to himself. He soon sobered up when he remembered that Edmund Ellershaw was at death's door. How could he feel so happy about someone else's misfortune? Still, it would be good to be in charge until either Ellershaw came back or the pit was sold. Either way, he'd make the most of it. He couldn't wait to tell Eliza when he saw her later that evening. Hopefully, with this responsibility, he would show her that he was equal to her in business and a good catch, with no mother to interfere with their courtship this time.

Victoria looked at herself in the long mirror in her bedroom and caught her breath. Eliza had just unwrapped the dress that she had lovingly made for her niece to wear at the Guild Ball and was admiring the beauty of her own workmanship while Victoria stood beaming at her reflection as she stood the perfect model for the frivolous dress.

'Just perfect, Victoria, you will be the belle of the ball. No one on that dance floor will shine as bright as you.' Eliza titivated the skirts and sleeves and glowed with pride at her skills as both a parent and seamstress. 'In a few years, the eligible young men of the district will not be able to take their eyes off you. I used to dream of having a dress like this and attending balls to find my Prince Charming. He will be out there one day, Victoria, a perfect man just for you.' Eliza kissed

269

her niece on the cheek and whispered, 'I love you, my dear.'

'You don't think I look too much like Grace, do you? She likes purple and now I know that we have the same father I can see we share some of the same features.' Victoria sighed.

'No, it's just that you are both blessed with thick dark hair and purple brings the best of it out. Besides, you are far younger and far more beautiful, so don't you worry about anyone linking you with the Ellershaws. Grace will be there along with George, although I don't think either of them will be looking for a sweetheart, do you?' Eliza smiled.

'I don't know, there could be a good-looking young man for George. He could be the scandal of the ball,' Victoria teased. 'Are you sure that you still want to take me to the ball? I can wait until I'm older. I couldn't help but notice that your old friend Tom has brought a look of happiness to you, and the poor post-boy is run off his feet going back and forward with your notes that you send one another.' Victoria was happy for her aunt. Since Tom had visited her, she had heard her singing to herself and quickly checking her looks every so often in the mirror.

'I don't know what you are talking about. We are just catching up on old times. But no, Tom would not thank you to attend the ball. He wouldn't know what to do with himself at such a posh do. Besides, I want to show you off.'

'Will Mr and Mrs Ellershaw be there? I hope not. I'd find it embarrassing, knowing what I do.' Victoria looked down at her feet and sighed.

'Don't you worry about them. He's never said anything or acknowledged your presence on this earth and he's not about to now. His wife would certainly have something to say if he did – after all, every penny that he has got is hers. It is most unfair that when women marry all their possessions and money becomes their husband's. I think that is why Grace has never married, she prefers to be in charge of her own life. Unlike that poor Priscilla Eavesham married to her brother. She is ruled by him and is a simpering wreck. Speaking of which, you should avoid William, he takes after his father. In the coming years, you need to be careful who you are seen with, Victoria, it will make all the difference to your future. Even now, if any of the boys at the ball ask for a spot on your dance card, make sure they are of good repute. But most of all, you enjoy yourself, life is too short to miss out on some fun.'

Eliza hoped that in the future Victoria could attract a husband of good nature and with some wealth. She knew little of hardship, not like herself who remembered the pain of hunger and the worry of having no money. She worried about her niece's place in society. After all, she had nothing to offer any suitor: an illegitimate niece of a seamstress, abandoned by her true mother and with a bastard of a father. Her family history and lack of money would not make her an ideal catch, but, hopefully, somebody would be attracted by her looks and personality.

'Now, I must go. I promised Tom that I would meet him once he had finished work at the pit. He is to give a talk at the Mechanics' Institute at

Allerton Bywater and I offered my support.'

In another hour she would be standing in the village of Allerton Bywater, amongst miners and their families all angry with their lot in life, and rightly so – they put their lives on the line every day for the pit owners. The pit there was unsafe and the pay was abysmal but it was the main employer in the area and people had to live. Things had come to a head when a woman had gone down the pit with a baby strapped to her back, working at the seam just to keep her family fed after losing her husband in a pitfall. Now, the miners were starting to demand better care and conditions and Tom had been asked to give his views.

Victoria glanced at her aunt. 'He sounds quite a reformist, does your Tom, from what you have told me of him.'

'He's not my Tom. But yes, he believes that no man is any better than the next and that being born into money does not give you the right to treat those less fortunate than yourself disrespectfully. I fear he has his work cut out, especially with pit owners like Edmund Ellershaw.' Eliza smiled and blushed.

'I think I like your Tom, even though I don't know him well.' Victoria smiled as she started to take her new dress off.

'Yes, he's a good man and I'm glad that he's made himself known to me again. We have a lot of catching up to do, but nothing more than that.'

Eliza left Victoria to change and made her way downstairs, thinking how true her words were. Tom was a good man and she was over the moon that he was back in her life. But she must hurry if she was to keep her promise of accompanying him to his talk.

'Oh, Tom, can you manage to run the Rose? It is a hell of a responsibility.' Eliza looked at the man on her arm and felt the determination that Tom was showing after hearing about Edmund Ellershaw's ill health.

'I can run it just as good as he's been doing. By the looks of his books, there's been more going out than coming in because he's been spending money like water, but not on the mine. That's had nowt spent on it for years.' Tom hastened his pace as they reached the outskirts of Allerton Bywater. 'If I had owt about me, I'd be making them an offer to buy it, because I bet they'd bite my hand off just to get rid of it now the old bastard's dying.'

'Tom, don't talk like that. He might be rotten to the core, but I can't help but feel for Grace, even though she knows he's no saint. He is her father, and Victoria's come to that, not that he has had anything to do with her. Perhaps if he does die, at least she will be able to tell her future lovers that her father is dead, without lying. I must be terrible wicked to think that, but Mary-Anne and I have wished him dead so many times, I've lost count.' Eliza looked up at Tom as he straightened his collar before entering the Mechanics' Institute where he was to give his talk.

'Aye well, if he does kick the bucket, it would do us all good. And I'm not going to hold back on blackening his name tonight along with the bastards who run the pit here. There's too many Edmund Ellershaws in this world, all looking to make money and take the food from our mouths and clothing from our backs. We both know what it's like to go hungry and worry about keeping a roof over our heads. If I owned the Rose, I'll not be one of them, I'll treat folk right. Not to say I'll be a soft touch, but I'd not see my workers go hungry.'

Tom's eyes sparkled with ambition. 'Anyway, lass, best foot forward. Let's give these owners something to think about and these poor buggers in this Institute a bit of hope. Because without hope all is lost.' Tom took Eliza's arm. He was drowning in hope, for both Eliza's love and to become the owner of his own pit, if he could just raise the money.

Chapter 28

'Well, what does it say? It must be something to worry about, by the way you are gawping.' A note had just been delivered by the post boy and Ma Fletcher was desperate to know what it said.

'It's from our Eliza, she's sent word that Edmund Ellershaw is in a bad way. He's had a stroke.' Mary-Anne sat down heavily in a chair.

'Couldn't happen to a nicer person, the old bastard. The devil will be stoking the fires for him as we speak because that's where he'll be going.' Ma Fletcher grinned. She might have resolved to

274

forgo her plans for revenge but that didn't mean she didn't feel pleased to learn of her old enemy's certain demise.

'Eliza wants me to tell Victoria. She thinks it's my place to do so, now she knows that he is her father. No sooner does she find out who her father is than she's losing him,' Mary-Anne sighed.

'Nay, she's never had him, it'll mean nowt to her, and in fact it's a blessing, if you ask me. She'll never have to look at him again, if we are lucky. I don't know why you are pulling that long face, you'd think you were going to miss him by the looks of it.' Ma Fletcher pulled her shawl around her and shook her head.

'William didn't say anything when I met him briefly last night, although he did seem upset over words that he had with him previously. I think his father had virtually disowned him over saying what he thought about his younger brother.'

'That's typical Ellershaw, they don't like to hear the truth about themselves. Don't forget Victoria is your blood, do right by her first. Bloody William must sort his own family out. He shouldn't mean anything to you, remember?' Ma Fletcher had noticed a change in Mary-Anne of late. William Ellershaw had taken hold of Mary-Anne's senses with his beguiling ways. She'd started singing around their home and talking as if she was starting to fall in love with him. This was not what she had planned, she had just wanted revenge.

'You are right, I'll make your dinner and then I'll go to Aireville Mansions. Victoria is on her own today because Eliza is at work in her shop. I suppose Grace Ellershaw will be in despair as well and unable to give support to our Eliza. What a carry-on! But, like you say, he's not worth spilling tears over. I hope he dies too, the world will be a better place without him.'

Mary-Anne busied herself preparing some bread and cheese for Ma Fletcher's dinner. Edmund Ellershaw had been like a dirty black shadow overhanging her life for so long. She looked down at the bread she was buttering and noticed her hands were shaking. Hopefully, the old bastard would die and then it was over. She could hold her head up high and forget the past. She wiped a solitary tear away from her eye, breathed in and thought of the world without Edmund Ellershaw. A better world. A world where, if she had her way, she would make his son her own.

'Mother, this is a surprise, Aunt Eliza didn't say you were to call.' Victoria rose from her chair in front of the window and put her sewing to one side.

'It was our Eliza who asked me to call. She asked me to tell you the news, about your father.' Mary-Anne saw her daughter's face cloud over.

'I don't want to talk about him, I hate him. I hate what he did to you.' Victoria could not make eye contact with her mother and sat back down in her chair.

'That's in the past. I wouldn't have been blessed with you if it hadn't happened. And you are a blessing, Victoria, don't you ever forget that.' Mary-Anne reached for her daughter's hand. 'Your father has had a stroke, quite a bad one. For all I know, he might have died overnight. Your aunt heard the news yesterday evening and asked for me to tell you today in a note that she sent. I know that you have no feelings for him, but he is still your father and you should know.'

'He means nothing to me, why should he? Aunt Eliza was both mother and father to me while you were in America. He could have offered her help but no, he did not even recognise that I was on this earth and would not have shown me any sympathy or affection if he had.' Victoria's voice was cold and unfeeling.

'I know, but you had to be told. One day, Victoria, I will make up for my absence in your young life, I promise.'

'You are here now, Mother, that is all that matters and I understand why you did what you did. At first, I felt it was because you didn't love me, but I know different now.' Victoria fought back the tears, she still felt slightly confused when it came to her feelings over her mother.

'You know you can come and stay with Mrs Fletcher and me if you wish? She's not a bad old stick, really.' Mary-Anne put her arm around her daughter.

'No, I'm fine here, Aunt Eliza needs me. Although I don't know how much longer for, she seems to have re-kindled a friendship with an old friend.' Victoria looked up at her mother and smiled. She was happy for her aunt, it was time she found happiness.

'That would be Tom Thackeray, I take it? You know she loved him dearly, and she should have married him. But he listened to the gossips and his mother and nothing came of it.' Mary-Anne looked across at her daughter. 'Happiness is everything, Victoria, remember that when you grow up, you grab it while you can. How's your friendship with George? You are a right pair, both of you have secrets that you have to keep to yourselves. Will he be worried about his father too?'

'George will be upset, but he's not been the best father to him either, money does not make up for love.' Victoria glanced at her mother. 'I know you love me and always have done. I remember Aunt Eliza reading your letters to me when I was too young to read and I could feel the love in your words. I'm glad that you are here now, I'm just sorry that poor John Vasey lost his life, he was a good man, he didn't deserve to die.'

'I know, he was a good man. I miss him. After all, we did love one another deeply once. I'd had enough of not having any security in my life but unfortunately it seems that I was the reason for him living. Life's been hard … but enough of this gloomy talk. You are a clever young girl with good prospects, thanks to Eliza. You should enjoy your life. Now, let us see what you are going to the Guild Ball in. I know Eliza will have made sure that you will shine.'

Victoria beamed. 'She has made me the most divine dress, Mother. It's purple with black roses around the bodice, I've never seen a dress like it before. I'll go and get it to show you.' Victoria rose to her feet and ran out of the room.

Mary-Anne was glad that her sister and daughter were so close and had a lovely home, she only hoped that the arrival of Tom Thackeray back into Eliza's life would not jeopardise Victoria's and her friendship.

'Oh, Victoria, it is beautiful, just look at the work that's gone into that.' Mary-Anne held the dress up and admired the creation.

'I know, I can't wait to wear it. I've never been to a ball before.' Victoria smiled as she held the dress next to her. 'It's a pity you are not going, Mama, it would have been lovely to have you by my side.'

'I would have loved to have attended, but I'm not important enough, unlike your mother and Grace. You enjoy the evening, live every minute, my love.' Mary-Anne kissed her daughter on the cheek, remembering how she had stolen her ticket only to return it when Eliza had cottoned on to her game. She was glad that she had now, it was right that Victoria had a chance to enjoy the party. She'd been mean and desperate when she had stolen it from under her nose. Besides, now she didn't need to make herself known to William, she already had him under her spell and the good Lord was making sure Edmund Ellershaw met the fate he deserved.

William Ellershaw rode his horse hard to his old home at Highfield House. The news of his father's illness had reached his ears through a tradesman saying that the Rose Pit was being run by Tom Thackeray and might have to close. Until then, he had no knowledge of his father's sudden decline in health, with not one of his family contacting him. He rode into the driveway and dismounted his horse around the back of the house next to the stables, leaving the horse saddled and still in its harness as he made for the kitchen door.

'Master William! You are here.' The cook looked worried. 'Does your mother know?' The gossip within Highfield House had been raging with everybody questioning why Edmund Ellershaw's eldest had not been informed of his father's illness.

'She will now! Is the old bugger still alive?' William asked as he made his way past the nosy old cook and through the kitchen doors.

'Yes, he's still with us, thank the Lord. But he's not … taking visitors.' The cook's voice trailed off as she watched William walk through the house and run up the curving stairs, still in his riding boots, to the room where his father lay with his family around him. There was going to be trouble in the Ellershaw household, she thought to herself.

'Now, isn't this a nice family scene. When exactly were you going to tell me that my father is ill?' William looked around him at the three faces of his closest relations and then at his father looking ashen, but still alive, lying in his bed.

'William, hush, your father is gravely ill. Come, follow me onto the landing and then I can speak to you in private.' Catherine Ellershaw walked over quickly to her son and took his arm, as he looked back at his brother and sister and noticed the disdain on their faces.

'Why didn't you tell me, Mother? Is he dying?' William looked with concern at his mother.

'He's still here, that's all I can say. He's lost the use of his legs and his right arm and can't speak.

However, he can hear you and he does know what you are saying. He gets upset if he thinks you are doing something that he doesn't agree with, hence the reason why we didn't send for you. His health comes first and he needs no more upsets. It was the words you had together that brought on this stroke.' Catherine sighed and blew her nose and sobbed.

'I will not be blamed for the state that he is in. It is his own doing, you know that as well as me. He's no saint, Mother, you know he isn't. And as for telling him the truth about our George, he should know what his son is about. After all, it is as clear as the nose on his face that George will never bed a woman and does not have the same family traits as father and me.' William shook his head and stared at his mother.

'Hush, hold your tongue. The servants will hear, do you want them all to know our business?' Catherine whispered.

'Here we go, keep it secret, don't let anyone know the truth! How much have you put up with from that old bastard I have the dubious honour of calling my father? Just how many women has he bedded behind your back in his late nights at the club? No wonder I am like I am. It is truly a miracle that our Grace turned out a lady; perhaps it is just the male heirs that are corrupt.' William's eyes flashed.

'How dare you!' Catherine raised her hand and slapped her son across the face. 'Your father is a gentleman, unlike you. He's been the perfect husband and father. It is you that has ruined our world, taking everything my father gave you and hardly acknowledging any thanks for what we all have done for you. It is yourself you are talking about, you and your whore. Poor Priscilla, I ignored her when she cried and told me about your time spent in other women's arms. I can't believe what my first born has turned into. Get out of my house and don't come back. Your father's right, you are no longer welcome here.' Catherine raised her hand to slap her son again, for him to grab it before she made contact with his face.

'I wouldn't stay here a minute longer. You deserve my father, you are both deaf and blind when it comes to your family. I hope the old bastard survives just for him to see his sons and daughter live their lives their way. We are all out of his control now, we will do as we want, my dear mamma.' William let go of his grip on his mother's arm and stood for a second looking at her before bounding back down the stairs and nearly knocking the cook over as he made for the kitchen door. Outside, he grabbed the reins of the tethered horse and mounted it before looking back at his family home, a home that he had never felt part of. He kicked his heels into the side of the horse and galloped to see Mary-Anne and ask her just how many times had she gone with his father and if she truly did have any feelings for him.

Mary-Anne was shocked to see William tether his horse to the garden railings and march his way up to knock on the door. 'William, I'm so glad to see you. I was wondering if you would send word to meet me, as I have heard that your father is ill. I thought that with your commitment to running your mills and your father's illness, we should perhaps not be seeing one another for a while. But here you are.' Mary-Anne stood on the doorstep and spoke loudly so as to make Ma Fletcher aware who her visitor was and for her to make herself scarce behind the dividing curtain.

'Ay, the old bugger is in a bad way. But I had to come and see you, set something that he said to me straight in my head, before I get in any deeper with you. Now, are you going to let me in, or do you want the whole neighbourhood to hear what I've got to say? It would give 'em all something to talk about or days.' William had no time for being held on the doorstep and the words of his father were starting to burn a spark of doubt in his mind about the woman who was quietly winning his heart.

'Of course, come in. I'm sorry to keep you on the step, I thought perhaps it was only a quick visit. Come through to the sitting room.' Mary-Anne held the door open, with her back facing the curtain partition and hoped that Ma Fletcher had retreated behind it, or at least made herself look like a respectable visitor. She glanced around her quickly and noticed the curtain being pulled as William crossed the threshold. 'Please, go through, whatever it is that's troubling you, I will answer and if I can, put your mind at rest.' Mary-Anne watched as William stepped through the kitchen into the sitting room that she had spoken to him once before in. He looked dark and scowling as she sat down next to the window overlooking the late spring garden and balanced his hat on his knee before speaking to her.

'Damn it, Mary-Anne, I've been besotted and entranced by your looks, and aye, I've been bloody blind to the woman that you really are. But looking at you now and looking around this house, my father's got to be wrong, with what he says. He's just got to be!' William shook his head and glared at her, trying to see who and what exactly was sitting in front of him.

'William, what has your father said to make you act this way?' Mary-Anne felt her heart race, wondering what William was going to say. 'Is there something wrong?'

'My father says that your mother was his whore and that he had you also and that I'm a fool to even look twice at you. I'm sorry, Mary-Anne, there is no easy way to say these words to you. Is it true? Have you bedded my father as well as me and was it for his money?' William looked at Mary-Anne and could see the pain that his questioning had brought into her eyes.

Mary-Anne bowed her head and then raised it to look at the man she was in love with. 'What your father tells you is true. I can't lie to you because I find myself starting to love you and you would have to know sometime. I didn't mean to fall in love with you, but it would seem my heart will not listen to my head because, believe me, it is in love that I am. As for your father, being bedded by him was not willingly undertaken by my mother or by myself, we both did it to survive.' Mary-Anne's eyes were filled with tears as William sprung to his feet.

'Then I've been a fool. I knew you were worth nothing when you left to find a new life with that useless Irishmen. You hadn't a penny to your name when you left with him. The poor bugger – I bet he had to work bloody hard to set you up in a house like this. It would seem that you take after your mother and have just seen me as a way to have easy brass in your pocket. Did she wine and dine with my father while my poor dear mother sat at home? Did she take my father for every penny she could get out of him, with you following in her shoes after her death, and then latching on to me, thinking that I was fool enough to keep you in a decent lifestyle? I see it all as it is now. I've been played like a fool.' William glared down at Mary-Anne.

'No, no you are wrong, you couldn't be further from the truth. My mother asked for nothing from your father, but for him to keep a roof over our family's heads. The only reason that she lifted her skirts for him was in payment of the rent, which my stepfather had spent in drink at the Boot and Shoe. She died because of your father, her and his baby. As for me, he took my innocence away from me, using me just in the same way as my mother. We were penniless when my mother died and my stepfather left and he took advantage of his power. Taking me to his gentleman's club for his amusement and for that of his friends, if I had not made good my escape. Please, William, I am no whore, nor was my mother. We were just taken advantage of. Your father was in control of our lives and we had no say in our own unless we wanted to beg on the streets.' Mary-Anne stood beside William and pleaded, pulling on his arm and sobbing.

William shook her off his arm and looked down at her. 'You could have done something, I thought you were making good money at the dress shop you and your sister had. My sister spent a small fortune with you both.'

'That was after the ill deed was done. She was our saviour, her and her friends, including your wife. Eliza and I will be eternally grateful for her support. We would have had to go into the work-house if she had not come to our rescue because I would never, ever have lowered myself to your father's abusive ways again. He is an animal and there is not a minute in the day that I don't regret that terrible night that I spent with him.' Mary-Anne could see William begin to soften as he realised what had exactly gone on between the Wild family and his father.

'I know my father is a monster to women, I too can sometimes be that way inclined as well you know. But with you, I thought I had found my perfect lover, that I'd not want for another whore to satisfy my needs. I even had thought, God forbid, that if anything happened to my wife I'd … well, I'm not even going to think about it let alone talk about it.' William sighed and looked at the sorrowful woman that stood in front of him.

'But nothing changes the way we feel about one another, William. Don't let your father win again. If it hadn't been for him last time, I would have been more accepting of your advances, but I couldn't stop thinking of him when we were together.'

'Hmm, perhaps you were thinking of how well he saw to your needs?' William grinned.

'No, no, no, I hated every minute and then he expected me to submit myself to him every month. He had complete control over our survival and then when I found myself with child, he cast me aside, not wanting his dirty secret to be disclosed,' Mary-Anne sobbed. 'I was in exactly the same situation as my mother, except I had no husband.'

'With child? Are telling me that you had a child to my father?' William sat back down in his chair.

'Yes, but he didn't recognise her for his. He's not paid a penny for her education or upkeep. I was too ashamed to name him as the father and I knew that the authorities would not believe me,' Mary-Anne whispered in tears.

'I have a sister? No wonder he wants to keep us apart.' William could not believe Mary-Anne's confession and stared at her.

'Yes, indeed you have. I left my daughter Victoria in my sister Eliza's care when I went to make a new life for myself in America. Victoria is your sister, and your father is all too well aware that she is, that is why he wants to part us. Victoria and I are his dirty secret that could bring his world down, that along with his regular abuse of my mother and other women, I suspect. You would need to ask the miners at the Rose, they would notice all of the women that visited his dirty little office to pay anything owing to him.'

'Does Victoria know who her father is? And does anyone else know the truth of her parentage?'

'I told her on my return. I had to, she was getting too friendly with your brother, although it

287

seems that I need not have worried on that score.' Mary-Anne couldn't help but smile gently at William. 'As for others knowing, only those who needed to know. Our old next door neighbours; John Vasey, he had to as he thought the same as you, that I was a loose woman.'

'Grace, does Grace know?' William leaned forward pressing Mary-Anne's hand hard.

'No, but there is beginning to be a family resemblance between them now she is growing up,' Mary-Anne sighed.

William stood up and put his hat on his head and said nothing as he made for the doorway.

'Don't go! Please, believe me. I was young and innocent. Your father used me.' Mary-Anne pulled on William's arm but to no avail as he stamped through into the kitchen.

'I've nothing more to say to you. Leave me be, woman, I need to think things through.' William pushed her away, slamming the door behind him before mounting his waiting horse. Mary-Anne watched as he rode it hard down the cobbles of Speakers' Corner, not even giving her a backward glance.

'Well, tha's done it now lass. That's your dreams gone and with it any hopes of being well to do. Why you had to tell him the truth, I just don't know, you silly bugger. You've only yourself to blame,' Ma Fletcher growled from behind the curtain.

'Shut up, just shut up. What else was I supposed to do? It's time he knew, else I can never love him properly. I wasn't going to start out with any secrets between us. My feelings towards him have changed, I no longer look at him as a way to get even with his father. Why should he pay for his father's actions? Besides his father has told him everything and has put paid to any further relationship, the bastard. You are right, I have probably destroyed my hopes of future happiness.' Mary-Anne stood in the centre of the kitchen and cried. Would she ever see William again? Had she just put an end to any happiness that she so wished for, just when she thought that she had it in the palm of her hand?

Chapter 29

George looked around him, hoping that no one had spotted him leaving the Molly house on Lands Lane. He didn't usually frequent the premises in daytime, preferring the cloak of night to hide his pleasures, but today, with numerous worries on his shoulders, he had escaped for an hour or two to be in the presence of his lover, a blond-haired, seventeen-year-old youth who satisfied his every need. There he had enjoyed the pleasures within with the aid of a good bottle of gin.

His brother's words, shouted out and heard by all his household as his father lay near death's door, had hurt him. He knew what he was. His love of men was much stronger than that for women, but up to then he had rather stupidly thought that no one else knew his preferences. Now, all the servants tittered behind his back and his mother, although she had not said as much, looked ashamed of him. Only Grace had accepted him for what he was. It was she he was going to see now, at her shop on Boar Lane.

He hoped Victoria would be there too. Though Victoria was only a little girl and probably didn't know of his proclivities, she seemed to accept him as he was and he felt the need to be with friends willing to do that. He stepped out in his blue breeches and embroidered waistcoat, his swagger stick tapping its way along the cobbled streets to the corner of Boar Lane, where he admired himself in the reflection of the shop's window. His ego had been restored due to his recent romps in the Molly house and now he was able to be George again, a young man who could fit into society.

He entered into the shop, his nose assaulted by the smell of women's perfumes and his eyes catching the sight of women's fineries. As he swaggered around the shop he secretly wished that he could be let loose to inspect and examine the fripperies his sister sold.

'George, I didn't expect to see you today. Will mother be all right on her own with father?' Grace stopped in her tracks as she saw her brother making his way to the bottom of the stairs, hoping to find her in her office, no doubt.

'She's got the servants, besides my father is not going anywhere. He seems to be stable at the moment, he even attempted to talk yesterday evening, as I'm sure you know. I couldn't make out what he said apart from the word "pit", which is just like him because, let's face it, all he loves is there and not at home.'

'You really should be more understanding, George. It is all father knows, it is his meaning in life – that and our mother.' Grace took George's arm and walked with him up the stairs and into her private office, not wanting anyone else to hear the blatant disregard for her father's health by her brother.

'Bah, I don't think he even has a love for our mother from what William was saying, but then again, he is just the same, no respect for anybody or anything unless there is something in it for him.' George sat in the chair opposite his sister and twiddled with samples of material that lay on her desk. 'Our family is a disgrace. I swear, sister, there is only you who is respectable. As for myself ... well, everyone heard what the world thinks of me.'

'Oh, George, don't you give me that sorry tale. Besides, just look at you, dressed to the nines and a gin to the worse, no wonder William abhors you, you act like a spoilt child, while we, dear brother, work to make a living. Perhaps now that father is ill you will take on some responsibilities. The Rose will need all of your attention if father is not going to improve.' Grace sighed. She knew all too well her brother's flaws and knew that the likelihood of George fulfilling his responsibilities would be slim.

'Tom Thackeray will see that the pit runs right, I don't want to visit the filthy place more times than I have to. I suggest that we get mother to put it up for sale if father dies. Until then I will look to keeping the accounts in order but nothing more.'

'Do you know what you need to do? I think that you'd do well to marry, George, just to stop these vicious rumours. Find a wife and settle down.' Grace looked coyly at her brother, she'd never mentioned her thoughts on the matter of George's behaviour before, but now she decided it was a good time to say what she thought. 'You seem to get on well enough with a young girl like Victoria, so surely you can find some other older woman who would be a good catch. Someone with not many assets, who would be grateful to catch the eye of such a wealthy man, and as long as you are discreet, well, you wouldn't be the first man in our family to seek his pleasures outside of his wedding vows. Take your chance at the Guild Ball, find a suitable woman to entertain and make your courtship of her public, and that will stop the gossip.'

'Perhaps your friend Eliza Wild? She fits all that you are telling me, although maybe she is too old. But surely you would not want either her nor I to be caught in a loveless marriage. A marriage that I could not commit to fully.' George looked at his sister, he thought her more respectful of her best friend. 'As it is, I use her niece as a shield in polite company to quell any suspicious minds. To marry her aunt would be a step too far, even for me.'

'Perhaps not Eliza, there are more women in the world than the Wilds. It was just a thought, a thought to protect you and our family.' Grace smiled and watched George fight against his obligations to his family's name and his own desires.

'But I'd not be happy. I don't see you rushing to get married. You will probably die an old maid. So how can you preach to me?' George hissed.

'Because as a spinster I am accepted in society, albeit thought of as strange for joining the man's world of business, but you, dear brother, are not accepted. Besides, I'm not about to give my wealth away to a man who would expect me to stay at home and play nursemaid to him and the children that he would no doubt expect me to carry and raise. I enjoy my independence and as a female this is the only way I can retain it. At least you would not be reliant on anyone once you have received Grandfather's inheritance. As long as the woman you chose was well clothed and well fed and kept like a lady, I'm sure she would be happy. She would learn to live with your indiscretions and be thankful that she was not at your beck and call each night. I think my idea is superb and I had a feeling that's why you have always been so friendly to young Victoria.' Grace glanced across at her brother and could see that he was pondering her suggestion. 'You could wait for her to grow up, I suppose...'

'I'll see. Is Victoria here today? I wanted to check if she is going to the ball next week, and not for any matchmaking reason you're plotting for when she's old enough...'

'Yes, she is with her aunt next door. I'm only thinking that it would appease everybody. At least you would please Father if you had a lady on your arm,' Grace smiled.

'I don't know, I'll see.' George rose from his

seat and sighed. 'I'll go next door and see Victoria. Only as a friend, so you can stop plotting.'

Grace watched as George left her office. She wasn't happy with her suggestion but she knew it would at least give George the cover for a life of his own. She shook her head. Why couldn't people let everyone live the lives they wished to live, instead of judging others? She sat back in her chair and thought about her father fighting for his life back at home and the look of despair on her mother's face as she sat beside his bedside day and night, despite his past transgressions. There was one thing that she was sure of: she herself would never marry; she'd made her own way in the world so far and would continue to do so for as long as God permitted.

Victoria raised her head as the cutting room door opened. 'George, how good to see you. Come, tell me how have you left your father today? Grace says that she can make the odd word or two out now and that he is able to drink broth.' Victoria smiled at her visitor and pretended to show an interest in her friend's father, even if really she had hoped that he had come with news of his demise.

'Yes, he is holding his own. Mother is tending to his every need and I am keeping an eye on his business interests.' George sat down on the seat next to Victoria.

'We hope that he recovers, George.' Eliza smiled knowingly at Victoria. 'Your mother must be terribly worried, no one wants to be left a widow at any age.'

'No, indeed, although he will have made provision for her after his death. But money is not everything, I suppose. His companionship is what she would miss most, as in any good partnership.' George looked at Victoria and saw her blush slightly. 'Marriage is about living with someone you can get along with, regardless of their flaws. I'm starting to realise that. My father, God bless him, is not an easy man, yet I'm sure my mother still loves him.'

'Love should be everything in a marriage. I could not marry without it,' Victoria said as she fingered her way through the latest pattern book, not realising the looks that George was giving her. 'I wouldn't marry a boy that I did not love.'

'Just listen to you two,' Eliza said hastily, realising that George was staring at her niece in a most odd way. 'Will you be attending the Guild Ball, George? I don't suppose your mother will be showing her face without your father on her arm?' Eliza stopped drawing the new design she was sketching and looked at the young, pompous Ellershaw.

'Indeed I will. I'll attend with my sister, providing that my father is still on this earth, of course. However, I do hope that you will have room for me on your dance card, Victoria? I can think of nothing better than escorting you around the dance floor at your first ball.' George grinned a sickly smile at Victoria. Perhaps his sister's words were to be heeded and he should be looking for a wife. If he made young Victoria his intended, it would be years before she'd be old enough to be a bride, while he still enjoyed the protection of

295

having a fiancée.

'I may have a few blank places, I may be able to fit you in.' Victoria smiled. 'Aunt Eliza has made me the most beautiful dress, she really has spoilt me. I don't deserve anything so fine.'

'Nonsense, child, the dress is nothing to the beauty of the wearer. You could go to the ball in rags and your beauty would still shine. There will be an army of young suitors lining up for your attention, of that I am sure. I will have to keep a close eye on you and see that you are not lead astray, especially as you're really too young to be attracting that sort of attention. Do you not think George?' Eliza looked at the plump, gaudy young man and saw in him traits of his father, the man all three of the Wild women hated.

'You may be surprised who will admire you, Victoria.' George sat back and stared at Eliza as she looked at him curiously but Victoria gave his words no heed. 'Anyway, I must be away, I need to get back to my father, give my mother some relief.' He rose from his chair and made for the door. 'Until next week, Victoria. I will look forward to you giving me the pleasure of at least two dances. That is, if I can fight my way through your admirers. Good day, Miss Wild, I will pass on your good wishes for my father's health to return to him soon.'

George closed the cutting room door behind him, breathed in deeply and then shook his head. Could he go through with Grace's plan? Perhaps not, there were no women of marriageable age that he even thought attractive; he'd rather be in the arms of his blond-haired lover in the Molly house, but that would never earn him the respect that he craved. But for now, he would have to return home to suffer the twitterings and jibes of the servants as they watched his every move.

'That dandy is up to something. Mark my words, Victoria. And as for his father, well, we will throw our own party when he's six feet under and stoking the coals of hell – the sooner he's gone out of our lives the better.' Eliza bent her head down and concentrated on her sketch. 'Let the devil take him and then we can all have some peace.'

Chapter 30

'For God's sake, Priscilla, stop this stupid game and get dressed.'

It was the night of the Guild Ball. William had been made aware of the state of his wife and his patience was wearing thin. William snatched the bejewelled dress out of the quivering maid's hands and threw it at his wife. 'I'm getting tired of this simpering idiot act. Just for once be the wife that I need and accompany me to the ball and be my equal in society.'

Priscilla sobbed as she lay crumpled up into a heap in front of the dressing table in her bed-room. Every year it was the same, every year she had to be cosseted and begged to join him. William had spent several pounds on her new dress and jewellery and now she was going to let him down again.

'I can't, I just can't. I can't face all those people and have all their eyes on me as we are announced and have to walk down the stairs and talk politely to everyone as they whisper about us behind our backs. They think I don't hear what they are saying, but I do, they hate me and they despise you … I just know they do.' Priscilla wept, raising her face to look up at William dressed in his best evening suit, his hair slicked back and his small dark moustache and sideburns groomed to perfection with his favourite twinkling ruby stud highlighting his cravat around his starched shirt collar. 'They do, William, they hate me … especially the women, because they want you for their own, they dream about how you could take them and bed them.' Priscilla's blond ringlets fell over her distressed face, leaving her maid's work of over an hour tangled and unsightly. She rubbed her hand over her eyes and mouth, the powder and rouge mixing in with her tears and smearing across her face, giving her an almost comical effect. She folded her hands over her dressing table, knocking the bowl of hairpins onto the floor as she laid her head down upon her arms and sobbed yet again.

'For God's sake. How much of that stuff the doctor gives you have you taken? You are not in your right mind, woman, just look at you.' William walked forward and lifted his wife's head in his hands for her to stare at herself in the mirror. 'You are a mess. No man in his right mind would want you on his arm tonight.'

He looked at both their reflections in the dress-

298

ing table mirror before summoning the maid to help him get his wife into bed.

'You never want me, William, you never did. You are like your father and you'll end up like your father or perhaps in your case, the devil will take care of you because that's who you are in partnership with, the devil, not me.' Priscilla slurred her words as William and her maid escorted her to her bed and pulled back the covers before placing her, still corseted between the sheets.

'Well, the devil makes a better bedfellow than you this night.' William looked around him and caught sight of the small bottle of tincture that had been the cause of Priscilla's condition on the bedside cabinet. He picked it up and threw it at the fireplace, smashing it against the polished marble, making the maid scream in horror. 'Shut up you stupid bitch! Look after your mistress and make sure she survives the night.'

William stalked out of the bedroom, leaving the maid in tears and his wife lost in her own world. He strode down the curving stairs of Levensthorpe Hall, paying little heed to the portraits hanging on the walls and the servants that tried to make themselves scarce to escape his wrath. 'You, boy, wait, get yourself a horse and deliver me this note.' William spotted his young houseboy and stopped him in his tracks as he scribbled a hasty note upon the hallway table. 'There's a florin in it for you if you can get a reply to me within the next hour. Tell the groom to get ready with the team. I still aim to attend the ball tonight, with or without my wife.'

William watched as the young boy left as fast as

his legs would carry him before going into the drawing room and pouring himself a stiff brandy. He stood next to the blazing fire and looked at himself in the full-length gilded mirror that showed his reflection on the opposite wall. He was the image of the perfect gentleman and to-night, by God, he would have a woman of beauty on his arm as he made his entrance at the Guild Ball.

'Are you feeling any better? Should I get the doc-tor?' Mary-Anne sat at the side of Ma Fletcher as she lay in her bed.

'Nay, lass, I'm all right, it's just these old bones of mine. A doctor can do nowt for me, so we needn't waste any money on him to tell me what I already know.'

'But he could give you something to ease the pain.' Mary-Anne held the old woman's hand. She knew Ma Fletcher would not want to tell her just how bad the pain was.

'What pain? I'm just tired. Now, whisht, and stop your fretting. Old Mr Tibbs is looking after me. Aren't you, my old faithful pal?' Ma Fletcher stroked the head of her old tom cat with her skeletal hands as he lay next to her, content and purring.

Mary-Anne released her hand and tucked it under the covers, leaving the other on Mr Tibbs as she watched the old woman close her eyes. Only to open them quickly as she heard a knock on the kitchen door.

'You've not sent for him without me knowing, have you? I told you I don't want him,' Ma

Fletcher groaned as Mary-Anne made for the door.

'No, I haven't sent for the doctor, if that's who you mean. I don't know who this will be!' Mary-Anne pulled the dividing curtain back and made for the door, opening it to find a dark-skinned servant boy looking anxiously at her. His dark eyes seemed full of fear as he asked for her to reply immediately to the note his master William Ellershaw had sent her. Mary-Anne unfolded the note and read it.

Accompany me to the Guild Ball this evening. I am in need of your company and I can't think of anyone more beautiful to be on my arm this evening. Please, I need you. I will send you a carriage on your acceptance, please don't say no.
William

Mary-Anne read and reread the note. Had William lost his senses? He couldn't take her. It would have to be his wife on his arm. The scandal of her accompanying him would have all the gossips talking for days.

'What is it, lass? Who's at the door?' Ma Fletcher asked in a soft voice.

'Try to sleep. It's nothing for you to bother about. It's just a young lad with a note from William, I'm going to send him on his way.' Mary-Anne glanced at the young lad on the step who looked worried that he had not received an answer as of yet.

'What's he say, lass, is he sorry for his outburst? Can I sleep without worry tonight, knowing that

301

he is still smitten by you?' Ma Fletcher whispered.

'It's more than that, Ma. He's asking me to the Guild Ball. I can't possibly accept, he must have lost control of his senses.' Mary-Anne crumpled up the note.

'You go, lass, this is your chance. Get yourself done up in all your finery and show him how you feel. He wouldn't be asking you if he didn't think anything of you. Get gone!' Ma Fletcher spoke as loud as she could, her breath ragged.

'But I can't leave you.'

'Mr Tibbs and I aren't going anywhere. We will both sleep until you return. Tell him yes, and be gone. Go on, don't let the lad wait any longer else it'll be the worse for the poor little bugger, if I know William Ellershaw.' Ma Fletcher closed her eyes and imagined the faces of the good and great as William Ellershaw was announced to one and all with his lover on his arm. How she wished she could be there.

Mary-Anne looked at the note again and at the poor lad who was counting the seconds for her reply. She looked down at Ma Fletcher and kissed her on her brow.

'Say yes,' Ma Fletcher whispered.

'Ooh, I don't know. He asks too much.' Mary-Anne looked at the note again.

'Please miss, I need a reply!' The young lad wailed.

'I must be mad, but yes, tell him yes! I'll be ready in an hour.' No sooner had the words left Mary-Anne's mouth than the young lad vanished into the night. He'd no time to wait for her to change her mind.

'There, the deed is done. Now go and stun them.' Ma Fletcher smiled with her eyes still closed. 'And give this old woman some peace.'

Mary-Anne stood and looked down at her old friend and pulled the curtain back into place. She'd no time to waste if she was not to let William down and get tongues wagging. But leaving Ma Fletcher as ill as she was tugged on her heartstrings and filled her with guilt as she climbed the stairs and took out the red dress that she had altered for the ball. She smiled. The sheen of the velvet caught in the candlelight and she held it next to her and admired herself in the mirror. Should she wear it? Or should she wear one of the gowns that she had stolen from New York?

She stood for a moment undecided, realising that her time had come, but yet again she was to turn her back on someone who needed her to pursue her own happiness. She breathed in deeply and whispered to herself, 'Just once more, and then I promise to behave and look after those I love.'

She quickly stepped out of her everyday dress, sprayed on eau-de-cologne and arranged her hair, fixing it up high on her head and adorning it with fake paste diamonds. She fastened a long ruby necklace around her white, swan-like neck. When Ma Fletcher had given it to her to go with the dress, she had said: 'That'll catch him. Just like a thieving magpie that is attracted to anything that shines, you wearing it will catch his eye.'

She stepped into the full skirts of her red dress and struggled to fasten the back of it before standing back to admire herself in the mirror of the oak wardrobe. She felt like Cinderella transformed before her arrival to the ball, only she knew that William Ellershaw was no Prince Charming and that perhaps she was about to begin a life full of regret. After all, he was still married, and the wagging tongues of the gossips would slaughter her with scathing words and looks. Was he really worth it? Did she really want to go through with all that and what it entailed? Too true she did; she'd be his mistress, just to cause pain to his father. While the old man lay on his deathbed, he deserved every bit of hurt. Besides, she was not just doing it because of him. Her love for William was growing stronger with every day and she had to make him hers.

Any doubt was cast to one side as she heard the clatter of hooves and her carriage drawing up outside the house. There was no time to be worried, William and the ball were waiting and she was going to make every moment count. She hoped that Victoria would understand and forgive her for perhaps spoiling her first ball by taking away the attention from her attendance. She justified her act of selfishness by consoling herself that if she won the affections of William and he provided her with the lifestyle she desired, that Victoria and herself would want for nothing.

She glanced at herself again in the mirror, held her head up and whispered to herself 'For Victoria and a better life.' She walked down the stairs and glanced quickly behind the curtain at Ma Fletcher asleep with her cat before placing her fur shawl around her shoulders and closing the door behind her at Speakers' Corner.

Eliza and Victoria arrived in their carriage at the bottom of the steps that led to the Guild Hall. It was a warm late spring evening and the air was full of chatter and laughter as they alighted down the carriage steps to join the great and the good of Leeds.

'I'm sure there are more people here than ever before.' Eliza glanced around her, smiling and acknowledging fellow business people and colleagues.

'I didn't know it was this busy, Aunt. Just look at the ladies in their finery and the men in their suits. I feel quite humble to be attending this event. There are so many important people here.' Victoria pulled her black and lilac wrap around her shoulders as she lifted her long purple skirt up to climb the steps into the Guild Hall.

'Hold your head up high, Victoria, you are just as good as them, if not better. You look very pretty. Remember your manners and try to be polite at all times.' Eliza walked up the steps of the hall, keeping in step with her niece and cooling herself with her lace fan decorated with hummingbirds that matched her hair piece and the embroidery on her blue satin skirts. They both stopped as two footmen asked for their names as they stepped into the hallway before entering the main hall itself.

Victoria looked at both the men in their powdered wigs and crimson coats with gold braided waistcoats underneath. With their breeches tucked into white stockings and black buckled shoes on their feet, they were indeed straight out of a fairy tale.

'Miss Eliza Wild and Miss Victoria Wild.' The voice of the younger of the two footmen carried clear and loud above the music as Victoria and Eliza made their way down the marble stairs into the main ballroom with all eyes upon them.

Victoria felt the colour come to her cheeks as she heard some of the ladies comment upon their apparel and smiled as she noticed groups of single young men whisper to one another as they made their entrance. She concentrated on every step as she demurely made her way down the steps onto the ballroom. Her stomach filled with butterflies as she noted the many faces that her aunt acknowledged and she smiled politely.

'There, that's the worst bit. You've no escape making your way down those stairs from the eyes that take in your every move and make note of every stitch of clothes that you are wearing. I think we impressed, judging by the looks on one or two ladies of note.' Eliza smiled at her young niece. 'Now let's help ourselves to some refreshment and then we will seek out Grace. She's bound to be already here, unless her father has taken a turn for the worse.'

'Don't mention him tonight, Aunt, let's forget that he exists. I just want to have the perfect evening and forget who I am.' Victoria took a deep breath and followed Eliza to a table adorned with flowered wreaths and swags. In the middle of it, huge crystal glass punchbowls were brimming with claret-coloured punch that was being ladled out into small crystal cups by man-servants dressed in the same dress as the footmen. No sooner had Eliza passed her niece a small cup of the punch, than an eager, dark-haired young man – who looked scarcely sixteen – edged his way towards Victoria, egged on by his group of friends who had pushed him forward to make himself known to her.

'May I be the first to ask you for a dance, Miss Wild?' He hesitated, not confident that his request would be accepted.

Victoria looked at her aunt for her permission.

'Go on, give me your punch. Go and enjoy yourself.' Eliza could see no harm in her niece enjoying a dance. She knew the young man in any case – he was Stephen Sanderson, the son of a well-respected corn merchant from near York, and if he was anything like his father, her niece would be safe in his arms. 'I've spotted Grace and George near the window. Join us when you need a breather.' Eliza smiled as Victoria took the hand of the young man. It was a night for the young and Victoria should make the most of her hour at the ball. She made her way to where Grace and George were sitting, balancing both cups of punch in her hands. She only wished Tom Thackeray could be by her side. Perhaps one day he would be if his dreams came to fruition.

'May I have the next dance, Miss Wild?'

No sooner had Victoria finished her first dance with Stephen Sanderson than another hopeful young boy was asking for her hand. Victoria placed her dance card in her hand and smiled as she wrote down the names of the squabbling suitors on her little notebook that was attached to her wrist. She had no idea that she would be so popular given how young she was, but the music and attention made her head spin as she waltzed around the dance floor. All eyes were on her and the beautiful dress that she was wearing as she tripped and swirled and politely made conversation with her besotted partner.

'Just look at your Victoria. Why, she is the belle of the ball. Just look at the young men that are queuing for her attention. You must be so proud, Eliza.' Grace noticed the glow of pride on her friend's face as her eyes followed her young ward around the room.

'Yes, she's a perfect young lady. I think I can truthfully say that my job is nearly done. I've said she is to stay only an hour with being so young but she looks so happy maybe we will stay a little longer.' Eliza felt satisfied with herself as Grace and George watched Victoria glide gracefully around the ballroom, until she had to return to them exhausted and out of breath.

'I've never had such a glorious evening, Aunt. My head is buzzing with excitement and I just must have a minute to cool down and catch my breath.' Victoria sat down giggling next to George, reaching for a drink of her punch while watching other older couples take to the dance floor. 'Isn't it wonderful, George? I've never been to such like before.'

'You seem to be popular,' George said and looked at the flush upon the young girl's cheeks as she politely refused another offer of a dance from another ardent admirer.

'Yes, I do, I can't quite believe it!' Victoria

tapped her toes as the ballroom came to life again to the tune of one of her favourite waltzes.

'Victoria, perhaps you would like to cool down on the balcony outside.' George looked serious but she paid little attention to his request, too intent on the gaiety before her.

'Later, George. Will it not keep? I must go back on the dance floor. Join me for a dance?' Victoria rose from her seat and pulled on George's hand. 'Come on, stop looking so serious and grumpy. You'll enjoy yourself. My dance teacher has taught me well, don't you think?' Victoria giggled and looked across at Grace and Eliza as she pulled the hesitant George from his seat.

'Victoria, have a dance with George and then we may have to think about returning home. You are too young to be here the whole of the night.' Eliza looked up at her as she pulled on George's arm.

'But I don't want to go home, I want to dance all night,' Victoria giggled as she forced George to join her.

George followed her reluctantly – he wasn't exactly nimble on his feet and he felt awkward as he put his arm around Victoria's waist as she pulled him onto the dance floor. 'Victoria, I really can't dance. I've got two left feet. Shall we go outside to get some fresh air?'

The couple moved around the dance floor and as they reached the bottom of the stairs George could wait no longer as the dance came to an end.

In a loud voice just as the music faded he said, 'No more, honestly, I cannot!' He stopped suddenly in mid-sentence, realising that all eyes were not on them but on the couple who had not waited to be announced but were walking down the stairs towards them. A hush came over the room and then the sound of the women gossiping as William Ellershaw and Mary-Anne made the most spectacular entrance down the stairs to stand next to George and Victoria.

'Mama, what are you doing here?' Victoria gasped, oblivious to the words that George had been in the process of saying to her. She looked at the finery that her mother was wearing and then glanced at William Ellershaw, who was grinning at the reaction of the tittering crowds. She felt herself blush with the embarrassment of the situation and knew exactly why the dance floor was reacting like it was.

'William was short of a partner, so I have accompanied him. Much to everyone's amusement and gossip. I hope you will forgive me, my darling.' Mary-Anne looked around her while linking her arm through William's, snubbing the ladies that she could hear saying 'disgraceful, brazen' and calling her a tart. 'We were once quite close, so when Priscilla could not attend he asked me. You look beautiful, darling. Are you enjoying your evening?' Mary-Anne kissed Victoria's cheek and gave George a quick glance.

'Very much so, Mama.' Victoria blushed as she noticed William look her up and down. She couldn't show her disdain of her mother being accompanied by him but she realised it was wrong and that it would bring back the memories of who she was by birth, and that like her mother, she would also be being whispered about throughout the room. Victoria felt sick inside as all eyes were upon them as they pushed past the full-skirted ladies of the ballroom to where Grace and Eliza sat.

The band decided to quell the noise of the scandal that had erupted and struck up with a new tune to get everyone back on the dance floor.

Mary-Anne just smiled at Eliza as she sat down next to her. Grace pulled William beside her, making everyone aware of the words that she was saying to him in chastisement at not bringing his wife to the ball.

'What do you think you are doing? Do you realise that you have completely ruined my and Victoria's evening?' Eliza hissed at her sister, hiding the words she was saying behind the fluttering of her fan. 'Why did he bring you here? The whole of Leeds will be gossiping about you tomorrow. And you are wearing red, like the scarlet woman that you are!'

'They'll get over it, the hypocrites. I hadn't planned to be here but William insisted that I attended. Priscilla is not fit for anything after taking laudanum. Besides, I always have wanted to see what this great ball was about. I just wish Victoria had not been here. You said you were taking her home after the first hour.' Mary-Anne smiled as William had obviously heard enough of his sister's views on his choice of partner as he walked back over to her.

Eliza snorted her contempt and watched as William held his hand out for Mary-Anne to take. 'She was enjoying herself so much, I planned to

311

let her stay a little longer. Now you have ruined her evening and broken her heart.'

'I'm doing this partly for Victoria,' Mary-Anne whispered to her sister.

'Mrs Vasey, may I have the pleasure?' William bowed and took Mary-Anne's hand.

'Indeed you may, sir. In fact, I think I will dance with you all night if I get the chance.'

William grinned. 'Indeed I am all yours for as long as you wish because it would seem that I am a cad and of very little standing, even though I am worth more than half the room's inhabitants put together. That is what my darling sister has just told me.' William pulled Mary-Anne into his arms and Victoria, Eliza, Grace and George watched in despair as the dancers in the ballroom gasped at the brashness of the couple, who were not in the least concerned by the dirty looks and taunts that they were receiving. They watched as they laughed and danced around the room with only eyes for each other.

Victoria was nearly in tears. 'Aunt Eliza, Mama is ruining the evening. How could she do this? I am so embarrassed.'

'Because she is a selfish self-centred woman. Since she came back from America she has had one thing on her mind, and nothing will distract her from getting what she wants no matter who she hurts. My sister has changed and perhaps her previous life and misfortunes have consumed her soul. Don't you worry, my love, this should not reflect on you. Most of these people here do not know the connection between us and your mother. It will be William that they gossip about.

Did you enjoy your dance with George? I saw he was trying to talk to you when your mother and William made their appearance.' Eliza knew Victoria was upset, this night would put the relationship with her mother back to where it had been when she had first reappeared in Victoria's life. 'Do you want to return home or should we stay just a little longer?'

'George has two left feet – I prefer dancing with boys my own age. Could we stay just a little bit longer? I think I will go out upon the balcony for that spot of fresh air with George. I feel quite faint and upset.' She looked at George who had gone strangely quiet since he had sat back down next to her with not a word said about his wayward brother.

'Of, course, but we will not stay much longer. Mary-Anne has spoilt my night as well,' Eliza sighed.

Victoria sat next to George. 'Forgive me, George, I had quite forgotten with your brother's and my mother's entrance that you were in the middle of asking me to join you on the balcony for some air. Would you like to accompany me now?'

'I don't know.' George looked down at his feet. 'Our William seems to have upset the apple cart yet again. I'm sure your mother is a decent person but she is causing controversy by attending with my brother. Perhaps it is best that we don't join one another outside, people might talk about us too. The Eaveshams are still respected in Leeds, it should be Priscilla who is with my brother tonight. My parents will disinherit him for sure.' George looked at his brother frolicking

313

with his mistress.

'I know, I'm quite ashamed. I only hope that people don't think that I'm like her. Aunt Eliza has always brought me up with manners and values.' Victoria nearly sobbed but then spotted Steven Sanderson making his way through the crowds towards her.

'You can't be responsible for your parent's sins, Victoria. You can just live the life that you want and hope that it doesn't cause hurt to anyone.' George stood up. 'Excuse me, I'm just going to grab some fresh air by myself, I'm afraid it is rather warm for me.' He bowed his head slightly as Victoria's younger admirer made himself known to her yet again and wandered off to where the long, tall open windows led out onto a balcony.

'Will you dance, Miss Wild? This one is my favourites. Do you know it?' Steven Sanderson held out his hand.

Victoria looked up at the young man. 'I believe I do, Mr Sanderson. My mother taught it to me just recently. I'm not perfect with my steps but we can practise it together.' Victoria took his hand and she smiled to her aunt over her shoulder as she wandered onto the crowded dance floor.

Grace sighed and reached for Eliza's hand. 'Well, that leaves two old maids sitting on their own, worrying about our siblings.'

'Why, Grace, less of the old maids, we still have life in us, and besides, I'd rather be an old maid and have money than be tied and beholden to a man, no matter how much I love him.' Eliza smiled.

'I was thinking, Eliza, we need to branch out, perhaps open a new shop in the arcade. What do you think? We are always busy and there are some shops not yet taken, I'm sure we could get one in time for Christmas.'

'I'm in agreement with that. Orders keep coming in; a second shop to serve the very best of society. Like those who are here tonight.' Grace and Eliza looked around them at all the couples on the dance floor and burst out laughing. 'Some couples just cannot dance, although William and Mary-Anne look so graceful together, they make a good pair. Poor Victoria, she must be so ashamed of her mother making such an entrance. I'll take her home once this dance has finished,' Eliza said.

'Oh, I think William has met his match. Let us see just how far this new tryst between your sister and my brother goes. He has never been happy with Priscilla, perhaps Mary-Anne will be good for him, despite the scandal. He was not backing down from his forthright views about his love for your sister no matter what I said.'

'Love, it is that deep?' Eliza sighed as she sat back and admired the view. So, Mary-Anne had finally got what she had aspired to, but no doubt the road ahead would be a bumpy ride, of that she was sure.

Chapter 31

George and Grace Ellershaw looked at one another across the breakfast table. Both had little appetite. They had not yet told their mother about what had taken place at the previous night's festivities, as they did not want to add more worry to her shoulders. Catherine had not yet come down to breakfast, as she kept to her husband's bedside.

'It is typical of our William. He thinks only of himself and never of the consequences.' Grace spread her toast with marmalade. 'Do we tell mother this morning or do we wait until one of her gossiping friends tells her? I'm sure she will have plenty of visitors queuing up to give her the bad news. I think it is better that we do so ourselves when she comes down from seeing Father.'

'Whatever we do we will be in the wrong, especially me. Although I couldn't stop my mad brother acting like a fool even if I had wanted to. Even I didn't think that he would go so far as to show his latest conquest off, and besides, it was a bit of a smack in the face for Victoria. I take it neither she nor her aunt had any idea that Mary-Anne was going to be there?' George sighed and bade the servant offering him poached eggs to take them away. His stomach felt queasy, both from the excess of drink and the fear of the news that his mother was about to hear.

'I know Victoria was totally shocked and she seemed more than a little upset, that was until that young lad from over near York came to ask her to dance with him. Eliza just took it in her stride, though she was clearly worried that her sister was the talk of Leeds and was the scarlet woman in more ways than one. That was until I told her that William had told me that he loved Mary-Anne, then she seemed more accepting of the situation. What did Victoria say? You disappeared for a while on your own and I never got chance to talk to you again, and then when I did you were so drunk you could hardly get into the carriage home and made no sense whatsoever.'

'Don't ask, I made a fool of myself dancing with her and then she went on to dance with every Tom, Dick and Harry until her aunt decided to take her home. She was like a summer's butterfly, flitting around the room.' George sat back in his chair and sighed again.

'Oh, George, you are just the opposite of our William.'

Grace went quiet as she saw her mother coming along the hallway after visiting their father who was still in his bed.

'I suppose you two are feeling worse for wear this morning. You must have been late, I never heard the carriage return with you both in it, so, I presume a good night was had?' Catherine Ellershaw spread her napkin on her knee and looked across at her son and daughter who were looking very sheepish.

'How's Father this morning, Mother? Is there any improvement?' Grace looked across the table

317

and skirted around the question.

'He's as well as can be expected. He managed to eat a little porridge and is still attempting to speak a little. But I must confess I can't make out many of the words and he gets so frustrated with himself. The one thing he still seems to possess is his temper. Now, how was the ball, who was there and who was not? It is the first time I have not attended in over thirty years, I must admit I envied you both slightly last night. Oh, to be young again, they were such good times.' Catherine looked across at both her children and realised that something was not quite right; neither of them was full of the usual chatter that they indulged in after the biggest night of the year. 'Well?'

Grace looked across at George and realised that it would be up to her to tell her about the night's events. 'It was rather eventful, Mother, and neither of us wants to tell you why, but no doubt someone will not be as kind as us and will gloat with the news when they knock upon your door.' Grace took courage and looked at her mother who seemed worried as she waited for her to tell her the worst. 'William attended the ball without Priscilla. He made his entrance with Mary-Anne Vasey – Eliza's sister – on his arm. It seems that they have been seeing quite a bit of one another.'

'What are you telling me? That William was foolish enough to take another woman to the ball in his wife's stead and parade her around in front of everyone like a prize dog, or should I say bitch in this case? We will be the scandal of Leeds. What was he thinking of? Why are we so interlinked with that abhorrent family? You lifted one of them out of the gutter and William, it seems, is willing to put himself and his reputation back into it. Oh, my Lord, how can I show my face to anyone? Bring me my smelling salts!' Catherine yelled at the servant who tried not to look as if he was listening to the gossip. She fanned herself with her napkin.

'Mother, you know that William has not been happy in his marriage. Priscilla is so frail, I can understand William looking elsewhere for affection, but I know that does not make it right. Also, I believe Mary-Anne has come back from America and is quite wealthy.' Grace tried to justify her brother's actions and also to make a stand for Mary-Anne Vasey, who had looked every inch the right woman for William to have on his arm despite him being married.

'You keep your whore in the bedroom, you don't flaunt her for everyone to see.' Catherine scowled at her daughter as she breathed in salts from a shaking servant and regained her thoughts. She glared at George. 'And I suppose you, the useless leech that you are, stood and said nothing about it, or were you too busy with the young men that you seem to admire? No wonder your father is dying in his bed, you have all driven him to it. Now get out of my sight and leave me in peace. I am truly ashamed of each and every one of you. Even you, Grace – I blame you as well – as you have brought this common, gutter-ridden family into our midst.'

Both her children pushed back their chairs and bowed their heads.

'I'm sorry, Mama, someone had to tell you. I know perhaps I have encouraged a friendship with Eliza, and Victoria, but I think you will find that Father knows the family a lot better than I. After all, he owned the cottage they used to live in and I think perhaps it is not the first time the Ellershaws and the Wilds have been so close.' Grace threw her napkin down and glanced across at her brother as they both made their way out of the dining room, closing the door behind them.

George caught hold of Grace's sleeve as she walked along the corridor. 'What did you mean by that? Why should our father come into it?'

'I looked at young Victoria Wild last night as she danced around the dance floor and I couldn't quite understand where I had seen her features until I looked in the mirror this morning. Yes, she has the looks of her mother, but she also is the spit of me, George. Now, I understand why Father hated the family so much and why he has thrown William out of our home. Either Victoria is his child or she belongs to William, but both have bedded Mary-Anne Vasey, of that I am nearly certain, so Victoria is one or the other's. Mother always has kept her eyes and ears closed when it comes to Father's way but I remember hearing raised voices when Eliza and Mary-Anne's mother died, then she questioned him once about the sisters still living in a pit house when their step-father left them and his answer made no sense.'

'That can't be right, you must be wrong? But he has always warned us about the family. He also shows no pride in you and your business; in fact, he always dismisses it when anyone talks about it. God, if you are right, it'll kill him if he finds out that William is flaunting Mary-Anne Vasey around Leeds.' Victoria was either his niece or his sister, depending on whether his brother or his father had sired her.

'It could be that he already knows, and it already nearly has done so. Which would mean that our mother knows it too.' Grace stood at the bottom of the stairs. 'It's what will happen next we have to worry about. Priscilla is nothing like our mother, she can't stand the rigors of living with our headstrong brother and the shame that he has brought her. As for Mary-Anne Vasey, she'll do as she pleases of that I'm sure, she's her own woman.'

'Oh, my Lord. I thought I was the black sheep of this family,' George whispered.

'You, dear brother, are whiter than white.' Grace smiled and left a disbelieving George standing alone in the hallway. He'd nothing to worry about except his hangover.

'I could have danced all night, I enjoyed every second.' Victoria leaned back in her chair and smiled as she ran her silk scarf through her fingers and thought about the dances and the handsome young men that had asked for her hand.

'I did notice that you were enjoying yourself but you weren't the only one. I suspect your mother will be the main topic of gossip today and for the next few weeks. What she was thinking of I do not know, she could have been more discreet.' Eliza looked across at her niece. 'How do you feel that your mother is having a dalliance with William? It must feel strange.'

'I sometimes wish that she was not my mother, especially when she was making it no secret that William is her new lover. I was embarrassed not only for myself but for her. All the women were talking about her and staring. Did you know Aunt Eliza that she was that enthralled by him, and him her, come to that?' Victoria scowled and crumpled her scarf in her hand.

'I think that initially she was thinking of getting some satisfaction in hurting your father by attracting William and making him her lover. However, I fear that she has been caught up in her own web of deceit by losing her heart to him. The heart is a fickle thing, Victoria, as you will learn when you grow up. You can never control it, no matter how hard you try.'

'I suppose I should be happy for her, but William is married, she is never going to have him as her husband. I'm never going to be a man's plaything. I will marry the perfect gentleman and will not share him with anyone.' Victoria remembered the arms of Stephen Sanderson around her waist and his charming smile as he guided her around the dance floor.

'Well now, young lady, you can put your head into a book and do some studies, your French tutor will be here tomorrow and he will expect you to have learnt what he set you last week. I'm going for a walk with Tom. So just stop your daydreaming – you're a long way off being old enough to take a husband. As long as I know that your mother has not hurt you yet again. She does love you, she just doesn't think sometimes.' Eliza kissed her niece on the cheek before walking to the parlour door.

'I know, Aunt. I also know that she only does things that will benefit me but I just want her to be happy and not to always do what she thinks is right for me. She doesn't know me, not like you. I won't be too young for ever and I'm well educated and will be my own woman, thanks to you. I can never thank you enough.' Victoria watched as her aunt fought back a tear before leaving the parlour.

Victoria sat for a second and recalled her mother's happy face as she danced and flirted with William Ellershaw. Why did it have to be him? Had she not had enough of the Ellershaw family and their sordid ways? Had she not thought it strange, her courting her daughter's brother with him already married, and with her own experience of William's father? Her mother's lack of morals was not to be applauded, she thought as she picked up her French books. What was the French word for a love triangle, she pondered as that was what her mother was in and she just hoped that she would not get hurt.

Eliza linked arms with Tom as they walked out on their usual Sunday stroll together. The sun shone down and the warmth of the summer's day made them both relax as they stood on the railway bridge at the bottom of Pit Lane.

'Do you remember when we first walked here? We were both young and worried in case our parents found out and then you returned home to the terrible news of your mother's death. I thought then our love was perhaps not meant to be.' Tom looked at Eliza.

'Do you still think that, Tom? I couldn't blame you, what with our Mary-Anne being the talk of the town and you knowing the truth about Victoria. We aren't the sort of family your mother would want you to be involved with.' Eliza looked up into Tom's eyes and saw the love that had always been there for her.

'But they aren't you, Eliza. I love you and I should have said these words years ago.' Tom held Eliza's hands tightly. 'Marry me, Eliza Wild. Be my wife and then I can always love you. We can build a home together and Victoria can still live with us but we will have one another for ever.'

'Oh, Tom, I love you too. My answer is yes, of course, I would love to be your bride.' Eliza wiped the tears of joy away from her face, she too had got her man.

Mary-Anne lay back in the arms of William and gazed at him while he lay sleeping. She noted the greying hairs in his once jet-black hair and the worry lines on his brow, but he was still a handsome man, one that anyone would be proud to be seen with. She thought about the previous evening and how foolish they had both been to cause such a scene. She'd heard the comments from the various well-to-do ladies. It's always the women that are the worst, she thought as she felt William stir beside her.

'Are you all right, my love?' She stroked William's face as he awoke and kissed him on his lips as he held her tight and began to kiss her neck and caress her body.

He smiled and said nothing, intent on having

his way with her again after enjoying a night full of pleasure in the room he had rented above The White Swan. His hands followed the contours of her body and his lips kissed and fondled her breasts.

'No, William, we must return to our homes. Think of Priscilla, she will be worried.' Mary-Anne looked up at the man that lay on top of her, his smiling face beaming down at her as he tempted her again to be his. 'I mean it, we shouldn't, it's already mid-morning, and Priscilla will be worried.'

William fell down back beside her and ran his hand through his hair. 'Damn that woman, I don't love her. I just need you and your wicked ways. I swear you are a witch and that you've entrapped me in your spell. All sense has left me as I know that what you say is right.'

'We must go home. Our exploits will already have given the gossips of Leeds enough fuel to last them all year. Go, and make sure Priscilla is well and we will meet again shortly, my love. I'll not abandon you, I'm here for as long as you need me.' Mary-Anne kissed him gently before stirring from his arms and quickly dressing. Even if he was in no hurry to get home, she was. Ma Fletcher was on her own with only her cat for company and she had already missed her breakfast.

William sat on the edge of the bed and slowly dressed as he watched Mary-Anne make herself presentable before returning to her home. 'Shall I get you a carriage? You are not exactly dressed for your walk home.' He placed his watch in his waist-coat pocket before putting his arms around Mary-

Anne's waist, holding her close to him and smiling at their reflection in the dressing table mirror.

'No, I'll be back home in a few minutes. I'll be fine.' Mary-Anne caressed his face and kissed him again before pulling her fur around her. 'Next Monday?'

'Next Monday at the music hall, I'll see you there.' William nuzzled her neck and then let her go as she made for the bedroom door. 'I'll be counting the minutes.'

Mary-Anne blew him a kiss and then made her way out of the room. The landlord and the serving maid smiled and tittered as she made her way out of the inn. They all knew who William Ellershaw was, but not the brazen woman who had spent the night with him. She paid them no heed as she walked quickly through the streets of Leeds, ignoring the looks and jibes of those who commented on her dress.

At the same time that she was worried about getting home to make sure Ma Fletcher was all right, she was thinking of her lover, and also Victoria, who she had hardly spent any time with at the ball, being so intent on securing William's love if she was to be the scandal of Leeds society. She must go and see her daughter, make sure she was all right, that she had not spoilt her evening and caused too much scandal. She hadn't realised that she would still be there, another half-hour later and she wouldn't have been, as Eliza had taken her away from the ball early. She only hoped that no more hurt would be caused between them when she realised why William had to be part of both their lives. Her heavy skirt, delicate shoes and tight bodice impeded her progress as she hastily walked through the cobbled streets, finally turning the corner into Hyde Park Corner. She noticed immediately that the curtains were still drawn at her home but thought nothing of it as she turned the key in the lock and walked into the darkened house.

'I'm home, Ma. Sorry I'm late,' she shouted as she pulled back the curtains to let light into the still house. The bright morning light filled the room, showing an un-lit fire and the curtains of Ma Fletcher's private quarters still drawn. 'Ma, Ma, I'm home.' Mary-Anne quickly pushed back the curtain and looked down at the grey-haired old woman still asleep in her bed. She went over to her side and shook her gently as Mr Tibbs twined his body around Mary-Anne's legs. Mary-Anne caught her breath as she realised that her dear old friend was no longer in the world and that she had not been there as she had passed from one world to the next.

Mary-Anne sat on the edge of the bed and sobbed. 'I'm sorry, Ma, I'm sorry I left you, I knew you weren't well. I never should have left you.'

A pang of guilt came over her. She had been selfish and uncaring and had let her own needs and pride come before anything else. She bent down and picked the demanding cat up and stroked him. She usually had no time for the creature, nor it her, but he was now purring on her knee as if he knew that his mistress had gone and he was going to have to make the best of the one he'd been left with.

'Well, that's it, Mr Tibbs, we are left with one

another. We are both adept at change and using people, perhaps we will show more love and care to the ones we love.'

Mary-Anne looked around the room and house that had become her home and a fresh sadness swept over her. She reached out for the cold hand of her old friend and whispered 'God Bless', then fed Mr Tibbs with the food he was demanding.

She walked over to the drawer that she knew Ma Fletcher kept her will in. She had been told to go to it upon Ma Fletcher's death. Nervously she opened the envelope contained within, as she sat on the bed edge next to Ma's dead body. Her hand shook as she unfolded the document and she read her dear friend's last wishes. She sobbed as she read each line over and over again. The house, contents and all Ma Fletcher's money were to be hers on one condition: that she looked after Mr Tibbs until his last days on earth.

Mary-Anne couldn't help but smile between the tears and watched as the old cat climbed up onto the bed and made himself known to her yet again. 'So you are like me too, going to whoever is best for you. We will survive, won't we, cat? Life has made us hard.' Mary-Anne stroked the old feline and then glanced around her. She had a home, money and the wealthiest lover in Leeds. She'd come a long way from the thief escaping her life in America. Now she must pay more attention to her daughter Victoria and secure her a future of happiness and not one of hurt and degradation. 'Life's just beginning Mr Tibbs, we will both live it well.'

The publishers hope that this book has given you enjoyable reading. Large Print Books are especially designed to be as easy to see and hold as possible. If you wish a catalogue please ask at your local library or write directly to:

Magna Large Print Books
Cawood House,
Asquith Industrial Estate,
Gargrave,
Nr Skipton, North Yorkshire.
BD23 3SE